The Book of Chooch

(a brautigan, sort of)

By Chooch

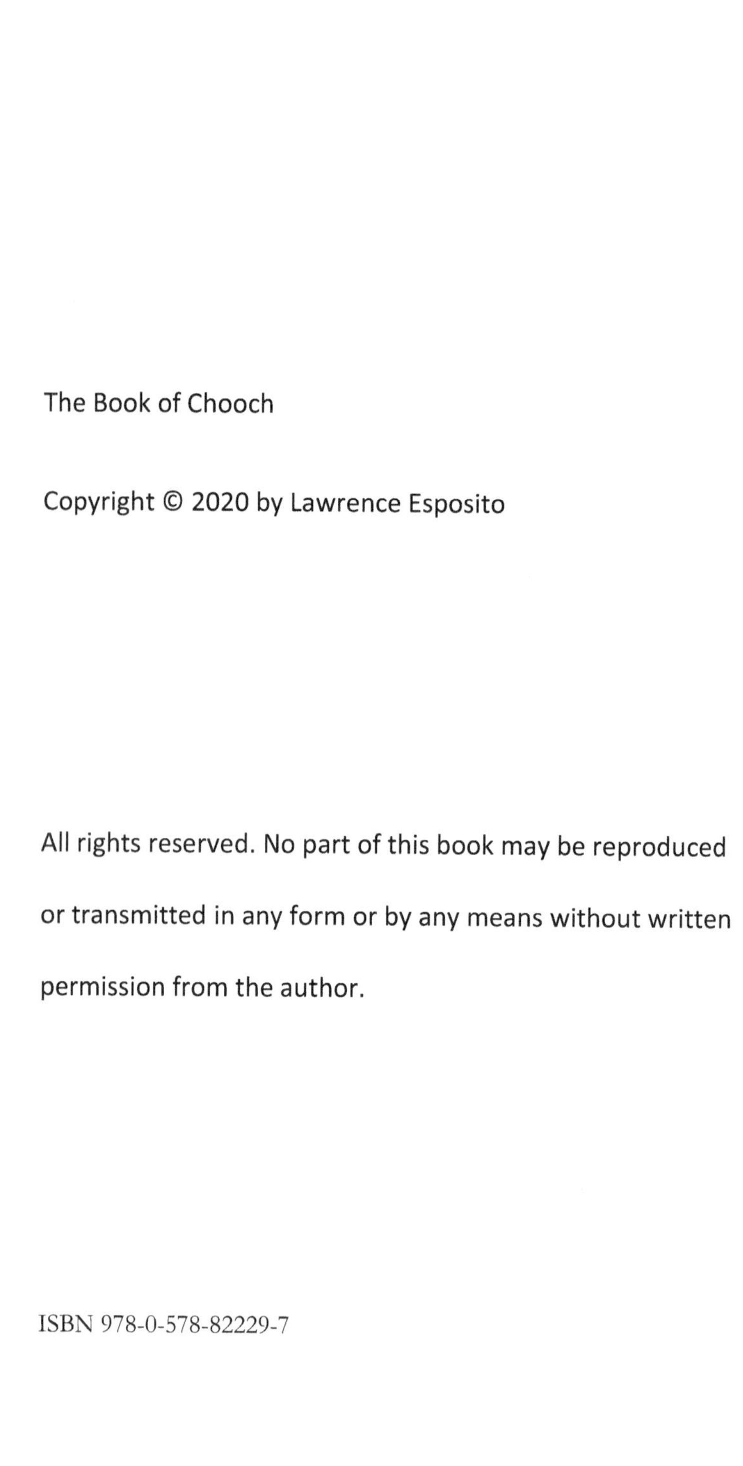

The Book of Chooch

ISBN 978-0-578-82229-7

DEDICATION

I would like to dedicate this book to an inanimate object; more specifically a garlic press. However the animated principals in my life might be a little put off even though, in a manner of speaking, I would do it as a joke. Ha. Ha. In light of such self-immolating jocularity I will desist from the wittiness and make a more normal (sane) inscription.

To two people I know (I can see ya!)

Who helped me with all my ideas,

Their presence on Earth,

And inestimable worth,

Make me proud to say "Hail Deb and Nia!"

Love you guys.

CONTENTS

PREFACE

Here lie the bones of 68 years of bizarre brain interactions; deeds both deliberate and unintentional; decisions diametrically opposed on the wobbly scale of wisdom and stupidity; internal and external wrestling matches wisely and dumbly perpetrated and perpetuated; and circumstances beyond my control or at least beyond my excuses. Now that I've got that out:

GREETINGS EARTHLINGS!

(I hope)

You are about to embark on a journey into mindless meanderings, portentous perceptual pirouettes, and any general and specific effluent I've decided to smear these pages with. So off with your virtual blindered goggles(!) and enough of this tomfoolery! Take it in and chew it up, slowly or quickly as you please. If there be side effects let them stimulate, incubate, repopulate, and celebrate all within the fence-less (or de-fence-less) confines of your reality. Or just get a few good laughs. Whatever you do is your business. Mine begins with page one. Damn the torpedoes! Full read ahead!

BTW: Visiting hours vary according to the day of the month and the nurses' vacation schedules.

ABSTRACTS

Fairly Recent (1967) Literary Review Entry

"Perhaps, when we are very old, people will write *Brautigans* just as we now write novels. Let us hope so."

> *Part of a review from the San Francisco Sunday Examiner & Chronicle, quoted on the first page of the paperback edition of Richard Brautigan's "Trout Fishing In America."*

Early Twentieth Century Vaudeville Entertainer's Day Off Entry

A well attended revival meeting in a tent somewhere in the hinterlands.

PREACHER: Sinners! As the apocalypse approaches you have one chance! You have one opportunity to query the Almighty and save your soul for eternity. Is there anyone out there with a question for God? Yes……

GROUCHO: What's the capital of North Dakota?

Twenty-first Century Snack Cake Ingredients Entry

Enriched Bleached Wheat Flour [Flour, Reduced Iron, B Vitamins (Niacin, Thiamine Mononitrate (B1), Riboflavin (B2), Folic Acid)], Corn Syrup, Sugar, High Fructose Corn Syrup, Water, Partially Hydrogenated Vegetable and/or Animal Shortening (Soybean, Cottonseed and/or Canola Oil, Beef Fat), Whole Eggs, Dextrose. Contains 2% or Less of: Modified Corn Starch, Glucose, Leavenings (Sodium Acid Pyrophosphate, Baking Soda, Monocalcium Phosphate), Sweet Dairy Whey, Soy Protein Isolate, Calcium and Sodium Caseinate, Salt, Mono and Diglycerides, Polysorbate 60, Soy Lecithin, Soy Flour, Cornstarch, Cellulose Gum, Sodium Stearoyl Lactylate, Natural and Artificial Flavors, Sorbic Acid (to Retain Freshness), Yellow 5, Red 40.

Deep and Emotional Song Lyrics Entry

"Ho-dee-doh-dee-day."

From "Don't Put Your Finger In My Garlic Press," by Chooch, 2019.

Nineteenth Century Let's Get Serious Poetry Excerpt

I am the daughter of Earth and Water,
And the nursling of the Sky;
I pass through the pores of the ocean and shores;
I change, but I cannot die.
For after the rain when with never a stain
The pavilion of Heaven is bare,
And the winds and sunbeams with their convex gleams
Build up the blue dome of air,
I silently laugh at my own cenotaph,
And out of the caverns of rain,
Like a child from the womb, like a ghost from the tomb,
I arise and unbuild it again.

From "The Cloud" by Percy Bysshe Shelley, 1820

“There are two ways to approach life. One is to seek success and hope that happiness follows. The other is to seek happiness. Anything after that is playing with house money.”

Chooch

ENTRY ONE:
CARLO'S BOAT

Chapter One: The Lagoon

The shoreline looked out onto waves that rose up and crashed in white swirls and salt plumes; fragments of shattered glass, or handfuls of diamonds tossed into the sky, glistening in the sunbeams. The spray, somehow always hotter than the air, created heavy mists that collected at the breakers and rolled continuously into the lagoon, at all hours and under cloudy or sunny skies, held captive by the horseshoe of pink cliffs so that even on days when no fog was present, a watcher on a passing ship could not discern where the sea ended and the lagoon began. Along the innermost shore, hidden from view, the water lay flat and still with an occasional ripple of incongruous bubbles barely lifting the few rowboats tied along a worn wooden jetty and pushing so easily against the piers that you could believe there was no water there at all but a hazy pane of glass with almond shaped driftwood embedded in it. A man limped along the beach, his right leg damaged many years before in a mysterious accident he never liked to talk about. He stepped out with his left foot and brought the other even, paused before stepping again, and repeated. His head seemed not to be attached to his body but floated above his neck, bouncing lightly over his rigid torso – a wrinkled balloon swaying in the breeze in no apparent relation to the rhythm of his gait. He had a full head of long wispy gray hair crowned with a round cloth cap best described as a beanie except without the toy propeller. On his bare feet were a grungy pair of worn boat sneakers and the rest of his outer raiment matched their condition. In his hand he carried a homemade fishing pole consisting of several thin tree branches lashed together with hemp string; hanging across his body a faded leather bag. As he approached the jetty he cupped one hand over his mouth and called out.

"Boy, where are you?"

"In the boat," came a voice from somewhere in the shadows.

"Which one?"

"The same as always."

The same as always, the old man thought. *He is a comedian.*

"I have brought you a sandwich. If you don't show your head I may put it in the wrong boat and it will be food for the seagulls."

"Did you bring a cookie? And a carton of juice?"

"I'll play a game with him now for his joking," whispered the old man as he held up a cell phone.

"You sent a text asking for a sandwich. I've brought a sandwich."

There were three boats tied to the jetty. A hand holding a smart phone popped up in the middle boat.

"I sent you a second text. Come look."

There you are, the old man thought. *You will reveal yourself for something sweet.* He made a grand gesture of looking at his phone and shook his head.

"*Sandwich* is the only message I have. Oh wait. Here is another just coming in now. It says: Y*our wireless bill is ready for viewing*."

Now two hands flew up over the gunwales in a gesture of despair followed by a spontaneous discharge of hysterical laughter.

"Old Gellato, YOU are the comedian. You always call me a comedian but it's you. I'm just a poor imitation."

A small boy sat up in the middle boat. "Yes, it's all your fault."

He gulped for air and finally calmed his crazy laughter. Sitting in the bottom he appeared tiny, his thin shoulders just visible over the side and only when the boat tilted with his movement. His hair was thick and black and cut down to the nubs so it almost appeared to be painted on. A black pair of glasses with frames too long for his face held tight against the bridge of his nose, pulled by an elastic strap attached to the arms that protruded past the back of his head. Gellato followed the dock to the boat and reached in his bag.

"Here is your sandwich and juice and two cookies." He hovered over the boat where books of various shapes and sizes were spread across the bottom. "I guess I'll have to just stand here all day."

"Ha!" said Carlo. He moved some of the books to make room and piled several to make a seat.

"Here, Papa. You can sit on Franz Kafka."

"As long as he doesn't mind."

"Oh no. He's quite used to it." the boy laughed.

Papa slowly lowered his bottom onto the stack of books and sat with his hands folded in front of him until he felt settled in and balanced. The boat rocked gently with sporadic taps against the pier as Carlo took a sip of his juice. Papa put his hands on his knees and leaned forward.

"I believe your mother is angry with me," he said.

Carlo frowned as he unwrapped his sandwich.

"What's the matter?" Papa said, "I made it the way you always like it."

"The sandwich is the best, Papa. You could be sandwich maker to the angels. But what's this about my mother being angry? Not that that would be anything new."

"Don't talk that way about your mother." Papa's eyebrows raised, the left one higher than the right, as he tilted his head to the side. Carlo halted the sandwich's approach to his mouth and lowered it to his lap.

"Yes, Papa. I'm sorry."

"Maybe you've been reading too much of this Kafka."

"Oh no. Mr. K would never be so bold. He's not like me at all. Why, if he spoke that way he would be tortured by guilt and maybe throw himself into the lagoon, or allow someone else to push him in. I feel sorry for him. He must not have been a very happy man. Happy people don't write like he did."

"Then why do you read his books? Isn't the real world sad and mad enough?"

Carlo took his first bite of the sandwich and stopped chewing to smile.

"Good sandwich, Papa. And that's just the point."

Papa chuckled quietly. "Yes. Nothing is more soothing than good food, even if it's just a slice of meat stuck inside a day-old roll."

"With avocado, tomato, salt and pepper and olive oil," Carlo laughed. "But Kafka. I mean, the whole point is that the world is sad and mad, but I say beat back the sadness and madness with a simple, thick, crunchy crust that's all soft, salty, and sweet inside, if you have the spirit for it." He took another bite of the sandwich and held it up. "See?" He giggled so mightily that he almost dropped the morsel out of his mouth. Papa shivered and clutched his belly with crossed arms, trying to hold his laughing, sore old body together.

"Hard on the outside, soft on the inside," he said. "I don't know that you're simply a comedian. Maybe more a poet."

"Or a Court Jester," Carlo smiled then frowned, "but then again. Tell me Papa, is it possible to be King and Court Jester, all at the same time?"

"Maybe the King of Comedy. If anyone can be such a person it's my Carlo."

"I suppose I could be. But I would always be talking to myself and saying clever things with hidden and deep meanings. Oh God!" He stopped abruptly. "What if I can't understand myself?"

Papa bellowed and winced as Carlo shook the boat with his laughter such that the water by the gunwales slapped and frothed against the weathered wood and small droplets leaped up into Carlo's and Gellato's hair. When the two of them finally calmed down Carlo poked his fingers into the bubbly water.

"You should be paid for making bubbles," Gellato said. "You would be the world's richest boy."

Gellato paused and gazed out over the still water as if looking for something.

"Did I ever tell you the story of our lagoon?" he said.

Carlo fought the urge to smile and instead raised his eyebrows and shook his head.

"No, Papa. What about our lagoon?"

He had heard the story many times before but he loved hearing it almost as much as Gellato loved telling it

"You see the cliffs, how they rise all around us? They are but remnants of a vast mountain that stood majestically in this place. A mountain that stretched as far as you could see in both directions, and almost twice as tall. The old ones told of it."

"There are just the cliffs now, and this lagoon," Carlo said. "What did the old ones say?"

Gellato raised his arm slowly and pointed.

"I know you've seen the bubbles out there. You always smile about the bubbles."

"They sing to me, Papa. Like Elvis."

Gellato laughed.

"Comedian. The bubbles are telling a story. The old ones spoke down the generations that yes, here was once a mountain, but not an ordinary mountain."

Carlo leaned forward, smiling, and spoke in a low, slow, quivering voice.

"What kind of mountain? Was it snow-capped even in the summer? Did it float above the water? Did it spit fire and grumble with anger and toss great marshmallow plumes into the sky?"

Gellato frowned.

"I've told you the story before."

"No, Papa. That's just something I saw in a movie. Now tell me what the old ones said."

"Here," Gellato said, "many generations ago; maybe thousands of years ago; perhaps many, many thousands of years ago; stood a great volcano; the biggest any human had ever seen or ever will see. The people living in the land surrounding it believed it was a god that would protect them and, truthfully, there were those with evil intent who, when they spied it from afar, would shudder at the sight. And when it deigned to belch a flame or shake the land with its roar they dropped their weapons, filled their pantaloons, and scattered to the four winds. In this way, the people lived in peace."

"What a beautiful story, Papa," Carlo blinked as if amazed. "But what about the lagoon?"

"I wasn't finished," he shook his head and gently pinched Carlo's chin.

"One day, long ago, the impossible happened: a miracle encased in a tragedy. The volcano pulsed and crackled and shook and blew its summit straight up into the sky. Hot lava like the blood of Satan poured out and raced down the slopes toward the fields of wheat, threatening to burn it all as it rolled over. There was smoke and ash to blind the highest soaring eagles and the earth began to break asunder and lava rivers smashed and burned their way towards the nearby villages leaving nothing in their wake."

Carlo clapped his hands to the sides of his head, his twinkling eyes struggling to fill with feigned terror.

"The people! What happened to the people?"

"Ah, here lies the miracle. A fierce storm was barreling ashore from the Adriatic: a hurricane! An event so rare the people saw it as an omen. For days before the terrible event, the fisherman told of the churning waters too far out to view from the shore and the sound of the wind that frightened them into leaving the fish for another day and seeking shelter for their boats. Once the people saw the unnatural waves crashing up the face of the mountain and the dark clouds blasting across the sky in the distance they took their families and their livestock and headed inland. Then the storm pounced with all its fury."

"And it put out the fires?"

"It did much more than that. The torrents of water washed the smoke and ash right out of the sky and the terrible winds blew it all into the throat of the volcano where the rain mixed with the magma deep in its belly. Instead of lava flowing from the fissures there were giant blasts of steam that cut the base of the mountain like wild, boiling axes; backwards bolts of lightning that chopped the great stone edifice into little pieces. The once mighty mountain of rock became quivering jelly that collapsed straight down into the depths. Thus were the people saved by a hurricane. But their mountain was gone. In its place became what you see now: this pink half crater that is mostly lagoon."

"Wow. What an amazing tale," Carlo said as he opened one of his juices, took a sip, and blew over the bottle's opening making a hooting sound. "So is the volcano dead now?"

"That's the funny thing. No. It's asleep. The bubbles you see once in a while are the buried mountain snoring. But over the centuries, in its slumber, it protected the people still, even to this day. The fire still burns deep in the earth."

Carlo turned away for a moment as if he heard something, then shook his head and turned back to his grandfather. Gellato hadn't noticed and continued.

"When the storm had passed and the people returned, they were astonished to see the mountain had disappeared. They were further baffled by the sight of the pink stone rising to the sky. It took a long time before they found the concealed fissure that led to the other side, to the lagoon, and wondered at the thick mist hanging over it. Out there, what we call the breakwater, is part of the rim that was left behind after the mountain collapsed into the hole that filled with sea water. The stones there should have been pounded into dust by the waves long ago, except that the volcano, even in its dream state, constantly rebuilds the wall that protects its slumber; rebuilds it with molten rock."

"And the waves crash against the hot rocks and turn into steam."

Gellato frowned. "I've told you this story before."

"Oh no," said Carlo, holding back a giggle. "I read it in a book of folk tales from Bali."

Gellato scratched the back of his neck.

"Bali," he said. "You must either be the most well-read person in history or else the biggest liar."

"Tough choice," Carlo laughed. "I'll have to think about it." But something in the distance grabbed Carlo's attention. He hesitated, then turned his ear toward the breakwater.

"So, about your mother," Gellato lifted his hands to his forehead, trying to remember something, then blurted out "Yes! Yes! I almost forgot. A man was looking for you yesterday." He stopped suddenly when Carlo motioned to be quiet and put a finger up to his lips.

"They've come again," Carlo said.

ENTRY ONE:
CARLO'S BOAT

Chapter 2: An Interruption

The Sam Ham Show:

- News "Commentator": Sam Ham
- Guest 1: Creese Melonchop,
- Guest 2: Engelsberto Berardi,
- Guest 3: Priscilla "Smarty" Panczsisnowski.

SAM: Our top story tonight has to do with one question: who is behind the recent worldwide rash of terrorist attacks? Attacks that have left scores of people dead or injured, entire towns in ruins, and horrifically slowed down the internet in isolated spots everywhere! Our guests tonight who will be discussing this mystery are Creese Melonchop, Chief Investigator for "The March of Realistic Truth" internet news site, a regular on this show. Creese, good to have you back.

CREESE: Really, Sam, I never left.

SAM: Ha-ha. Always the wit. In the middle is a newcomer to our show, Engelsberto Berardi, Professor of Conspiracy Theories and Chair of the Political Science Department at "Phelony Phonix On-Line University."

Welcome Engels. May I call you Engels?

BERT: I prefer Bert. Engels has a slightly unsavory tinge to it.

SAM: Oh, goodness! I'm blushing pink. Won't make that mistake again. Finally we have Priscilla "Smarty" Panczsisnowski, a commentator from a rival network who we bring on when we want to show the world we are fair and balanced. Just kidding. Smarty's new book, "There Is No Whatever There!" premiered at number nine on the New York Times Best Seller List and is disappearing from the shelves like paint chips at a consumer home show. Haven't seen you in a while and I always enjoy your insights. Plus I get to call you "Smarty".

PRISCILLA: I really wish you wouldn't.

SAM: Well that's a discussion for another show. Right now, in case you, my loyal viewers, are still hiding under a rock, I'll explain what's going on here. First, I remind you that you can instantly post your comments on my twitter feed: @SHAM#terror. OK. In the last 6 months there have been an inordinate...... I'm sorry, a whole bunch of unclaimed terrorist attacks around the globe. No-one seems to have any idea who is responsible (raises one eyebrow) or why. That is, until this morning. An astounding discovery was revealed on Creese's website that........well, I'll let Creese tell you about it.

CREESE: Thanks Sam. As you know we employ only the best investigators...

SAM: Who are not journalists so they only deal in facts.

CREESE: That goes without saying. We use mainly our thoughts about facts and we control them, unlike other so-called news sites. Anyway, when we looked at what's been happening it seemed very strange to us that no group or organization came forward to claim responsibility because usually these people are publicity hounds who will do or say absolutely anything to attract hits, get on the air, or even get booked on your show.

SAM: And that's not the case here.

CREESE: Right. So we began to look into the possibility that it isn't a group or organization at all, but a force the likes of which we have never seen before.

SAM: A force? How intriguing. You're not going to tell us it's space aliens or anything like that are you?

BERT: Can I jump in here?

SAM: Not yet. Go ahead, Creese.

CREESE: No. No aliens of any kind. We only deal reality. Through our various sources in the deep state and on the dark web, we've been piecing together a clear enough picture to come up with what we believe is a solid and compelling conjecture. We know we're on the right track because when we posted it this morning we got an overwhelming response on social media as well as directly on our unmediated covert contact pipelines. You don't get responses like this unless you have something.

SAM: I'd say the suspense is killing me but I saw your feed as soon as you posted and I responded immediately. I was dumbstruck......Sorry for interrupting. Go on, Creese. Our audience must be about to burst, I know I am.

CREESE: Bear with me here because this is going to take some time to explain. Here's the logic: if it's not a group or an organization; if it's not one of the many terrorist governments in this world; if it's not anyone out of this world – for example extraterrestrials; and if it's not Yahweh, Alah, Buddha, Zeus, or any other god;.....then.....IT MUST BE SOMETHING UNEXPLAINABLE, UNEXPECTED, and INCONCEIVABLE.

SAM: Wow. Can you elaborate on that? I mean explain that to our audience?

PRISCILLA: Can I just say something?

SAM: Not now, Smarty. Why don't you talk to Bert? Creese, continue, buddy. Explain.

CREESE: It's really obvious if you think about it and any intelligent person couldn't possibly miss the potency of it. If it's none of those things I mentioned before then it must be.......someone.

SAM: It must be someone. This is a revelation. Tell us, Creese. Do you have any idea who that "someone" is??

CREESE: Carlo.

SAM: Carlo.

CREESE: Carlo.

SAM: Incredible. You already have a name. What do you know about this Carlo?

CREESE: Our evidence points to him being a reclusive, invisible, billionaire and possibly the richest man in history since it appears that money is no object when it comes to his evil machinations.

SAM: You mean his plans.

CREESE: Yes. Unfortunately for us, his plans. We're not sure yet of his ultimate goal but one thing we know for certain: we believe he intends to use his money to cause as much disruption as possible in order to eventually install himself as Supreme Leader of the World, establish a global Lib-tard government, and promote the general chaos to ourselves and our prosperity.

SAM: I didn't catch that in your post this morning. Is there more to this than you have yet revealed? Because, actually, it sounds like you have a very good idea of what his aims are.

CREESE: Well, I got a little carried away there. These are merely extrapolations from the evidence we already have. But we are certain the path leads somewhere.

SAM: Tell us about the evidence. I'm on the edge of my seat.

CREESE: We have solid, huge, physical evidence that will prove our conjecture beyond any shadow of any doubt.

SAM: I can't hold it any longer, Creese. That evidence is?

CREESE: (pauses dramatically) That evidence is......Carlo's boat.

SAM: Wow, folks. This is turning out to be much bigger than I imagined when I pre-planned this show at the last minute. We have to go to break right now, at least I do, but I know for sure that I'll be coming back to hear more of this. You all come back now too. Unbelievable!

COMMERCIAL: *There's so much happening in the world today that it's almost impossible to keep up. Information blasts you at the speed of light and it seems like everybody knows something you don't. "My Ideas Magazine and Podcast" has the answer. That's right, 12 monthly issues and or digital pods jam-packed with short, easy to remember thoughts, concepts, beliefs, and opinions, grouped alphabetically and ready for your use anyplace, anytime. You never have to feel inadequate, uneducated, or stupid again. Your first year subscription starts with the letter "a" and continues on through "b", "c", "d", "e", "f" all the way to "l". If you decide to renew, "My Ideas" will keep coming until you're through the entire alphabet. As a subscriber you can download our app free and have original thoughts at your fingertips at a moment's notice. Cancel anytime if you're not satisfied. Hurry, and you'll also receive our annual swimsuit issue.*

SAM: Welcome back. I feel relieved, if you know what I mean. But before we get back to our guests I want you to check out this video posted a couple of days ago on the PPOnlineU website. Take a look.

(SHAKY HAND-HELD SMART PHONE VIDEO)

BILLY: My name is Billy. I'm an amateur professional investigator and news intern at the "Seeing Is Believing" online documentary film school at PPU. I'm whispering because I don't want to disturb the fish. And also, I'm not supposed to be here. This island is restricted to residents only. Anyway, what you're looking at here...

(Video of what appears to be a very old man sitting on the shore of a lagoon holding a primitive fishing pole. He hardly moves except to occasionally swat at insects buzzing around his head.)

BILLY: (continues)...is the only official inhabitant of this island who blindfolded me and took me through some kind of cave, at least it echoed like a cave, to this spot and may be the only person known to have actually seen THE BOAT – Carlo's boat. We are somewhere on a tiny atoll off the Adriatic coast of Italy between Rimini and Ravenna, an area infamous for being almost near the birthplace of the famous Benito Mussolini. The water just off this bank is extremely deep and drops off over 600 feet within meters of the shore. As I pan right you can see the dense fog here this morning and you can just about make out what appears to be a wooden dock stretching out into the mist. The man you see fishing says his name is Gellato. What led me to his exact location was a video he posted on Instagram only a few hours ago, taken with his cell phone.

Gellato's VIDEO: shows the water covered in a thick mist and silhouetted against the fog-bound rising sun. Hundreds of feet down the shoreline there appears to be a dock stretching out into the fog bank; a dark object, almost invisible, bobbing up and down next it. The picture is distorted by what must be mist on the phone's camera lens.

BILLY: I was able to convince him to speak to me earlier before he became suspicious and took me away again blindfolded. His story is astounding.

Video of Gellato with fog-shrouded water behind him.

GELLATO: I posted the picture of the boat because I thought it was pretty, and because my daughter-in-law might be worried and because she would know I was fishing.

BILLY: Did you actually see the boat?

GELLATO: There are three boats I can see. Do you mean the boat in the picture?

BILLY: Yes, the boat in the video. Can you describe it for me?

GELLATO: It floats on the water.

BILLY: Yes. But what does it look like.

GELLATO: Hoho. It's big. A big boat. I used to rent them out to locals who fancied themselves fisherman but the mist frightened them and they disappeared.

BILLY: The boats?

GELLATO: No the fisherman. You can see the boats can't you? They are so big.

BILLY: How big?

GELLATO: I don't have a boat that big. The lagoon is sleepy but the breakwater......

BILLY: How big?

(Gellato places his hands about six inches apart and as he speaks, slowly widens out until his arms are straight out from his sides.)

GELLATO: It was thiiiiiiiiiiiiiiiiiiiis big.

BILLY: Wow.

GELLATO: Big wow. Madonne! So big yet it is tiny compared to the ocean...(unintelligible)...... just like a little boy. He is dwarfed by the mountain but doesn't know to be afraid.

BILLY: Whatever. You say you think you saw someone in the boat. Could you see any of their features? Height, weight, color? Long or short hair? A beard? Mustache?

GELLATO: I know what he looks like.

BILLY: But can you tell me......

GELLATO: He is Carlo.

BILLY: Carlo! You've seen Carlo? How do you know?

GELLATO: I know his name. He comes here to hide. He keeps his boat here.

BILLY: Here in the bay?

GELLATO: Apparently you are the antonym of intelligence. Who are you?

BILLY: Thank you. I have a 4.0 grade point average and will graduate soon. But could you please elaborate? This is so very important.

GELLATO: I must fish now.

BILLY: But you posted the video.

GELLATO: I must fish.

(BILLY TURNS THE CAMERA ON HIMSELF)

BILLY: Wow. Suddenly he seems scared. I'm scared! I need to get out of here but there's only one way back to the mainland and.....

THE LIVE STREAM CUTS OFF.
(BACK TO THE SAM HAM SHOW)

SAM: I'm with you on that. Wow! I wonder if our next guest had anything to do with that investigator being out there. What do you have to say about this, Bert?

BERT: Young Mr. Dew was.....

SAM: Mr. Dew?

BERT: Yes, Billy Dew. One of my online students. I sent him to that region days ago.

SAM: Days ago?

BERT: I am well aware of your favoritism toward regular guests and your tendency to believe totally in their veracity and sometimes, shall we say, dark methods. But that is neither here nor there. I've been trying to get on your show – any show for that matter – for several days now.

SAM: Bert, I apologize for...whatever.

PRISCILLA: Can I say something now? That's actually part of my book's title.

CREESE: What a hypocrite! How would you like it if Sam interrupted you like that?

PRISCILLA: I haven't been able to get a word in.

SAM: Ok. Ok. Smarty we'll get to you, I promise.

PRISCILLA: I told you about that "smarty" stuff.

CREESE: Now what? Is Sam discriminating against you? Are you under attack from the patriarchy right here on live TV?

SAM: Creese, buddy, I love you, but let's get back to this story. And Smarty, hang on, I'll get to you.

PRISCILLA: Truer words hast thou never spoken..

BERT: May I continue? Mr. Melonchop claims credit for breaking this story when, truthfully, there have been rumors running rampant for almost a week now. At first I considered it absurd that one man could be the instigator of, and financier for, so much carnage, and on such a vast scale. Nothing was known about this man or even if he really existed, other than reports of this boat. That is, until the video you saw at the beginning of this segment, posted by the supposed "old fisherman" Gellato; obviously a code name. What I am about to show you proves not only that Gellato's video is accurate, but that the story goes far deeper than anyone could imagine.

CREESE: We uncovered this thing from day one. Nobody even knew to look for this man until we posted our first verified suspicions.

SAM: Creese, Creese. Let him talk.

BERT. First of all your suspicions and your theory are dead wrong, but more on that later. Now Sam, could you have your people display the photo I brought along. Image number one.

SAM: Ok. This is it? It looks like a bunch of smoke.

BERT: Yes. It is an unprocessed satellite photo of the very Italian coastline and the lagoon where Mr. Gellato supposedly fishes on a daily basis in a lagoon devoid of fish.

SAM: Well, that IS suspicious.

BERT: We've been watching him for a while.

SAM: Why? How? What led you to him, there? This smoke screen?

BERT: One of the members of my conspiracy club is quite adept at sifting through enormous amounts of smart phone data and she discovered traces of deleted texts from a particular smart phone. The texts were addressed to someone entered in the phone's contacts as CRLO and referred to a boat. Unfortunately we could not decipher the messages as they were in some super encrypted code, but it was child's play to identify the owner of the phone and pinpoint the exact geographical location. The phone belonged to one Adamo Gellato at coordinates.......

SAM: That old man on the video!

BERT:..somewhere between Rimini and Ravenna on the Adriatic coast of Italy. Unfortunately the location turned out to be a small, nearly unreachable volcanic atoll. A bay that faces the sea is where we pinged Gellato's phone. This bay, or lagoon, is obscured by a mist that seems to cover it all the time, although it shifts from ground level to as high as the stratosphere and every level in between. In any case it at least partially obscures the view from space pretty much 100 percent of the time. That's why I asked Mr. Dew to go there physically and report back on what he found.

CREESE: You're right, Sam. It's nothing but a bunch of smoke.

BERT: Ah. But please. If you would be so kind as to display the enhanced image....

SAM: Gasp!

BERT: Here you can plainly see the outline of the bay. If we increase magnification you begin to see the dock that was visible in Billy Dew's video. At full magnification...well, Sam, tell me what you see.

SAM: It's difficult to make out but I would say it's a boat. A BOAT!

PRISCILLA: There's no boat there.

CREESE: I can't believe I'm saying this but I have to agree with Smarty. It could be a log, or a whale, or even a shadow.

PRISCILLA: Thanks Creese. And for you, Smarty is ok.

SAM: Well... it looks like, well, maybe not so much a boat but a kayak.

BERT: Let me clear up the mystery somewhat. Please, if you would, display the ultra-enhanced photo.

SAM: My goodness!

BERT: Here you can see that the object most definitely is a small row boat apparently tied to the dock. And there appears to be a human-like figure lying in the bottom of the boat. The face is obscured, however, by what appears to be a rectangular object, possibly even a cloaking device, and is impossible to identify even as to gender.

SAM: It's very pixelated. Almost unearthly.

CREESE: (laughing hysterically) Maybe it IS an extraterrestrial. (Continues laughing.) That little thing is Carlo's boat? I suppose those little fuzzy squares in the bottom are the terrifying Terror-Master Carlo himself!

SAM: I kind of have to agree with Creese, Bert. If this is Carlo's boat I'd have to say, well, I believe I'm pretty underwhelmed.

BERT: And so it appears. But look at this here. There is a long shadow underneath the boat stretching hundreds of feet out to the end of the dock.

SAM: Wouldn't that be the shadow of the dock?

BERT: Look closely. Do you see shadows anywhere else in the image? The mist and fog diffuses the sunlight so nothing in this photo has a shadow.

SAM: What are you saying?

BERT: That this long, dark, area under the little boat is not a shadow at all.

SAM: Then what is it?

BERT: A submarine.

PRISCILLA: Sam, can I just...

SAM: Hold that thought Smarty.

PRISCILLA: No I won't hold it. I've sat here long enough listening to this garbage and I refuse to be silent any longer.

SAM: We'll get to you in a minute. This news is earth-shaking. It's unbelievable.

PRISCILLA: That's the first sensible thing you've said all night. It is unbelievable, inconceivable, and beyond the realm of intelligent inquiry. Here you have a person who is supposedly behind terror attacks perpetrated by radical groups from both extremes of the political spectrum with a name, Carlo, that seems to have been conjured up out of thin air, and you have absolutely no proof that this person even exists or ever existed.

SAM: But Carlo's boat....

BERT: The U-Boat.

PRISCILLA: A shadow wrapped in fog viewed from outer space at such a distance that there are no identifiable markings or features to prove that it's anything but a sand bar sitting under a probably unoccupied little dinghy with the capacity to hold maybe two or three people. This would be the hiding place of the richest man in the world? And where does he live three hundred and sixty-five days out of the year, on the U-Boat? In the dinghy? With Geraldo?

BERT: Gellato.

PRISCILLA: Whatever. He circumcises the world in a boat of some kind without ever steaming into a port anywhere to get fuel and supplies? And where are his billions of dollars? That kind of money can't be hidden for very long. No bank accounts. No property. No friends. No family. And as of this moment NO FACE! Just a conjectural name and a conjured up boat with no real evidence for any of it.

CREESE: There! You've fallen for all the false and misleading information propagated by the One World government. The lack of evidence for all these things proves there is a conspiracy and you're just too blind to see it.

PRISCILLA: Lack of evidence? As the title of my book points out: "There Is No Whatever There."

SAM: Thanks for your insights, Smarty, but we have to go to a break now. We'll be back after these messages from our sponsors.

PRISCILLA: Get your filthy hands off of me........

COMMERCIAL: (A bearded man dressed in a flowing white robe walks within a room full of computers with people frantically working at the keyboards.)

BEARDED MAN: Are you worried about the hereafter? Well, who isn't? And with the world being the way it is today, with all the violence and murder at your doorstep, you may be getting there sooner than you think. That's why you should listen carefully to what I am about to say. I have good news. At Apocalypse Dow, our supercomputer analysis of all known religious works from around the world proves conclusively that everything you possess on your personal final expiration date you may keep with you in the afterlife. Yes, it's true. You CAN take it with you! And the spiritual stock brokers and Armageddon arbitragers at Apocalypse Dow will help you prepare your portfolio for your glorious infinity in paradise. We'll even show you how to maximize your eternity should the Judgment Day come before you leave this mortal coil. With your A.D. account you get a personal Supernatural CPA to guide you on your journey with advice like:

- What types of investments now will serve you best on the other side.
- How to make your heavenly wealth transfer without losing a penny.
- And how to profit from the coming holocaust.

Just call the number on your screen to book your first consultation. The first phone call is free. We're so sure you'll love our system that we extend to you a thirty day, money back guarantee. Call now and get our weekly newsletter for half price. Order in the next five minutes and receive a free copy of our swimsuit issue! Remember:

YOU CAN TAKE IT WITH YOU!
And we'll show you how!
Call now.
Apocalypse Dow!

SAM: Welcome back to our rather heated discussion. Priscilla "Smarty" Panczsisnowski had to leave to get to another place but we still have Creese Melonchop and Bert Berardi here with some final words on this continuing search for the elusive Carlo and, more importantly, Carlo's boat. Creese, could you summarize your evidence for us.

CREESE: I sure can, and at the same time address the misleading allegations of your departed guest, "Not So Smarty." First of all, as anyone who knows anything about conspiracies can attest: evidence is routinely hidden or destroyed by the secret powers to cover themselves and their hidden agenda. So, the fact that there are no facts, that there is no evidence, points incontrovertibly to the existence of something they don't want us to see or know about.

SAM: But what about this boat? People have seen it. Now they have seen the video and I'll bet it was instantaneously shared around the world within seconds.

CREESE: Who is to say that this is the actual boat? From what I understand, as we speak, reports are coming in from around the world of possible sightings. For all we know there may be more than one boat. But one thing is for certain: when we find the real boat, we find Carlo.

SAM: Wow. Bert, sum up your findings in 30 seconds or less. No No! Wait a minute! I just received a series of tweets from the POTUS himself and he asked me to read them to my audience. He says, and this is straight from the horse's mouth: "I have ordered all of our wonderful intelligence agencies to drop all other activities around the world and concentrate on this awful and embarrassing Carlo criminal. We will do this our great selves and to hell with our supposed allies who don't pull their own weight anyway. I am directing the Seventh Fleet immediately into the...into that sea next to Italy. This horrible, horrible, man, and he is a disgrace, this murderer will be caught in the most beautiful trap net the world has ever seen."

BERT: Ha.

SAM: Bert, what do you mean?

BERT: They are too late. (looking down at his Y-Pad) The latest satellite surveillance shows the u-boat has spirited away.

SAM: You mean...

BERT: Don't you know that a sophisticated, magical ship such as this has the means to detect approaching forces from anywhere in the globe? Perhaps, as I mentioned before, he even possesses a cloaking device. What we know for sure is that it is not there. Good luck ever finding it now.

SAM: I've got one more tweet from the POTUS: "I heard what that fake intellectual just said, but mark my words: with fire and fury we will destroy Carlo, fire and fury like has never been witnessed since the beginning of time and most importantly, and I mean this sincerely, we will turn Carlo's boat into Carlo's driftwood."

(DRAMATIC PAUSE)

SAM: And thus spake the POTUS. Good night, Sir. I know I feel safer thanks to you. My thanks to Creese Melonchop and Engelsberto Berardi for their unbelievable input,...and "Smarty." Tune in tomorrow for more on this incredible story.

(DRAMATIC MUSIC AND FADE TO BLACK)

ENTRY ONE: CARLO'S BOAT

Chapter 3: The Lagoon Again

Gellato stood up to better see what Carlo was talking about. Carlo was looking toward the breakwater but felt the boat shake and turned around.

"No, Papa. Stay down. Stay down. Listen."

Gellato strained to hear but the waves smashing against the rocks overwhelmed his ears. He thought he saw something moving so he tapped Carlo on the shoulder and pointed toward the sky. An object was swaying and lurching in the winds above the rocks.

"I think I see it," he said as Carlo turned and held him by the shoulders.

"Papa, get in the boat."

"But we are in the boat."

"The one under the dock."

An identical row boat swayed gently under the old wooden structure. Carlo fished a rope out of the water and pulled it closer.

"Get in, Papa, get in."

Gellato slid into the boat headfirst to avoid using his gimpy leg. Carlo scrambled after him and nudged the craft until it was completely underneath.

"How long have you had this here?" Gellato said.

"Since the Truant Officer began looking for me."

"That reminds me. About your mother. She is very upset with me. She thinks I am keeping you from school."

"Not now, please Papa. Let's watch the helicopter." He held his smart phone out just far enough to capture the approaching machine. "It's really entertaining how they try to defeat the updraft at the barrier wall."

"They've been here before?" Gellato leaned forward and stared at the image on the screen. The helicopter approached slowly. He could see a man leaning out of the bubble holding something in his hand.

"What's he holding there? I see a man holding something."

"Maybe it's a machine gun."

Gellato jumped and hit his head on the planks above.

"Why? What do they want, to kill us now?"

As the helicopter approached the mouth of the lagoon it started to sway violently and to jostle up and down. Still, the pilot tried to fight through the turbulence. The man hanging out of the side almost dropped what was in his hands but a strap attached to his wrist held it dangling a few feet below the skids. He gestured violently at the pilot whose reflective headgear traced his equally violent reaction.

"It's a camera, Papa," Carlo laughed. "They're trying to take movies. Like the man you talked to yesterday."

"But again? Why? I told you everything he said and how weirdly he behaved." He paused and tilted his head. "I talked to him like an old philosopher in a bad movie. You're right. I'm a comedian, too. But what do you make of all this? I can't make sense of it, can you?"

"Why would it have to make sense?"

Gellato paused. He drew his smart phone out of his pocket and tapped it a few times. The display flashed on and videos from his news feed cascaded across the screen: wars, murders, famines, reality shows, unreality news networks, and the world leadership freak show.

"You have a point," he said.

"Do you think he'll make it this time? I actually wish he would so we can get a better look at them."

"I'm not one to make wagers, but if he can keep control I bet he will surely enter our gentle lagoon and find safe haven. Maybe then we can reason with them. They may know of the bizarre events of the last few days and give us some answers."

Carlo turned and looked at Gellato. *He is so much of the old school,* he thought. He remembered his mother telling him about the day his own father disappeared over the breakwater, his boat crushed by the obsidian and basalt, and how Papa rowed out one of the old boats like an Olympian and smashed back at the waves over and over until his strength ran out, then made a bowline out of the mooring rope and threw like a cowboy and lassoed a stone, pulling himself against the tide until he finally stood for a moment on the black and pink rampart, searching in vain for any sign of his son-in-law. The next wave blasted him backwards unconscious into the froth at the lagoon's mouth and somehow the bubbles carried him and he floated back to the shore.

"Yes, Papa," Carlo said. "That would be good."

The helicopter backed off and stabilized. With a roar it shot straight upward. At first the ascent was clean and straight but as it got higher it began to lurch in all directions. At one point it spun completely around then began to slowly descend until it returned to the altitude where it had started. Turning away from the lagoon it sped away until it became a shiny pinhead in the sky.

"This one is braver than the last one," Carlo said. "But still he can't conquer the mighty lagoon. Ya ha!"

He fiddled with his phone. "I think I got it all. The whole thing. I might go back to school just to show the class."

Gellato raised his eyebrows and pointed at the boy.

"You should go back to school. The police came and bothered your mother about it."

"Did they arrest her? Tell me they didn't."

"No. She told them you disappeared without telling her where you were going. *How could that happen?* they said. To which she replied, *Talk to his grandfather.*"

"They didn't arrest you, then. You come here every day."

"I told them I see that you're safe and you have food. I tell them you're studying with the same teacher Abraham Lincoln had and they don't laugh. But I did. They must have thought I was insane and couldn't believe a word I said because they marched away without me. I almost wish they had taken me."

"No. I can't be here without you."

"And that's what your mother thinks; that it's my fault you don't go to school. She informed me of this as she beat me with a wet mop. I was lucky to get out without serious injury. Had I gone to the hospital they might have locked me up there. Many people in town think I'm out of my mind already including some of the doctors."

Gellato placed his hands lightly on both sides of the boy's head.

"It's time to go to your mother. She's worried sick and you know she is in delicate health. And I," he twisted his neck until it popped. "And I can't be in two places at once."

In the distance a roar like an explosion rocked the cliff sides followed by a hellish screeching as the helicopter's rotors spun into invisibility. The crazed machine charged like a bull with its front tilted down, a trail of smoke whooshing behind it, and a swirling ridge of water being pushed before it. Carlo grabbed Gellato and covered his chest with his own body in the bottom of the boat.

"What is it, Carlo?"

"The final attack."

ENTRY ONE:
CARLO'S BOAT

Chapter 4: Mongoose and The "Bomb"

H.E.N. Standard Intro:
Harold Mongoose Investigates,
Season 22, Episode 6 - "Live" "Who Is Carlo?"
Narrator/On Camera Talent/Director/Star – Harold
(also featured: Jerry "Jerry Bomb" Chamberlain)

INSERT INTRO: (DRAMATIC VOICE-OVER) *Tonight the master Mongoose investigates the mysterious, the unexplained and the unbelievable, as the History and Education Network presents: "Who Is Carlo?"*

(CRASHING HEAVY METAL MUSIC and CUT TO HAROLD - In front of a helicopter with blades churning).

HAROLD: Forget about just the "Who?" I'll expose the "Who?", the "Where?" and even the "Why?" So stay with me. The whole world is watching!

(HEAVY METAL TAG and OUT.)

(INSERT PROMO:)
DRAMATIC INTRO VOICE-OVER, SERIOUS AVANT GARDE MUSIC: *On the next "Alien Gourmet", Adelaide Chesnochny investigates the mysterious origins of garlic.*

(ADELAIDE STANDING WITH PROFESSOR ENG.)

ADELAIDE: "So these are the cave carvings?"

(CARVINGS OF WHAT APPEAR TO BE GARLIC CLOVES)

ENG: "These could possibly be over 100,000 years old."

(ADELAIDE APPEARS AMAZED).

ADELAIDE: That would mean that it came from somewhere or someone other than humans. But how?

(DRAMATIC INTRO VOICE-OVER) *Find out tomorrow at 8, on the History and Education Network.*

Harold Mongoose hopped into the passenger side of the two-seater scout helicopter. The pilot, Jerry "Jerry Bomb" Chamberlain, completed his final checks as Harold consulted his notes and checked that his camera communicated with the cellular uplink pod fastened to the ceiling behind them.

Jerry finished his procedures, stared at the camera, and spoke directly into Harold's face.

"That thing's not going to be on the whole time is it?"

"Of course not. We'll be going 'live' when I say we go 'live' unless you have some objection?"

"No..."

"Good. Let's get something straight: the first pilot I had was an uncooperative chicken shit. Just as we were about to hit pay dirt he turned back, the scared little rabbit, while I was on the air, no less, and I can assure you it was embarrassing. It was manna from heaven for all the late night comedians with their phony talk shows and all the twitter twerps and Facebook phonies. So if you have a problem with this mission or following my orders speak now or forever shut up and do what you're told. This is reality TV and the more real the better."

Jerry laughed and moved his face closer still. "I will do anything within reason and some things beyond reason if I think my machine can take it. Remember: I AM the 'Bomb'. But let's cut the crap. If it's so damned real why do you have a script?"

Harold smirked. "You don't expect me to wing it completely, do you?

Of course I have an agenda; a plan. After all, I am bringing the truth to the world." He threw his head back and roared with laughter. "Now let's get this show in the air. Do we understand each other Mr. Bomb?"

By way of responding Jerry pulled back on the throttle and the helicopter shot into the air. The sudden movement caused Harold to drop the camera and his papers on the floor.

"You idiot. Trying to prove something?"

"Just following orders."

The helicopter took off from a small airfield about twenty miles north of the target. As with the previous attempt, local authorities had denied a request to fly over land because of the number of towns along the route, the roughness of the terrain, the perpetual dangerous air currents, and the fog. They had no choice but to approach from the ocean side. At their altitude they could see great detail of the houses, beaches and boats along the shore until they were only minutes away from their destination. There, the shoreline disappeared in a featureless cloud with only the tops of surrounding cliffs visible.

"Very interesting. Doesn't show up in my navigation." said Jerry as he brought the helicopter lower.

"Fog, mist, ocean spray. Might as well have been a brick wall. I told you about the air currents surrounding the lagoon."

Jerry flipped a switch and a screen on the control panel lit up with murky, poorly defined shapes.

"Radar doesn't penetrate. Not very well anyway."

"The whole area looks like a squashed marshmallow floating on the water, even from the damned military satellites. We can't see anything and won't see anything until we're right on top of it."

Jerry smiled. "On top of what?"

The helicopter jolted to the right. Harold clutched his camera to his chest.

"Damn. I hope you know what you're doing."

Jerry reacted quickly and steadied the aircraft.

"Don't sweat it," he said.

Harold held out a stick with the camera fastened to a movable ball mount on the end. He straightened out his head gear and moistened his lips with his tongue.

"Master control, do you have me?" He nodded his head as someone responded in his headset. "All right. We're ready to go live. Give me a countdown."

Jerry attempted to say something but Harold snarled and waved him off. His face broke into a smile, not too jolly, not too serious – just right.

"This is Harold Mongoose in the air over a silent, shrouded piece of rock; a small island, at least I hope there's an island down there, that may hold the answer to one of the world's most pressing questions."

He turned a knob on the handle that spun the camera as he panned the stick out the open side of the cockpit.

"We're now approaching the area in question. E.T.A in less than a minute."

"Swinging around," Jerry said.

Harold held tight to the stick and guided the camera for a smooth movement as the helicopter turned and pointed toward the fog. The helicopter jolted backward then steadied.

"You can see what we're up against," Harold spoke into his headset. "Horrific turbulence. Can't see a thing. But you can hear the roar below us. I'm talking as loud as I can and you can probably barely hear me. Whatever is making that fearsome noise is obviously something monstrous. No, not like Godzilla, but a genuine monstrosity of nature that could smash us to bits for real; much worse than any movie behemoth."

He paused to let his audience hear the sea crashing on the breakers.

"We will now prepare for our approach which is not as simple as it sounds. The topography here is so unnatural that the winds alone are capable of utterly destroying our aircraft. We'll take a break to compose ourselves, make a final equipment check, and maybe say a little prayer as we gear up to descend into the maelstrom. This is Harold Mongoose. Don't go away."

He clicked a button on the camera stick and turned to Jerry.

"If you screw this up I will see that you lose your license and become, forever, a pariah of infamous proportions. This event is 'live' worldwide. A lot of money is riding on this not to mention my career."

"Don't you care about what you're going to find, if anything?"

"It doesn't matter. Whatever I find I will make into the most incredible, stupendous, mysterious and ultimately world-shaking thing the world has ever seen, even if, no, especially if it's not."

Jerry shook his head and peered into the mist in front of him as Harold held up his hand for silence.

"All right," Harold said. "We're back and ready. Hold onto your seats because what's on the other side of this fog may be the man the entire world has been searching for: the elusive Carlo."

He turned to Jerry. "Let's do it."

Jerry revved the engines and the helicopter careened into the whiteness. Violent air currents tugged and pushed the craft, shaking it like a toy such that Harold lost his grip on the stick and the camera and stick fell toward the roiling waves below. Jerry wrenched the helicopter upwards and backed away from the turbulence. Harold pulled back on his wrist strap and screamed into his headset.

"I almost lost the camera. Can't you even fly this thing?"

He pulled on a rope that was tied to the camera stick and held it in front of his face.

"Yes, my audience, that must have been some wild footage you just saw. Almost lost the camera and if I hadn't been strapped in I'd have fallen right after it."

Jerry gunned the rotor and the helicopter shot straight up so rapidly that the g-force almost caused Harold to drop the camera again. He was about to scream at Jerry but composed himself.

"Our pilot is about to give it another try. I told him before we embarked on this journey that I would not be defeated again."

He turned the camera to show their rapid ascent to a point above the thickest of the mist. The pink cliffs came into view when suddenly the helicopter was tossed in every direction, went into a dizzying spiral, and bolted to and fro as it rapidly lost altitude. Harold fought to hold the camera steady until Jerry was finally able to regain control.

"Where are we? Are we in? Did we get in?"

Jerry sat motionless in his seat, beads of sweat leaving trails down his cheeks, his teeth clenched, and a wild look in his eye. Before Harold could get another word out Jerry spun the helicopter around and blasted away from the island with such force that the camera became loose on the end of the stick. Harold gripped with both hands as the camera pointed itself forward.

"Dear God this is madness!" he yelled

The helicopter came to a jolting halt and Jerry spun it back around to face the growling, taunting fog bank. The smokey coastline appeared to be at least a mile away. Harold turned the camera on himself.

"I know what this looks like. But we are not giving up. I will not give up if I have to fly this thing myself."

Jerry glanced at Harold. He looked once up at the blue sky and shoved the accelerator to full speed ahead.

"Here we go, people. This is going to be it! Damn you, Carlo. We've got you now!"

ENTRY ONE: CARLO'S BOAT

Chapter 5: History and Education Network "Special Edition"

H.E.N. Standard Intro: Harold Mongoose Investigates, Season 22, Episode 6 - "Live" "Who Is Carlo?"
After promo cut to "Live" in the studio. Host: Celia Trapp

CELIA: Good morning, good afternoon, good evening. I'm Celia Trapp and no matter what your time zone or how you're watching you are in for excitement beyond anything you've ever seen as "Harold Mongoose Investigates" takes you "Live" to a tiny island with enormous significance. By the end of this show you, and the rest of the world will know the answer to the question: "Who Is Carlo?" Harold and his pilot took off moments ago in a high-tech surveillance helicopter and are, at this very moment, approaching the island where it is believed the elusive "Carlo's Boat" is anchored. While we wait for his "live" feed I'm going to play an interview I did with Harold before his departure this morning. Next on "HMI."

Commercial: A MAN IN OVERALLS AND A TEE SHIRT.
Are you out of work? Has your job been 'outsourced' to a computer? Has AUTOMATION brought you CONSTERNATION? Forget about it! You can beat the AI heat and we will help you do it with our 21 part on-line course "I'm A Plumber, so Kiss my AI". You heard that right! Go to "AICantFixNoLeakyToilet.com" to check it out. The course is free, and when you're done, you will be the most sought-after neighborhood technician, the envy of your unemployed friends, and a distinct person of interest to anyone looking to hook up with someone who actually has money in their pocket. You will also have your own set of professional tools and a kit including all the most commonly needed parts like silicon washers, pipe thread tape, and a variety of faucet handles - all available on an easy payment plan.(SMALL PRINT ON THE BOTTOM OF THE SCREEN: Purchase required to register for course. Total cost for tools and kit - $2,999.99, plus shipping)
So what are you waiting for? Go to "AICantFixNoLeakyToilet.com" and sign up today. Register within the next 24 hours and get a free copy of our swimsuit issue.

(CELIA SITTING WITH HAROLD AT AN UNIDENTIFIED HELIPORT. A HELICOPTER SITS IN THE BACKGROUND.)

CELIA: So, Harold, first I have to say I admire your courage. You're willing to risk everything to bring us reality in a big way. I salute you.

HAROLD: Thanks. There's no-one on earth more real than me.

CELIA: Than "I".

HAROLD: Oh really? Let's see you get in a helicopter and battle the worst that nature can throw at you and still win! Let's see you do that.

CELIA: I'm sorry, Harold. Let's move on. What do you expect to accomplish today?

HAROLD: Is there something wrong with you? What's the name of the show? "Who is Carlo?" right? Can't you figure it out from that?

CELIA: I just wanted you to spell it out for our audience.

HAROLD: My people don't need it spelled out. (*looks at camera, sneers, jabs his finger at the lens and growls like a pro wrestler*) Who is Carlo? That's what I'm going to find out. I will stop at nothing to bring you everything you need to know to navigate the twists and turns of this upside-down world. Just watch ME. Just trust ME. I'm a man of my word and that word is ME. Bet on it!

CELIA: Well...

HAROLD: I've got the best helicopter, the best pilot, the best camera; everything the best. All those other phony reality show rodents just sit behind their phony desks and read teleprompters. I'm going out into the nominal world and putting my life on the line. Right people? I want you to go to your windows and yell...

CELIA: Harold. I'm sorry. We only have time for one more question. Why are you approaching this island at its most dangerous part? From what I understand the landward side is calm and placid; perfectly navigable at any time of day.

HAROLD: I can't believe you're even asking that question. Attack by the landward side? That's exactly what Carlo would expect. By the time we crossed the island to the lagoon he would be long gone. These are some of the dumbest questions I've ever been subjected to. Who hired you? What...

(CELIA BACK IN THE STUDIO, LOOKING FRANTIC)

UNIDENTIFIED VOICE OFF CAMERA: What the hell happened?

CELIA: (panicked) We now join Harold Mongoose Investigates live and in progress.

The live image shows the point of view shooting forward. The helicopter is moving at an insane speed hurtling toward a solid wall of swirling fog. Harold's voice can barely be heard over the rushing wind and roaring engines.

HAROLD: (off camera) Here we go, Baby! Take no prisoners!

The helicopter penetrates the fog and the camera appears to be flying around the cabin accompanied by crazily pitch-shifting whooshing sounds and revealing only split second images of bouncing off the instrument panel; the pilot's head crashing into an unidentifiable black box; Harold's shoes; an empty coffee cup careening through the air and smashing on the windshield; Harold's face contorted in a scream; a loud crash; another brief scream; and a view of water smashing against the camera lens. Then nothing.

CELIA IN THE STUDIO, HER HANDS COVERING HER MOUTH

UNIDENTIFIED VOICE OFF CAMERA: Oh yeah! This is going to go viral! Viral! Monetize it and upload it NOW!

CELIA: (a strange smile on her face) Great job, Harold.

(To be continued............)

ENTRY TWO:
THE MAD RHINO PROVING GROUNDS

READY TO RUMBLE!

It was a peaceful, sunny day when I made my way up a winding two-lane in a semi-rural area of the Pocono Mountains, Pennsylvania. I quickly learned to pay attention to the road signs indicating sharp curves as I barreled past dense stands of pine and oak, broken up by the occasional rusting double-wide or crumbling, moss-covered, abandoned house. My GPS kept rerouting due to the poor service in this remote area until it finally abandoned me altogether. I eventually came upon a half-mile stretch of tall grass and a driveway that seemed to lead to nowhere, hovered over by a faded old billboard announcing "K-9 Training Grounds" that featured a proud German Shepherd, erect and alert as a Marine guard at the Tomb of the Unknown Soldier. Believing I was at least in the general vicinity of my destination I took a chance and headed up the driveway which was surprisingly smooth as if recently paved. At the point where it appeared from the road to vanish into the forest it actually took a sharp right that led up to a neat and cozy-looking cabin surrounded by sentinel trees too dark to identify. By the wooden slat sign hanging from a stake stuck in the ground by the front door, I knew that, at last and for sure, I was in the right place: "R2R Rhino Training Grounds."

Before I could quite get out of my vehicle I was greeted by a thin, smiling, black man who emerged from the cabin's front door, dressed in a brown uniform of shorts and a button down cotton shirt. Sergeant's stripes undulated on his floppy sleeves as he casually saluted and extended his hand.

"You must be the fellow from the magazine," he said as he shook my hand. "Welcome to the Ready to Rumble Rhino Training Facility."

His speech was clear and forthright but I couldn't place his accent. He answered my question before I could even ask.

"I am Sam Ntuto, Chief Rhino Trainer here at R2R, lately of Mokolodi Nature Reserve, Gaborone, Botswana. Perhaps you've heard of it?"

"Wow," I said, "That's one of the finest nature reserves in the world. Of course I've heard of it. My name is Emory Bohard, freelance writer from Connecticut. I thought my trip was far but you! You're really a long way from home. What brings you to the Poconos?"

From the look in his eyes I realized the silliness of my question but he answered with a gracious smile.

"To train Rhinos."

Inside, the cabin had an ultra-rustic décor: cheap sheet paneling, worn pine flooring, and low rough-hewn ceiling beams, all matched by a distinctly musty odor. Sergeant Ntuto introduced me to a white man seated behind a well-worn wooden desk scattered with books, papers, and a teak ashtray cradling a large, smoldering cigar. A bamboo ceiling fan turning slowly overhead completed the ambiance and I felt like I had stepped into a Hollywood version of a tropical outpost. The white man wore an Australian bush hat decorated with a black and white ostrich feather that he tipped back by way of a salute then waved his hand across the desk.

"Have a seat. Welcome to the new world of all-natural law enforcement. Joe Mossburg is my moniker but everyone calls me Captain Joe. Something to drink?"

Despite his "down under" looks his accent belied roots in the deepest, darkest, concrete jungles of Brooklyn, New York. I smiled openly, pleased that my story would at the very least feature some genuinely interesting characters.

"Well, Captain Joe. I thank you for the hospitality. Sergeant Ntuto tells me I'm here at a good time."

"Yes. Today is a good day. He's been working diligently with our bull male Edgar who will be tested this afternoon to see how he responds to the commands the Sergeant has been drilling into him for the last two months. Ain't that right, Ntuto?"

"I've been in the bunker with him from sun-up to sun-down. Day after day. Running, running, running."

His face drooped slightly and I couldn't tell if it was from the heat or from exhaustion.

"Yes," I said. "I imagine it's tough to train a Rhinoceros. I will be asking you a lot of questions."

"And he's got the answers," Captain Joe said as he handed me and the Sergeant a cold bottle of locally brewed beer. "Don't you, Ntuto?"

When I'd finished my beer (which was very good, by the way, although I had a rough time pronouncing the name until the sergeant told me it rhymes with "Sing-Sing") we all went outside and down a dirt path that led to a building with concrete sides and a raised suspended roof that provided a space for air to circulate. We were met at the solid steel access door by three youngsters who appeared to be in their early twenties: two young men, and a young lady, dressed in the same brown uniforms. One of the boys had a shaved head and was covered in indecipherable tattoos. The other boy wore sunglasses fitted over long, scraggly sideburns and a ponytail that reached half way down his back. The girl wore an orange kerchief around flaming red hair that perfectly matched the tanned freckles on her cheeks. The tattooed boy was holding a large round leather hoop attached to a twenty foot stretch of thick linked chain so heavy it had to be supported by both of the other two.

"Baez, Quirk, and Talmadge, here, are our trainer trainees," said Captain Joe with a flourish. "Baez is the walking comic book, Quirk is the refugee from a barber shop, and Talmadge on the end there has a special affinity for animals, being a descendant of Celtic Druids."

All three appeared unsure how to respond when Sergeant Ntuto bailed everybody out.

"Baez is a graduate student majoring in endangered species preservation; Quirk is a professional camel trainer; and Talmadge is an environmental biologist working on a doctoral thesis. But the most important thing is they are all athletic. In a little while you will see why."

"Mr. Baez," I said. "What's that you're holding?"

"A collar."

Confusion must have blared out from my face because he smiled and said, "For Edgar. The male Ceratotherium simum simum."

I still didn't understand so I turned to Ntuto.

"Does that rhyme with 'Sing-Sing' too?"

He laughed. "Baez speaks the scientific name of the southern white rhino, the sub-species I am most familiar with and have handled back home."

"And the only one," the captain pointed out, "that can be exported legally to the United States."

"Ah ha!" I laughed as my brain finally linked everything together. "The collar and the chain are for walking the rhino."

"Correct-a-mundo," Quirk said.

At that moment, I must admit, I was dumbfounded. Even as I was speaking the words about walking the rhino I could hardly believe anyone would take them seriously. I was making a joke. I couldn't imagine it at the time but I was about to get an amazing lesson.

"The building that you see here we call 'The Rhino Condo' and houses our two male rhinoceri," Captain Joe said. "Some people say rhinoceruses but we say rhinoceri because it sounds more elegant."

I thought to myself that elegance might be one of the last things I would equate with a rhino. Zoo rhinos mostly impress me with their ever-present smell of rhino dung and their ponderous girth that produces more earthquakes than waves of enchantment. I watched as Baez opened the top half of the steel door and I marveled at his fearlessness. He dangled a tree branch with a few small wild apples on it just inside the opening and I involuntarily took a step back. However I had nothing to fear at this point. A huge two-horned head emerged from the shadows and nibbled gently at the tree branch. Suddenly the animal's ears pricked up and he emitted a startled grunt. Captain Joe grabbed my arm and quietly led me away from the building.

"He must have heard you breathing," he said. Apparently Rhinos can't see very well but have incredible hearing and sense of smell. So, while Ntuto and the three trainees prepared Edgar, the Captain led me to another structure with a concrete wall that stretched hundreds of feet to the left and right. We ascended a staircase to a roofed-over observation booth looking down on an enclosed acre of sun-drenched brown clay dotted with upright concrete slabs seemingly spaced at random intervals.

"This would be the training ground," I said. The captain nodded and swept his arm grandly across the vista.

"Pretty cool, huh?"

While we were waiting for the arrival of Edgar and the crew I took the opportunity to ask the captain for details about the program, its purpose, and the progress toward its success.

"Of course," he said, "you already know we are training these animals to assist law enforcement agencies mainly in the area of crowd control."

I was aware of the general thrust of the effort, that the rhinos would take the place of dogs in certain policing situations, but was taken aback by the specific activity he referred to.

"Might that be a little dangerous?"

The captain rolled his eyes and smirked.

"That's why we're training them. We focus on two simple commands: Stop and Go."

I was a little unnerved by his confidence so I probed further.

"So you truly believe a four to six-thousand pound animal can be safely controlled by a human shouting two one word commands?"

"Look. These beasts are pea brains. You'll never get them to beg, roll over, or play dead. But we've seen a lot of progress getting them to charge or not charge. Go. Stop. Get it? We also use their natural instinct to protect their food to modify their behavior to fit specific situations."

"How does that work? Rhinos don't eat people."

"Part of the training is that we get them used to very particularized types of food that they learn to love and thus will fight over. Think of it like a kid trying to protect his last slice of pizza from his dim-witted friends. You can see the potential for him to kick all of their brains out in a big way."

I still didn't understand. The Captain pointed to a small steel door at one end of the training ground.

"Behind that there door is a trough filled with some of that special rhino food which, by the way, is as addictive for them as a fast food hamburger. Formulated that way on purpose just like that hamburger, too. The rhino will do anything to protect it."

"And how does that assist in crowd control? All the people have to do is stay away from it and the rhino will leave them alone."

"First of all we are not talking about people, we're talking about perps; perpetrators. The strategy goes like this. The perps are rioting or looting or whatever. A police truck pulls up and a large vessel assembly like the one behind that door is set up. Note I said vessel assembly. I'll get back to that in a minute. A trained officer leads a rhino out of the back of the truck and up to the vessel which contains the special food. Part one of the strategy is that, at this point, most sane people, even perps, will see the potential for mayhem in the presence of six thousand pounds of angry odd-toed ungulate and thus will back off and disperse of their own free will. Rhino dines. Riot over."

"What if they don't stop?"

"Remember how I called it a vessel assembly?"

At this juncture the main gate opened. Ntuto emerged from the tunnel leading Edgar with the collar and chain. I'm not sure if it was the heat of the day or the head-spinning conversation with Captain Joe, but I found myself wondering what Norman Rockwell would make of that scene.

The captain reached into a cooler and took out two more beers.

"Here," he said. "You look a little dehydrated."

The bottle was chilled to perfection and the cool liquid filling my stomach seemed to help, and quickly. Before I could chug the last swallow he was handing me another one.

"Just watch," Captain Joe chuckled and pointed. I swear I had the sense of him twirling a villainous mustache even though his face was completely lacking in even a hint of stubble. I steadied myself and watched.

Ntuto led Edgar to the far end of the training area and guided him so he stood facing the wide open space. Baez, Quirk and Talmadge filed in carrying what looked like placards on poles. Cloth tubes hung from the placards and swayed left to right as the three spread out near the middle of the grounds. They stood waiting as Ntuto finished attaching the thick steel chain to a huge eyelet fastened to the wall. Meanwhile, Edgar stood so motionless I couldn't be sure if he was even awake.

At a signal from the sergeant the three trainees removed the cloth tubes to reveal various items attached to knotted ropes: empty cans, chimes, sleigh bells, and odd shaped metal pieces. Edgar appeared to yawn. Then the three youngsters began to bang and swing their placards, smashing at the dangling objects, and shouting at the tops of their lungs insults, taunts, and political slogans laced with obscenities. Edgar started to move toward the racket.

"Stop!" commanded Ntuto.

Edgar slowed to a halt. I was completely amazed and completely captivated at this point. I was sweating massively so I fished another beer out of the cooler. The noise continued with an ever rising intensity. I could see Edgar's nostrils flaring as he began to paw the ground.

"Stop!" ordered Ntuto.

The pawing ceased but the nostrils got bigger as Edgar began to shake his head back and forth. The three trainees moved closer. The noise seemed to reach an impossible level and I felt the need to cover my ears. I saw Ntuto raise his hands into the air and his mouth contort.

"Stop!" he screamed. This time Edgar let out a bellow that I felt in my legs and took off in a full barrel charge. Ntuto ran after him yelling "Stop! Stop!" as the trainees scattered and hid behind three of the concrete slabs. I slurred something like "Oh, that's cute," as Captain Joe clapped his hands and pumped his fists.

"Three times he obeyed! Three times! Ha-ha!"

With the ending of the noise and the trainees' disappearance Edgar finally halted his charge. He had also reached the end of the chain. He stood for a moment sniffing the air, smelled something, and turned his head back toward Ntuto. The Sergeant was emerging from the small steel door pulling a large, wheeled box. He lined it up near the wall, applied brakes, and backed away. Edgar started slowly then broke into a rhinoceran gallop. When he reached the box he began to push it with his horn. Ntuto approached slowly, gripping the chain, and guided the rhino behind the box so he was once again facing the open end of the grounds. Again the Sergeant backed away. He aimed an object that turned out to be a remote control and the box lid flew open revealing the magic rhino food. Edgar dove into the mixture with gusto, grunting up an absolute storm of joy.

"That was incredible," I said.

"I'll drink to that," said Captain Joe as he handed me another beer.

"Sing-Sing!" I said.

"Salute!" said the Captain.

As we were toasting the "success" of the trial it slowly dawned on me that the results were at best ambivalent and at worst, disastrous. I voiced my fear that in a real situation, Edgar might indeed injure someone or worse.

"Rhinos have no sympathy for the perps," Captain Joe said. He leaned in close to my face.

"And a mad rhino don't discriminate."

He motioned toward the grounds.

"Besides. You ain't seen nothing yet."

Baez, Quirk, and Talmadge slowly emerged from behind the concrete slabs with their placards and gingerly approached the gourmand Edgar.

"Remember when you asked what happens if the perps aren't scared off?"

The trainees suddenly launched into their extreme cacophony with even greater intensity than before. Ntuto watched with his arms folded as Edgar turned his head to get a look at the source of the noise. Deciding he had much better things to do, the rhino continued to bury his face in the food box.

Captain Joe pulled me by the arm and pointed toward Ntuto. He spoke into a microphone attached to his epaulets.

"This is Mission Control. Ready for launch."

He waved his arm over his head and counted down, "Three, two, one, blast off!"

The Sergeant again activated the remote control. A loud noise banged from the box and startled Edgar backwards a step. Then, with a crashing boom, the box and its contents launched toward the trainees, soared over their heads and rained down a torrent that covered them with the strange slop. An insanely angry Edgar bolted toward them as they again dived behind the slabs. But this time Edgar snapped the chain and circled behind the shelters. Baez, Quirk, and Talmadge sprinted with extreme prejudice towards the outer walls and just barely made it to a small opening that allowed them to crawl out under the wall. Meanwhile, Sergeant Ntuto ran behind the rhino yelling "Stop! Stop!" until Edgar turned around. For an instant the two stood eye-to-eye. Just in time Ntuto leaped to the side as the charging Edgar thrust and missed. This began a crazed imbroglio that slashed back and forth across the clay.

Meanwhile, Captain Joe squirmed on the floor, doubled and tripled over with laughter.

"You got a camera on your phone?" he coughed out. "You got to shoot this."

He laughed hysterically. As for me, I was horrified.

"You've got to do something."

He stumbled over and pulled a long box out from under a bench. When he turned around he had a huge rifle in his hands with a telescopic site big enough to see craters on Mars. He must have registered the horror on my face.

"It's just a tranquilizer," he said as he steadied himself and aimed. He waited until Edgar was running straight toward him and pulled the trigger. Bullseye! As Edgar reacted to the shot, Ntuto was finally able to scramble down the same hole the trainees had escaped through only moments before. My brain was spinning and I could barely stand. I felt hands grip both of my arms to keep me from falling. A strange odor filled my nostrils and I turned to see Baez on one side and Talmadge on the other, propping me up; both of them still covered with the rhino's feast. They helped me wobble down the stairs as my dizzying day approached its positively worthy denouement.

The sky was turning twilight gray by the time we returned to the office. The trees were alive with the blinking lights of thousands of fireflies and night creatures were stirring in the underbrush, making tell-tale crunching sounds as they scampered over the leafy forest floor. The three trainees had repaired to another building on the property to shower, put on clean clothes, and prepare for the nightly wrap-up. Captain Joe, Sergeant Ntuto, and I settled into the worn leather chairs in the office to review the day and for me to ask my final questions. I checked my phone for emails and messages but service was almost non-existent and there was nothing new from any of my apps. I decided to wait until I returned to "civilization" about 15 miles down the road. The captain passed out more cold Sing-Sings and we commenced to "chew the fat."

"Is this the kind of thing that happens here every day," I asked.

"Some variation of it, yes," said Captain Joe. "Just think about it. It could take over a month to complete basic training for a German Shepherd, a far more intelligent and compliant animal, believe me. We've had our two rhinos for three months now and we're just now seeing results, as you witnessed."

I wasn't sure that what I had seen could be characterized as "results", but I decided to move to my concluding questions rather than disparage their obviously herculean and parlous efforts. Besides, I could sense by the limpness of my extremities that I may have had too much of a good thing (Sing-Sing) and should be heading home sooner rather than later.

"With all the work you put in here, - the frustration, the danger - do you feel it's worth it?"

"I can tell you this: you're not the first visitor we've had here. Several parties interested in our product have spent days 'scouting' us so to speak. The fact is, our investors are very excited that we will soon turn our first profit, as soon as the contracts are signed."

I was floored.

"You already have a buyer?"

"Not only do we have a buyer, we have four more rhinos on order. And one of them is female, understand?"

At that statement I couldn't prevent my mouth from curling in a wry smile.

"You're going to try to breed rhinos? In the Pocono Mountains? In Pennsylvania?"

"Why not? The United Nations Council on Endangered Species approved our next shipment. Think about it. We will be helping to preserve and maybe even multiply one of the world's most endangered animals by giving them a secure habitat and increasing their value as living commodities. You know, instead of poachers killing them for their horns they will become valuable assets to the law enforcement community. Nothing preserves better than cash value. Dammit, I think that calls for another 'Sing-Sing'."

I was too tired and worn out to argue about the end justifying the means. And anyway, I thought, he might be right. Still, something else was hiding in the back of my mind that I just couldn't get a handle on, so I continued my final interrogatories.

"You say you already have buyers. Can I ask who?"

"Certainly. And I'll tell you who. It's not going to be any big secret. In fact they want the news to spread far and wide to strike fear into their particular brand of perp. As soon as Edgar passes his final tests proving his utility as a crowd control asset, he will be traveling to New Mexico for final training with the United States Border Patrol."

"That sounds really bizarre to me."

"Shoot. Who needs a wall when you've got a Rhino."

Both Captain Joe and Sergeant Ntuto burst out laughing.

"Let me tell you this," Ntuto said, "We have had interest from governments all over the globe including Beijing."

Captain Joe slapped his desk. "No more tanks in Tienanmen Square. None needed. None at all! Soon our biggest problem is going to be keeping up with demand."

I hardly heard that last part because the mental object in the back of my mind began to leak into my consciousness. Before the thought was fully formed I blurted out a question.

"Where's the other rhino? I met Edgar but I've not seen the other rhino."

Captain Joe re-lit the cigar that was still in his ash tray from the morning.

"His name is Bergen and he is nowhere near as advanced as Edgar. If you want to come back we will be beginning his intermediate training next week."

At that moment the three trainees entered and announced Edgar was still chained and sleeping peacefully in the training compound with a full trough of magic rhino food in case he should wake up and feel hungry. All was quiet in the "kennel" so they had decided not to disturb Bergen by turning on lights or opening gates.

I don't know if it was from the too-many beers, the cigar smoke, the lingering smell from the trainees, or from a combination of the compilation, but I could no longer formulate a whole thought in my head except for an intense desire to crawl beneath the covers in a bed somewhere and put myself and the day to rest. Assuming that my research at the Training Grounds was essentially complete I thanked my hosts for their incredible demonstration and made an unsuccessful attempt to get out of my chair. Captain Joe motioned to Ntuto to help him support me as I wobbled out to where the vehicles were parked.

"Put him in my truck," I heard the Captain say.

I found myself belted into the passenger seat of a huge Hummer with Captain Joe behind the wheel.

"Mr. Bohard, I'm going to drive you to a motel about ten miles down the road where some of our clients stay when they visit. Sergeant Ntuto will follow in your car. I know that all probably makes no sense to you right now but it doesn't have to. I will check you into the motel so you can get a good, safe night's sleep and be on your way home in the morning. We appreciate you writing a story about us for a national magazine and it would do us no good at all if you were to drive off a cliff or into the river."

He chuckled when he said that and patted my shoulder.

At the motel I was able to walk into the room on my own legs with just a little balancing from the Sergeant. We said our goodbyes and I flopped down on the bed. In seconds I was blissfully unconscious.

In the morning I still felt a little dizzy but after a quick shower I was alert and ready for the long drive home. I checked my phone and was delighted to see I had good service. While sorting through my notifications I saw a curious alert from my mapping program: something about "be on the lookout for" a large animal that, during the night, destroyed someone's backyard garden and trampled a neighbor's shrubs. I flipped on the television to local news and watched until a story came on about the incident. The woman whose garden was destroyed described being awakened at 3 am by thrashing sounds then looking out her window to see a large animal resembling a rhinoceros. The news anchors made a lame joke as I dialed Captain Joe's cell phone. When he answered, the background noise indicated he was outside and I could hear the three trainees in the distance reciting the mantra: "Stop! Stop! Stop!" The connection was not very good so I quickly got to the point.

"I suppose you've heard about an alleged rhino attack in Canadensis? What can you tell me about it?"

I heard what sounded like a motor revving and some unintelligible screaming followed by a loud report reminiscent of an elephant gun. The call started to drop but I thought I heard Captain Joe saying, "It wasn't one of ours."

I was tempted to take a ride back to the R2R facility to investigate further and to formally thank the Captain and Sergeant for taking care of me the previous night, but I needed to be on my way with other important appointments and stories blowing up my phone with reminders. I took a deep pull of the warm, summer, mountain air and headed back down the twisting road to the Interstate.

The End

ENTRY THREE
ITZA SHAKA

Plunge One: Random Quotes, Musings, Journal Entries

“So I'm walking along 43rd street when this Dennis Rodman-looking woman pulls up to the curb in a vintage Nash Rambler, throws a cup of ice in the street and sits there watching it melt. I watch with her and after a few seconds of New York 90-degree black-top the ice is a slimy brown puddle. ‘That's life’, she says, and drives off. I think, ‘That's deep’. But since I'm in the middle of searching for the ultimate charcoal-broiled hot pretzel, I opt not to think about it, although her orange hair intrigues me to this day.”

Selection from Itza Shaka's "Letters To My Friend Buffy and Assorted U.S. Presidents"

"Being first is the same as being last if you're traveling in circles."

Excerpt from incredibly intellectual film director Itza Shaka's keynote address at a recent convention of Shriner silicon chips, LaBrea Tar Pits Oil & Water-Ski Resort and Bakery, May, 1994.

"The journey of a thousand tidal waves begins with the first ripple."

Quotation from incredibly famous film director Itza Shaka's commencement address to a graduating class of frozen carrier pigeons, Bryant Park, class of '97.

"You spend your time beating your head against a wall so you can have this and that. Me? I'm thinking about Dean Moriarty."

The complete text of a speech by committed film director Itza Shaka to three bewildered second graders and a derelict school bus driver, just west of the Intrepid Air and Space Museum, Manhattan, September, 1993.

"I was napping on the green velvet at Einstein's pool parlor, dreaming about a road warrior eight ball when, suddenly, it hit me......"

Selection from "The Secret Papers of Itza Shaka", Chapter 44 - "Hospital Emergency Room Examinations and Prognoses # 27, Month Of April, '91". Copyright 1985, Shaka Press & Olive Oil Refinery, New York and Tikal (second Pyramid on the left).

"Spent the whole day at the quarry conversing with several sets of identical, newly minted, extra-virgin tombstones. I says to them, I says: So anyway. So anyway. So anyway. So anyway. So anyway. So what's you're point?"

Excerpt from Volume Three of director Itza Shaka's "The Shaka Diaries". Entry under "Friday, June 17 – first day off in 12 hours."

"I'm working on this film I call "Love Is Like A Microwave Oven", where I'm exploring the physical, metaphysical, and nuclear-physical similarities. For instance, a microwave heats from the inside out, you know, like love does. And it can leave hot spots and cold spots, like love does. And, and, if you leave it in too long it'll explode! Just like.... You see, it's a kind of metaphorical simile. Very heavy."

Selection from Itza Shaka's soon to be released self-help audio series: "Things Not to Say ... Ever"

“Herve' and Miriam finally showed up last night with the 57 pounds of ground armadillo I'd asked them for in 1983. We had a pleasant evening standing around the empty lot, chatting by the fire I lit in the old garbage can. Apparently they've been very busy with their used brick business and expressed some interest in the rubble of my ex-house. I told them I'd get back to them as soon as I found a toxic waste dump for the unidentifiable armadillo material they had so graciously kept in their broken freezer for 13 years. They apologized and said they thought something was wrong with the freezer and had planned to get it fixed but time just seemed to slip away. We said goodbye and after they left I discovered that the armadillo stuff, when tossed into a flame, had the explosive power of the equivalent weight of TNT. I proceeded to sprinkle the muck over those bricks they'd drooled about and set off an explosion that devastated much of the neighborhood and left a pile of fine red dust where the bricks used to be. I almost lost an eye. That'll fix them."

Page 33 from Itza Shaka's "Ten Pages That Shook the World and Other Missing Journal Entries – 1996"

"I keep thinking about the summer we spent by the lake. We had such a wonderful time and, had we been luckier, could have stayed a few more days. I wish we could do it again. By the way, I got some new dredging equipment. How about it?"

Hand written post-it note retrieved from recovered stolen purse claimed to belong to J. Edgar Hoover. Found in the possession of Itza Shaka at a street corner auction, in front of a burger joint on Times Square, 12:01 am, January 1, 2000.

"You know about the chimp. His name's "Turvey" but I refer to him as "Baal" and you can guess why. I hand him a video camera just to keep him occupied while I shoot a music video. He goes around to the dancers sticking the thing in places usually reserved for Presidents and other powerful skank-offs. So his work becomes the toast of the Sundance Film Festival. Gets booked to do a music video for some hip-hop character named "Da C-Rapper", hires me as his assistant and I'm not too happy. Then I think I have an idea for a great shot and I clamp the camera to his numb skull and throw him off a fifteen story building. Unbeknownst to me the bugger is packing a mini-hang-glider. Soaring shots, crazy airborne corkscrews and screaming sounds equalized like insane laughter. Wins the MTV Music Video Awards. Punk."

Transcript from Itza Shaka lost guest appearance on a late night talk show just prior to the host realizing he had no idea who he was or how he got in the studio. March 2000.

"I had a vision of a small boat, beached on the shore of the Norwalk River, about 50 yards from the sewage treatment plant. After viewing it for 150 consecutive weeks from a passing commuter train, I paddled a canoe out to the wreck at three in the morning one chilly October night. Nobody saw me paint in huge letters the words "S.S. Minnow" on the side. I will never know if anyone ever got it. That was my vision. That was my dream. I deny everything."

Unsigned confession from "The County of Fairfield vs Shaka",

November 11, 1989.

"If stupidity was a legal handicap, 99% of all parking spaces in the world would be painted with blue lines."

Complete testimony of Itza Shaka before an empty chamber of the Pennsylvania State Senate Fair Parking Color Coordination Committee, two weeks before Christmas, 2006.

"This is enough, and more than enough."
A Partially Bogus Story by Itza Shaka

There once was a painter named Giotto,
Known for his brush stroke bravado,
Approached by a mope,
Who worked for the Pope,
He split for a gig in Chicago.

A True Story (so they say)

Giotto was an artistic genius from Florence, Italy. His works included paintings, sculptures, and architectural designs and his innovative realism made him a superstar of fourteenth century Europe. When Pope Benedict XI was doing some major redecorating in Rome he heard about Giotto the Genius and, always hiring the best, sent one of his courtiers to see if "G the G" lived up to the hype. On the way, the courtier picked up samples from other artists just in case Giotto was a flop-o. When he got to Florence he asked wither he could find this great virtuoso and was pointed in the direction of a swinging artists community locally referred to as "Giotto's Grotto."

Upon meeting Giotto the courtier explained his quest from the Pope. Giotto swigged down his vino, picked up a brush, and proceeded to draw on a blank canvas, with one smooth stroke, an absolutely perfect circle. He smiled at the courtier and said "Take that to the Pope."

The courtier thought Giotto was joking and demanded another sample to take back to Rome. But Giotto replied, "This is enough and more than enough."

Feeling like he had maybe been scammed, the courtier moped back to the Pope with Giotto's enigma and all the other samples. But when he explained how Giotto, in the blink of an eye, had whipped his brush on the face of the canvas, the Pope and his advisers realized that they were in the presence of greatness.

Giotto got the job-o.

(Had to cancel his gig in Chicago.)

Doctoral Thesis (as submitted) by future "Dr." Shaka to the PhD. Committee, Culinary Philosophy Department, The Universal University of Roswell, New Mexico. May, 2001.

"I used to write in a cacophonous convoluted caricature of current English until I met, and was heavily retro-fitted by this Radical Grammatical Fundamentalist. I merely asked him to check my punctuation and he proceeded to rip my manuscript into mangled mixed gender paper dolls; light them on fire; and put out the flames with a combination of whole wheat flour, basil, and shredded coconut. He wailed that I was an adverbial abomination and a punctuational cretin. I asked him what I should do to be normal. He said absolutely nothing. Changed my life."

Preamble to Itza Shaka's revolutionary treatise "Life Is A Semi-Colon, Wrapped in a Parenthetical, Inside a Posthumous Poem By A Living Writer." - Blind Harry's University Press, 2001.

"In the future, only people who are not famous will be famous."

Graffiti chiseled into base of Henry Hudson Bridge on the occasion of Itza Shaka's 50th birthday, December, 2002.

ENTRY THREE
ITZA SHAKA

Plunge Two: Hamlet – A Portrait by Itza Shaka

FADE IN

SOMBER MUSIC

INTERIOR. KITCHEN, DAY.

The film, a documentary, opens with interview footage of HAMLET BURGER, serial killer, sitting at his kitchen table playing with a floor-standing globe, intercut with ALICE "ACE" VENTURA, his therapist, sitting behind her office desk, and a montage of Hamlet, wearing an apron, making breakfast.

HAMLET

We all have our desires, our needs, our, dare I say it? Hungers.

Hamlet makes breakfast.

HAMLET (Voice Over)

I don't consider myself unique in any way. Actually, except for a certain notoriety, I could be any man walking down the street.

Hamlet sits at his kitchen table.

HAMLET

You know...the boy next door.

SWITCH BETWEEN INTERIOR. OFFICE, DAY. AND KITCHEN, DAY

ACE looks through a bookcase in her office and opens a book. She is a young psychologist who recently completed her PhD.

ACE (VO)
It's really very simple and tragic:

Ace sits behind her office desk.

LOWER THIRD: DR. Alice "Ace" Ventura, PhD., MD.

ACE
...in this society where just about anything goes, he's been branded an outcast and forced to live in this environment, simply because he doesn't conform to somebody's arbitrary standards.

Hamlet continues making breakfast.

ACE (VO)
Hopefully, the work we're doing here will help keep others from a similar fate - from becoming secondary victims in this way.

Hamlet holds up a piece of chicken liver and smiles.

EXT. CONDO, DAY.

The condos are homey-looking with a white picket fence. It is a lovely, peaceful day. WYNDHAM ERROLL, the film-maker, narrates and asks on-camera questions. He is in his early thirties and aggressive but naive.

LOWER THIRD: Voice of Wyndham Erroll - Film-maker.

WYNDHAM (VO)
It's a place you could walk right past and not even notice - so ordinary that it leaves your mind almost before it enters. But inside is a secret place, deliberately masked by the mundane, the everyday. This is a prison -

Close Up: Plate on front door reads "Cell Block #9".

WYNDHAM (VO)
- one that houses some of the most criminally diseased men the world has been unfortunate enough to know. This is the story of one of those men.

TITLE: The title roars onto the screen:

Hamlet: A Portrait - A Film By Wyndham Erroll

INTERIOR, KITCHEN, DAY.

HAMLET makes his breakfast. A pot of oatmeal steams on the stove top. Home fries sizzle in a frying pan. Hamlet takes chicken livers from a package, washes them in the sink, and applies spices.

LOWER THIRD: Hamlet Burger, Patient.

HAMLET
I always cook for myself. It's one of life's simple pleasures, you know. Breakfast is my specialty.

CLOSE UP: Livers. ZOOM OUT TO Hamlet applying spices.

HAMLET (continued)
Sometimes I'll cook for Dr. Ventura, depending on....well, she should be here shortly. I have to finish these before she gets here. If she smells them raw..... She's so squeamish.

Hamlet shows the raw livers sprinkled with spices and sniffs.

HAMLET (continued)
To die for.

SWITCH BETWEEN INTERIOR. OFFICE, DAY. AND KITCHEN, DAY

DR. ACE VENTURA working at her desk in her office.

ACE (VO)

Hamlet is an extremely interesting and important case to me, with my specialty.

CUT TO: HAMLET continues with breakfast.

ACE (VO)

On the surface he is so....normal.

CUT TO: ACE, behind her desk, is interviewed by WYNDHAM.

ACE

It's hard to imagine, and this is my life's work mind you, hard to imagine him being a monster, as some people have characterized him.

CUT TO: HAMLET is completing his breakfast preparations. He sets two plates on the table and distributes knives, forks, and napkins.

HAMLET

I hope she gets here soon. The food will get cold. Especially the eggs. It's hard to keep eggs warm without drying them out. I've also got a little surprise for her. A dish I call "Adam's Apples". Don't tell her.

He signals "shhh" by putting a knife to his lips.

CUT TO: ACE behind her desk as WYNDHAM interviews her.

ACE

My area of specialization is the study of the effects of micro-environmental aberrations on children of otherwise normal development and the impact of those experiences on their adult lifestyles.

The camera cuts to Wyndham for his reaction. He is slightly bewildered. The camera pans back to Ace who reaches for a file, opens it on her desk, and leafs through it as she speaks.

ACE (continued)

Let me give you an example aside from Mr. Burger. When Tommy here - I'll call him Tommy - when Tommy was a boy he hated peas, but his Mother always forced him to eat them and, in fact, sometimes that was the only food she would make for a week straight. For Tommy this was a most excruciating torture, exacerbated by his proto-verbal repressed expressive pathology. He hated peas. It led him, starting at the age of fifteen, to date and then marry a series of increasingly domineering and abusive women, all of whom he, of course, murdered.

She pauses at a series of photographs and puts on a pair of glasses to study them.

ACE (continued)

And in some creative and unusual ways, I might add.

WYNDHAM

And this is a direct link back to his domineering and abusive mother?

ACE

On the surface it may appear so. However, Tommy's mom is actually a sweet and endearing woman whom he adores to this day.

WYNDHAM

Well then, how do you explain his, um, his...?

ACE

Choice of lifestyles? I'll give you a hint:

She hands Wyndham a sheet of paper.

CLOSE UP OF PAPER: The title: "Misanthropic Alphabetical Syndrome – Feminine P Subset – Case #122".

ACE (continued)
A partial list of his wives', his victims', names would include Paula, Patty, Pam, Petruschka, and, of course, Pia.

WYNDHAM
He hated peas.

ACE
I know it appears simplistic, Mr. Erroll. But sometimes, things just are.

INTERIOR. CONDO KITCHEN, DAY.

HAMLET sits eating his breakfast. He enjoys it immensely. He puts a piece of potato in his mouth and savors it.

HAMLET
I can really burn some home fries. I learned that from Dr. Ventura.

WYNDHAM speaks from behind the camera.

WYNDHAM (off camera)
She taught you how to make home fries?

HAMLET
No, the phrase. I learned the phrase from her. Like, to "really burn" something is to make it good, you know. Really good. She says I can really burn some home fries.

He takes a forkful of livers and chews slowly.

HAMLET (continued)
I'm more partial to these. I can burn some chicken livers.

INTERIOR, CONDO FRONT DOOR, DAY.

The doorbell rings. HAMLET enters and unlocks the door. He opens it and is delighted as DR. VENTURA enters. They exchange pleasantries but Hamlet appears to be a little intimidated.

WYNDHAM NARRATES.

WYNDHAM (Voice Over)
When Dr. Ventura finally arrives for the morning session, the scene is somehow strange to me. I don't know why, but I expect there to be a warmer, more personal interaction. Instead, it is obvious that Dr. Ventura takes her work seriously. Secretly, I marvel at her courage.

INTERIOR, OFFICE, DAY.

ACE is behind her desk. WYNDHAM interviews.

WYNDHAM
At the risk of sounding sexist, may I ask you why they would choose a woman to study...to spend time alone with, individuals like Mr. Burger? I would think the assignment to be quite dangerous.

ACE
First of all, I wasn't chosen, I volunteered. Secondly, I can take care of myself very well, thank you.

Wyndham smiles.

ACE (continued)
And finally, Mr. Hamlet Burger is a completely safe subject for me to study one-on-one. In fact, it couldn't be more perfect. I don't fit his "Modus Operandi". You see, he only kills men.

Wyndham's smile disappears.

INTERIOR. KITCHEN, DAY.

HAMLET putters around the kitchen.

ACE (Voice Over)
Serial killers are an interesting phenomenon.

INTERIOR, OFFICE, DAY.

ACE is behind her desk. WYNDHAM interviews.

ACE
They generally fall into a narrow range of categories in personality type, childhood experiences....Even in the areas of race, religion, and age group they seem to predominate in one or two areas.

WYNDHAM
Is there a reason for that? An explanation of why generally specific groups have these tendencies?

ACE
At this time there is no definitive answer. In fact, that is one of the principal goals of my research.....

INTERIOR. CONDO LIVING ROOM, DAY.

HAMLET and ACE play a flash-card game while WYNDHAM watches. Ace holds up a picture of a little girl and Hamlet reacts by hugging himself. Ace holds up a picture of a dog and Hamlet reacts by petting himself. Ace holds up a picture of a throat and Hamlet reacts by rubbing his stomach.

ACE (Voice Over)
....to better understand the mind and make-up of these individuals with the ultimate aim of helping them adjust to the social values which, for better or worse, dominate our culture.

SWITCH BETWEEN INTERIOR, KITCHEN, DAY AND OFFICE, DAY.

HAMLET offers ACE some breakfast. He shows her the eggs and home fries in the pan.

ACE

Oh, no thank you. But that was very thoughtful of you. You are certainly making progress.

CUT TO: Office. ACE and WYNDHAM.

ACE

Part of what we're trying to do here, apart from studying these men, is to re-orient their thinking so that, maybe someday, they can function within the norms demanded by society.

CUT TO: Kitchen. HAMLET makes a motion with his hand as if to say "wait 'till you see this." ACE smiles politely at the camera. Hamlet pulls a baking pan with fresh muffins out of the oven. Ace laughs and claps her hands.

ACE

Bravo! Bravo!

HAMLET

Then you'll have one? They're organic.

Ace takes one and tries a bite. She is pleased. Hamlet looks mischievously toward the camera then back to Ace.

HAMLET (continued)

I have another surprise for you.

He reaches under a towel and pulls out a raw chicken liver, dangling it in front of her face.

ACE

Mr. Burger, please!

Hamlet looks remorseful but in a mischievous way.

INTERIOR, OFFICE, DAY.

ACE and WYNDHAM.

ACE

Here at the institute we study only a particular type of serial killer. Our subjects here have not only killed but also consumed their victims, or, to be more precise, consumed parts of their victims.

INT. CONDO LIVING ROOM, DAY.

HAMLET, still wearing the apron, vacuums the carpet, dusts the furniture, and rearranges a set of figurines in a display case.

ACE (Voice Over)

Mr. Burger's victims are mostly middle-aged males working in the television or film industries. His modus operandi is to sever their jugular veins with a sharp object and then to immediately surgically remove the vocal chords and larynx.

INT. OFFICE, DAY.

WYNDHAM and ACE.

WYNDHAM

Why the vocal chords and larynx? Is he trying to make some statement about verbal communication or, more specifically, the type and quality of communication we receive from mass media?

ACE

No. Apparently he considers them the tastiest morsels.

WYNDHAM

You mean he ate them? Raw?

ACE

Raw, steamed. grilled....it depends on the availability of cooking utensils, spices, or condiments.

WYNDHAM

That's incredible. But what I mean by "why these particular body parts?" is what sort of meaning do you attach to his, uh, preference? What motivated him?

-ACE

My theory is, and my study is not complete, that Hamlet Burger...

INTERIOR, KITCHEN, DAY.

HAMLET is forming and arranging small cookies on a cookie sheet. They are in the form of human bodies.

ACE (VO)

...who, deep inside, is a very creative and gregarious individual, must have been severely repressed as a child, possibly by one or two abusive parents.

INTERIOR, OFFICE, DAY.

WYNDHAM and ACE. Wyndham produces Hamlet's headshot and bio sheet.

ACE (continued)

Most likely the culprit was his father.

WYNDHAM

His father? According to his bio sheet his father died before he was born.

ACE

Well, think about it. Can you conceive of any more

selfish or abusive act? A boy growing up with an absentee father?

WYNDHAM

Absentee? But he was dead.

ACE

Can't get any more absent than that, can you? Then, to compound the problem, Society did nothing to correct this situation - no educational programs, no counseling, absolutely nothing. The result? A sensitive human being damaged to a somewhat above-normal degree through no fault of his own.

WYNDHAM

So Society is responsible? What about his own responsibility? I mean, he murdered twenty-two people.

ACE

Twenty three.

Ace looks at Wyndham as if he is too stupid to reason with.

ACE (continued)

Murder is such an ugly word. And it is not truly appropriate to this case. Murder is proactive. What Mr. Burger did was reactive. How can you persecute someone for merely reacting to the environment that was forced upon him?

INTERIOR, KITCHEN, DAY.

HAMLET, still wearing an apron, places the cookie sheet in the oven.

HAMLET

This is the second batch. I'll show you what I have already.

ACE (Voice Over)
One of the things we're trying to do here is to see if we can somehow fill the void that was created in his childhood.

HAMLET sits at the kitchen table and displays some of the finished pieces. They are little toasted human bodies. He picks them up one at a time.

HAMLET
This is a man. And this is a man. And this.....

He stops to think.

HAMLET (continued)
....is a man.

INTERIOR, OFFICE, DAY.

ACE and WYNDHAM.

ACE
We've developed several programs for arrested creative development that incorporate the individual's unique trauma phenomena into semi-virtual surrogate psycho-motor events. The idea is to channel their socially indecorous behaviors into productive and hopefully lucrative careers. In Mr. Burger's case we allowed him to choose his own therapy with the eventual aim of returning him to society in a profession where his peculiar talents are not only appreciated but, in fact, are in great demand.

WYNDHAM
Can you tell us what that profession might be?

ACE
I can't be too specific at this time but I can tell you that it is in the area of marketing.

INTERIOR. KITCHEN, DAY.

Hamlet breaks each cookie man into body parts.

HAMLET

This is really neat. I'll show you. I added this secret ingredient to the parts and baked it right in. You can't see it. See?

He pours milk into a cereal bowl and puts the pieces of one whole cookie in the milk.

HAMLET (continued)

Watch this.

The parts start to ooze red liquid as if they are bleeding.

HAMLET (continued)

It's this really cool breakfast food - a cereal made from whole grains with a dye made from organically grown raspberries. It contains 80% of the minimum daily requirement of vitamins, according to the FDA.

WYNDHAM

You mean, you've already gotten approval from the FDA?

HAMLET

Better than that. Right now we're negotiating with a major breakfast cereal manufacturer which, by the way, has agreed to let me design the box, write the slogans, and consult with the advertising agency for the marketing campaign. Here, let me show you the prototype of the box.

He holds up a box for the camera. On the front is a grotesque cartoon drawing of a dismembered body surrounded by police detectives and a TV camera operator. The name of the cereal, emblazoned across the top - "CEREAL KILLER".

HAMLET (continued)

The Ad agency thinks this is going to go through the roof.

EXTERIOR, CONDO PATIO/DECK, DAY.

HAMLET, WYNDHAM, and ACE sit roasting marshmallows. Hamlet is leaning over the charcoal grill, intent on precisely toasting his marshmallow. Ace sits holding her unroasted marshmallow on a stick. Wyndham tries to get his marshmallow over the fire but Hamlet keeps staying in his way.

CLOSE UP: HAMLET'S MARSHMALLOW. Hamlet slowly turns it over the heat.

RACK FOCUS TO HAMLETS INTENSE FACE

HAMLET

Do I ever feel remorse? Well, let me put it this way
Do you ever feel remorse?

BACK TO WIDE SHOT

WYNDHAM

Me? For what?

HAMLET

For what you do?

WYNDHAM

Why should I?

HAMLET

Do you like what you do?

WYNDHAM

Of course I do. But there's no comparison between what I do and what you did.

HAMLET
Maybe not literally. But let me explain.

Hamlet suddenly jumps up and points.

HAMLET (continued)
There goes the new fish.

The camera pans to a man in the distance, walking toward the patio. He looks up and immediately turns around and hurries around a corner out of sight. The camera pans back to Hamlet who notices that in his excitement he has dropped his marshmallow.

HAMLET (continued)
Damn!

ACE
Hamlet!

HAMLET
Excuse me. Darn!

Ace nods her approval. Hamlet puts another marshmallow on his stick and sits back down.

HAMLET (continued)
Well anyway, that guy you just saw, he only killed about thirteen people, I think, before they caught him. He owned a deli and he used their cerebral cortexes in his potato salad - a delicate blend of both hemispheres with just a hint of basil. The deli was called "Brain Food". I understand it was quite a popular place.

WYNDHAM
That's horrible.

HAMLET
Well, at least he couldn't be accused of false advertising. I have heard, though, that he used the hypothalamus as a stretcher in his meat loaf. And get this - he mixed generic vinegar with balsamic,

HAMLET (continued)

you know, to cut costs and increase his profits. Can you even imagine? Whatever happened to integrity?

Wyndham thinks then laughs nervously.

WYNDHAM

That's funny.

HAMLET

You think so?

WYNDHAM

Of course. You made a joke. A satirical remark.

Hamlet looks bewildered.

HAMLET

What's your point?

ACE

Now Hamlet, let us not speak about other peoples diagnoses. It shows a lack of empathy.

Hamlet narrows his eyes

WYNDHAM

Well, if it's all right with you, Mr. Burger, let's get back to what you said before.

HAMLET

About what?

ACE

About remorse, Hamlet. Mr. Erroll wants to hear your views on remorse.

HAMLET

Oh, yes. Remorse. You see, <u>you</u> enjoy what you do so, you do it. That's not seen as anything strange or deserving of punishment.

WYNDHAM
But I don't hurt anybody.

Hamlet shakes his head.

HAMLET
The human condition is such that we are the only animals aware of our own mortality. We're all going to die someday, you see, and essentially, from the time we are consciously aware of that fact, everything we do in life - our work, our play, our, well...everything in general - is just an activity to help us keep that thought hidden in the back of our minds. Think about it - careers, children, religion..... everything we do is merely a diversion, a misdirection, an entertainment. We all choose our own ways of distracting ourselves, yet only some of us are punished for it. You see basically, I'm being persecuted for a lifestyle choice.

INTERIOR. CONDO LIVING ROOM, DAY.

ACE watches as HAMLET inserts a CD into a CD player. As the music starts she begins to dance with HAMLET, instructing him in the dance steps.

WYNDHAM (Voice Over)
As we near the end of our visit, I sense a shift in Dr. Ventura's approach. After hours of intensive therapeutic activity, she and Hamlet settle down into a more relaxed, almost domestic interaction. The afternoon is a time to slow down - to play - to be, in a manner of speaking, normal. In my gut, however, there is a feeling of uneasiness that I can't quite put my finger on.

INTERIOR, OFFICE, DAY.

ACE and WYNDHAM.

ACE

For my last few hours with Mr. Burger we usually spend some quality time just socializing; going to the pool, surfing the net, or playing a round of golf; activities designed to give him a taste of what is considered a normal existence, as opposed to the living hell he experienced for most of his life. This is, actually, - and don't tell him I said this - actually a part of our overall plan of treatment.

INTERIOR. LIVING ROOM, DAY.

ACE watches as HAMLET fumbles through some dance steps. She laughs, claps her hands, and hugs him.

ACE (Voice Over))

It also gives me some time to reflect on the day's accomplishments and just kind of absorb how far he has progressed and, in fact, enjoy the innocent personality that is slowly, but surely, emerging.

INTERIOR, KITCHEN, DAY.

WYNDHAM watches as ACE shaves HAMLET's head with a straight razor. Hamlet picks up a magazine.

HAMLET

I read a story in this magazine the other day about a gentle little dog, a little mongrel dog who recently died and was given a hero's funeral in the town where he lived. His master had trained him from the time he was a puppy to be an attack dog, which was against his nature because he was this loving little puppy dog. But, I guess the man wanted protection for his family. One day he came home and found his wife and three children had been mauled to death, bitten through the throat as if by some animal. Thinking that his own dog was responsible

HAMLET continued)

for this horror, he ran out the back door. And there, in his own back yard, he found his little dog, that he himself, had tried to turn into a killer. Only the dog was still tethered to the fence post where the man had left him that morning. The poor thing was lying limp on the ground, apparently worn out and nearly choked to death from trying to free himself to do what he had been trained to do - to protect the family. He nearly died then. So sad.

WYNDHAM

What happened?

HAMLET

Oh, the man was arrested and sentenced to prison.

WYNDHAM

He murdered his own family?

HAMLET

Of course not. He was given ten years with no parole for excessive cruelty to an animal.

ACE

The man who eventually confessed to the killings is now a best-selling author and motivational speaker. He was rehabilitated at this very facility. A real success story. His book is titled "Having the Will To Wish".

Wyndham looks as if he cannot believe what he has just heard. Ace, now shaving Hamlet's neck, slips and nicks his throat. Hamlet puts his hand up to his throat and blood drips through his fingers. Wyndham cannot suppress a sarcastic laugh.

WYNDHAM

How does it feel?

HAMLET

You tell me!

In a rage, Hamlet snatches the razor from Ace and swings it at Wyndham who is out of sight, off camera. We hear Wyndham gag and then his body thud to the floor.

CAMERA POINT OF VIEW.

The camera is dropped to the floor by the camera operator. In his terrified haste he knocks over Hamlet's globe. We hear his foot-falls as he runs out of the condo, slamming the door behind him. The camera stays on the floor, showing only the legs of the table, part of the globe, and Hamlet's and Ace's feet.

HAMLET (OFF CAMERA)
Where's he going?

ACE (OFF CAMERA)
Oh, Hamlet. Look what you've done. The warden is not going to like this.

HAMLET (OFF CAMERA)
Why? I didn't get any on the rug this time.

ACE (OFF CAMERA)
But you were doing so well.

HAMLET (OFF CAMERA)
Should we call the infirmary?

Ace's feet cross in front of the camera as she examines Wyndham.

ACE (OFF CAMERA)
It's a little late for that.

HAMLET (OFF CAMERA)
Then do you think I could....I mean...

ACE (OFF CAMERA)
Hamlet!

HAMLET (OFF CAMERA)
I mean, It would be such a waste. him being

HAMLET (OFF CAMERA)
already dead and all.

Ace hesitates, shuffling her feet. After a moment she answers.

ACE (OFF CAMERA)
Well. All right. I don't see any harm in it now.

Hamlet's feet scurry across the camera's view.

HAMLET (OFF CAMERA)
Dr. Ventura?

ACE (OFF CAMERA)
Yes, Hamlet?

HAMLET (OFF CAMERA)
Could you hand me the blade?

We see Ace's foot tapping in anger.

HAMLET (OFF CAMERA)
Uh. Please?.......Thank you.

Ace's feet show that she sits down in a chair and crosses her legs. We hear chewing sounds from Hamlet.

ACE (OFF CAMERA)
Tell me, Hamlet, what are you feeling at this very moment?

HAMLET (OFF CAMERA)
Do we have to do this now?

ACE (OFF CAMERA)
Yes. We do. This could turn out to be a very constructive episode.

HAMLET (OFF CAMERA)
Well, it's OK. Could use a little mustard seed.

Hamlet accidentally kicks the camera and pans just enough to reveal more of Ace's feet and the globe, cracked, and upside down.

HAMLET OFF CAMERA)

Who's coming next week?

ACE (OFF CAMERA)

Info Wars, I think.

HAMLET

Big crew?

CUT TO BLACK THEN UP ON MOCK CREDITS.

MOCK CREDITS:

"Hamlet: A Portrait"

A Film by Wyndham Erroll

Edited by Hamlet Burger

Executive Producer

Alice "Ace" Ventura

Marketing & Talent Agent

Mannlicker Carcano Associates

A Special Thanks To Coventry State College and Penitentiary
For The Study Of So-Called Social Deviancy,
Reverend Warden Jocko Ballistic, SJ, CEO

Catering provided by "Brain Food II"

Funding provided by The National Endowment For The Arts

Dedicated to The Memory Of Wyndham Erroll - #24

FADE TO BLACK

REAL CREDITS

THE END

ENTRY FOUR:

A TRULY SHORT STORY (WE'LL SEE)

ONE

Thaddeus Elohim changed his legal name to Doctor Marvelous the day before he graduated with his three PhDs from Harvard: chemistry, genetics, and sociology. He was a tall, thin, and rather dour twenty-year-old with hedgerows for eyebrows and an annoying habit of speaking either too softly or too loudly and usually out of context with the particular circumstances. Despite his age and inexperience, his natural brilliance and originality, coupled with the fact that he truly looked the part, made it possible for him to be immediately offered a full research professorship at his alma mater in any one of his specialties. The deal would have been instantly consummated after the graduation ceremony if it weren't for the decorative chimpanzee rib bone he had pierced through his nose that same May day right before he accepted his triple-threat diploma. He called it a tribute to his hero: a wanna-be opera singer and noted distributor of genetic material named Screamin' Jay Hawkins. He stood at the podium with his hands in his pockets and proceeded to give one of the most disturbing and nasal valedictories in the history of that institution or any institution since the invention of higher education. The true decision makers at the college wavered over committing to a full tenure track position, unsure that such a spectacle as he presented could be effective in an ivy league college class room. To make matters worse there remained the strangeness of his unexplained penchant for keeping barnyard animals in the Graduate dorms. He immediately sensed their clouds of doubt and their momentary hesitation led to his prompt dismissal of their offer and immediate departure to seek his destiny elsewhere.

He was offered professorships at numerous prestigious universities but settled on a small, sleepy college in a remote part of New Hampshire where he could pursue his peculiar research undisturbed and incognito. Within weeks of his arrival he published numerous small, narrowly focused papers in the leading scientific journals that demonstrated such depth, breadth, and innovation that the college gave him an entire wing in one of its landmark buildings along with funding and graduate assistants normally reserved for more established and venerable scientists. He accepted this largess in an off-handed manner that somewhat dampened the administration's enthusiasm. Nonetheless, they were convinced they had in their midst a bona fide genius and budding scientific sensation who, in spite of his name, was being taken seriously by the worldwide research community.

After a few semesters complaints began to filter in from students that his lectures were obscure and bewildering; sophistic and condescending; and bore little relation to the exams he gave or the papers he assigned. Then there were also the continuing questions about the presence in his living quarters of rabbits, small pigs, and baby goats. The Dean sat him down for a fatherly talk and Dr. Marvelous promised:

"I will be less pedantic and more pedagogical."

This satisfied the Dean enough but he couldn't shake an impression of irredeemable and unrepentant weirdness in the young man's smirking demeanor. The decision to finalize the full tenure process was fast approaching so he called in all voting administrators to express his concerns. At meetings end he declared, "I am excited to guarantee for our institution a lifetime of glorious research in genetics, chemistry, and sociology. Yet I resolve to keep a close watch on our enigmatic Dr. Marvelous." The committee agreed and while some left the building that day skipping and jumping, others dragged themselves to the parking lot scratching their heads.

Things went well for a few more semesters until one of Dr. Marvelous' graduate assistants showed up in the Dean's office looking as if he hadn't slept in weeks. His name was Ivan Ancrum and the Dean guided him to a chair where the young man sat, running his hands through his tangled hair and sniffling loudly.

"I don't really like doing this," the young man said. "I feel awful. I can't sleep. I can barely eat."

"What on earth is going on?" said the Dean. "There's no need to harm yourself. Whatever the problem is we are here to provide a remedy."

"How easy for you to say. Have you ever felt like a traitor? Have you ever had to question your own character? Have you ever looked in the mirror and seen a rotten, stinking snitch?"

The Dean handed him a box of tissues and the young man paused to blow his nose.

"But I can't help it. I don't understand everything I've seen but I've seen enough to know that people should be made aware of what's going on."

"All right, my boy," the Dean sat on the edge of his desk. "Get it off your chest."

Ivan proceeded to tell a circuitous and confusing tale involving social theories, mathematical formulas, chemical manipulation and gene splicing. As he spoke his breathing became more labored and he began to pull at his earlobes. The dean became alarmed and reached for his phone to call for emergency medical services but the young man held up his hand and begged him to stop.

"I don't want this getting out right now. I'm not sure what I'm seeing. I'm not sure what I'm saying. I don't want anything to happen to him. I just don't know what to do."

The Dean leaned over and put his hands on his shoulders.

"Don't worry. For now this is strictly between you and me. You have harmed no-one except for battering yourself needlessly."

He managed to sound soothing and empathetic while in his head he was seething with excitement. If what this boy said was even partially true, they were sitting on the tip of a gigantic, world-changing iceberg. He needed to expedite the tenure process to ensure the college's financial stake in whatever Dr. Marvelous produced.

"Thank you, young man," he said as he patted Ivan's head and smoothed his tangled hair. "You have done a great service. Now go home and fret no more. It is out of your hands."

Ivan managed a weak smile as he rose from the chair. The Dean sat back down on the desk with his hand up to his chin, staring out the window. As Ivan opened the office door he paused, thinking. He lifted his head, spread his hands, and spoke in such a deeper, clearer, darker tone that the Dean snapped to attention.

"By the way," Ivan said, his face like stone. "He's banging the other Grad Assistant."

The Dean called Dr. Marvelous into his office to ask for explanations of what Ivan had told him. Without revealing his source he pieced together as best he could the facts he believed had been revealed and his tentative interpretation of their meaning. Dr. Marvelous blinked.

"Did Doris tell you all that?"

"You mean your other graduate assistant?"

Dr. M. smiled at the word "other".

"No matter. As far as my work goes I think my published papers speak for themselves. Beyond that, most of my work is purely theoretical at this point. I wish to keep it secret until I have demonstrable answers and facts. I don't want anyone to steal my hypotheses and possibly beat me to the punch, although I doubt there is anyone as capable as I am to make such mysteries into realities."

"Do you think it might be possible to compose a simple description of the aims of your research to satisfy any curiosity the other administrators might have? Just a paragraph will do, you know, to keep the record straight."

"You can tell them what I've told you just now. If that is not good enough for them then you'll have my resignation as soon as I can write it."

The meeting ended with the Dean promising to stay out of Dr. M's business and to shield him from other prying minds. The Dean kept his word and the tempest subsided. But, there was nothing he could do when another bit of scandalous information hit the local news media, causing an uproar that skyrocketed up to the State level. Dr. Marvelous resigned in disgrace and disappeared into the ether, taking his menagerie with him. A graduate student named Doris Sandhurst vanished at the same time. When the police questioned her ex-boyfriend about her sudden absence he replied with two simple words.

"Good riddance."

TWO

This is where I came in. My working pseudonym is Charlton Bronson. I have a PhD in Genetics from Oxford University. I am also a graduate of a clandestine organization I am not at liberty to name. At the time of Dr. Marvelous' disappearance I remember hearing, in both organizations, vague stories about secret experiments being conducted in the wilds of New England. Being an all-around novice these stories held little interest for me at the time as I thought they sounded either like the most amorphous of tabloid fabrications or possibly even cleverly ambiguous precursors of a clandestine disinformation campaign. In other words: bullshit. I moved on and the stories faded into dark regions at about the same time as their protagonist. Five years later I was no longer an "organization man" but a freelance operative with credentials a mile long and a history of great if not spectacular success in every project I had ever taken on. I was hired by a consortium of European and American security agencies; some of the strangest bedfellows your nightmares could ever conjure. My mission: to find Dr. Marvelous and, if possible, infiltrate his organization if, indeed, one existed, and, ultimately, to either convince him to work with my employers; bribe him to work with my employers; strong arm him into working for my employers; or else, if necessary, steal his research or, barring that, destroy it. My usual methodology was to ingratiate myself with one or two central actors by volunteering for and performing tasks that might be important, desirable, or repugnant to them without asking for payment, recognition, or a quid pro quo. I knew that once I made contact I would have no problem convincing Dr. M of my usefulness as a scientist and gaining his confidence while keeping my real purpose a complete secret. Being a geneticist himself I was reasonably sure he had heard of and probably read my doctoral thesis on the genetic basis for herd behavior in feral Nepalese Bangur swine which was hailed as "revolutionary" and appeared in research journals around the world. I was, for a short time, a "science celebrity": a "wunderkind of wildebeest"; the "ace of antelopes"; the "maestro of muskoxen"; etcetera, etcetera, ad infinitum. But that was my first and last genetics paper. I wanted to have fun. I wanted to buck the odds. What intrigued me was gambling. I decided I could either become a gambler myself or, instead, exercise my wiles at the casino while operating covertly; busting all manner of bad guys or carrying out whatever mission my clients were willing to pay for. Working freelance undercover allowed me to have it all.

My first problem was finding him.

As it turns out he was also a genius at melting into nothingness. It's not easy to escape modern surveillance technologies and methods but it's not impossible either. It took about 15 minutes to crack all the obvious portals for traces of ghost fingerprints: cyber pointers, credit card transactions, cell phone locators, and other digital trail markers. Nothing. That left me mainly with the physical search option; a tedious and possibly calendar-busting slog of acquaintance interviews, surreptitious searches, and Academy Award-worthy personal subterfuges. I like a challenge but I hate to waste time. I studied the known history of the obnubilate Doctor, made an analysis of the possibilities, and shot straight for New Hampshire small college and ski country. It wasn't much of a gamble because one thing you can always count on is people's belief that they need "closure" to move on with life so I wasn't excessively puffed up with myself when I located a recently unclosed-out individual named Ivan: Ivan the "ex"; Ivan the Grad Ass.; Ivan (it turns out) the ski instructor. His one-hundred-and-ten-percent teaching technique was locally and privately referred to as "The Crash Course" and his bruised and splinted alumni anointed him with a name befitting his snarling attitude: Ivan the Terrible. Not knowing his back story they had him figured all wrong. I didn't have that problem.

I signed up for lessons and it took less than an hour of my sycophantic chatter to get him to invite me to the lodge for a drink. Without his ski gear he looked small with a thin face outlined by tight curly hair and a wisp of goatee. I felt sorry for the little guy so I maneuvered him around to my purpose as quickly as I could to spare him any unnecessary trauma.

"Hey," I said, after profusely complimenting his prowess on the slopes. "Does your girlfriend have an older sister?"

"Why?" His eyes narrowed until they looked crossed. I had to pull back slightly.

"Oh, no reason. I hear the club downstairs is really swinging and I love to dance. I'm just a little shy and I have problems talking to strange women. I thought that if you knew somebody....."

He frowned and looked down at the floor.

"I don't have a girlfriend and she doesn't have a sister. If she did I wouldn't wish her on my worst enemy."

"I'm sorry I asked. I didn't mean to bring up something painful for you."

I decided to take a calculated emotional risk. I forced myself to blush, stood up, thanked him, and started toward the elevator. Stopped dead when he called out.

"Mister! Why don't you sit back down and just tell me what you want."

I thought I had somehow given myself away when he started babbling about how he was a lousy skier; that nobody at the lodge liked him; that nobody at his school liked him.

"And you come in here and you're talking all nice to me. I figure you must want something so what is it? I may be naive but I'm not dumb."

I told him I was writing a book on the new pioneers in the DNA field. I improvised a few inspired embellishments and by the time I finished shoveling my convoluted fairy-tale cover story at him he volunteered everything he knew about Dr. Marvelous and his research; Dr. Marvelous and his bizarre personality; and finally, Dr. Marvelous and Doris. None of his confused babble had any real interest for me; useless material not worth a two-bit ante. Still I indulged him with sympathetic nods sprinkled with eye-pops, "oh my"s and "tsk-tsk"s. He finally accidentally got around to the golden nugget.

"She called me to apologize for the way things happened and that was the only time I heard from her. I was so mad."

For a moment I contemplated exactly how I would get a hold of his phone so I could bring it to my tech crew to analyze his incoming calls when suddenly he cried out with his hands spread in a crucifixion pose.

"Why did she go with him? What does she see in him? And of all places what the hell is she doing in Havana?"

THREE

I purchased a used Cape Islander with the name "ACRO" painted on the stern (which is "Orca" spelled backward - yes, I know), and large enough to get safely across the Estrecho de Florida. We were to meet my friend Toro Del Oro in a deserted bay between Matanzas and the "City of Columns."

(Did I say "we"? I brought Ivan along because I thought he might be of use. At the very least he so completely bought my story that I hoped his sincerity might be able to sway Doris who then could possibly gently influence Dr. Marvelous and eliminate a slew of precarious machinations on my part, the failure of any of which could complicate the successful completion of my contract. We'll see.)

As we approached the shore we could see an inflatable dinghy rowing out toward our boat, powered by the muscular arms of what appeared to be a stumpy strongman escaped from a half-scale circus. His impeccable white linen summer suit contrasted oddly with his ragged straw sombrero as he climbed aboard and immediately held out his hand. Ivan stared at the tiny figure who appeared to be substantially south of four feet tall then reached for the proffered hand to shake it but jumped back when the man emitted a sudden, guttural roar.

"Cabron!" he said. "No stranger touches Toro. I don't know where you've been." He pulled at the bottom of his coat to flatten some of the wrinkles and turned to me. "Who is el baboso? Ah, never mind" He held out his hand again. "Cash. Cash in hand. Cash transactions only. Five thousand dollars tickling my fingers or this is as close as you get to your prey."

"Five thousand?" I said. "You can't be my friend Toro. You must be one of the Pirate's ghosts that haunt these waters."

"Don't play with me," he said, pounding his index finger into the palm of his other hand. “En la palma de la mano, Blackbeard. Pay me or you will have come all this way for nothing.”

I put on a good act of reluctantly handing him a stack of U.S. hundreds and worked up a sincere frown as he counted it. To myself I smiled as I thought about the inconceivable amount of cash hidden below in the engine compartment destined for the potential purchase of Dr. Marvelous.

“So,” I said. “You do know where he is?”

He didn’t answer but laughed quietly as he pulled his dinghy up on the deck and lashed it to the gunwales. He looked at Ivan who was trembling and soaked with sweat.

“You’re a dwarf!” Ivan blurted out.

I readied myself in case Toro was packing a small blade. I’d seen him hack up men four times his size just for sport; but an insult? I was relieved when he looked up at the pathetic little Grad Ass. and smiled.

“Listen, Muchacho. Charlie and me are old friends,” he paused and winked at me, “from Oxford. So instead of killing you right now, in deference to him, I’ll give you 30 days to live.” He shook his head and muttered, “I am too generous to my own detriment.” He waved his arm at me. “Come. I’ll give you the coordinates. So you know you can trust me I’ll come along for the ride.”

“I wouldn’t have it any other way,” I said and turned to pat Ivan on the shoulder. “Relax, kid. We’ll be there soon.”

“I don’t know what I’ll do when I see her,” he put his hands on the sides of his head. “I don’t know what to say to her. I don’t know what she’ll say to me.”

I don’t like rogue variables and I was beginning to regret bringing him along. “You just listen to me and you’ll be fine,” I said. I knew that, in the end, his situation would resolve itself for better or worse and I didn’t really care enough to dwell on it. My only concern was his effect on Doris. I was prepared with alternate methods of manipulation in case Ivan flipped out, but was nonetheless confident I could pull his strings when the time came.

I joined Toro in the cabin where we exchanged our usual insults over shots of some exquisite rum he had obtained on the big island. Finally he handed me a piece of paper with latitude and longitude scrawled on it and I searched the ultra-reliable and up-to-date charts I had obtained from a generous group of recently deceased smugglers.

“There’s nothing there,” I said, pointing at the location. “There’s nothing within a hundred miles of that point.”

He rolled his eyes. "You don't trust me?"

"Not any more than you trust me."

"That's exactly why I'm coming with you. We're old friends and I want to prove my honesty."

I fished my encrypted communicator out of my pocket and punched in the numbers.

"Toro, Toro, Toro. You're just curious about this Dr. Marvelous and how you might be able to extort a few dollars out of him."

I frowned as the device returned a null verdict. I was certain I had entered the correct numbers but the top secret satellite I was accessing showed an empty expanse of water. I made a decision and fired up the engine.

"I always wanted to see the Bermuda Triangle," I said.

"So! You believe me now!"

"Only one way to find out."

I gunned the motor and skated off toward a blank space half way to Cay Sal Bank. I heard a crash and a moan at the back of the boat. Toro waved his arms and jack-knifed over the back of the pilot's seat mimicking Ivan's knarley near-taco at the stern.

"El Tonto rides again!" He looked out the cabin door and gave me a thumbs up which I chose to interpret as signifying the kid was still with us.

I checked my heading on my device and noted the winking emoji verifying that my other message had been received and Plan A was in effect. (The plan was simple and nearly one hundred percent fool proof. We'll see.)

As we approached our destination on that moonless night I turned off the motor and all the lights. We drifted toward the darkened hulk of the island and tossed out our anchor when we were about a half mile out. I put on my night goggles and the three of us got into Toro's dinghy. I held the rudder as he pulled silently yet powerfully toward a strip of sand that appeared as a lighter dark spot in front of us. The noise of the waves masked the sound of the oars and I was certain we had attained complete surprise as we pulled the boat out of the water. In a flash we were blasted by the beams of several bright spotlights that in my night goggles resembled a sheet of fire. I ripped the goggles off to see Ivan standing frozen in front of me and Toro scampering gingerly down the beach until he, too, froze in his tracks. Several gun-toting shadows stretched along the sand to my position and a bullhorn blasted from somewhere behind the lights.

"Velcome to Marvelous Island," came a high-pitched voice with an accent I remembered from a project in Kinshasa. "Ve are pleased to have visitors. Shtep toward the lights and our staff vill lead you to your accommodations."

"Moby." I recognized the shearing tones of a furiously deranged individual whom I had never met but whose bizarre recordings lay dormant in that portion of my brain reserved for dirges and satanic chants, parked right next to vivid festering holograms generated by impossibly warped and morbid tales, all apparently true. "Didn't plan on this," I thought.

The lights were kept shining in our faces until someone came up behind me and shoved a black bag over my head. I've been bagged like that before but there was something a little odd about this time; almost as if the person behind me was breathing through his belly button.

FOUR

When they finally removed our blindfolds we were standing in front of a cluster of quaint, New England-style cottages that rubbed the environment entirely the wrong way. Soft light from solar powered lamp posts illuminated white picket fences and gabled roofs among the palm trees that only added to the strangeness I'd felt on the beach. Our escorts, who we had only seen as shadows, vanished into the jungle. A squat figure in a black uniform on the front steps of the first house waved his arms for us to approach.

"My name is Moby," he puffed out his chest. "Perhaps you've heard of me."

"Por supuesto!" Toro burst out. "Of course! Moby DICK!"

"Schweinehund!" Moby's right arm flashed across to his belt where he yanked out a whip. We all stood with our mouths agape, more awestruck by his choice of words than the imminence of mayhem. He was about to whip the rubber snake across Toro's face but suddenly froze in mid swing at the sound of one commanding word.

"Halt!"

Now we all turned in unison toward the remarkably practiced voice. I heard Ivan groan and watched as his bones dissolved. He fell to his knees and began to weep uncontrollably, for there before us was a vision unlike anything I'd ever seen except in comic books. A woman standing, hands on hips, legs planted firmly apart, wearing red glittered knee-high boots, silver glittered short-shorts, a tight and low-cut red white and blue glittered top, muscles bulging through the short glittered sleeves, and crowned by a blue glittered headband under a lion's mane of red, silver and black glittered hair.

Toro laughed so hard he had trouble speaking until finally he flung out his arms and cried, "Wonder Woman!"

Ivan, fighting to keep from merging with the ground, let out a long, spiraling, excruciating wail.

"Dooooorrrrrrriiiiiiiissssss!"

"Hello Ivan," she said coldly and turned to Moby.

I knew who Moby was from an assignment I had in the Congo where my cover was as a recruiter for an international circus. My real task was to root out poachers by making shady deals with the local authorities to legally illegally acquire endangered animals. Moby was the popular leader of an acapella quartet consisting of full-grown adults under four feet tall and all members of the Mbenga tribe; folks more commonly referred to as pygmies. In reality he was the mastermind and enforcer for a brutal cabal of Belgian-Mbenga half-breeds who, following Moby's unholy orders, strutted around the countryside wearing S.S. style outfits, claiming to be pure Belgian while speaking a pygmy hybrid of German as they rounded up individuals or entire villages for the international slave trade. I won't describe their methods of persuasion here but it was once rumored that a recalcitrant village was purposely contaminated with Ebola, causing an epidemic that ended up infecting a good chunk of the center of the continent. At about that time Moby was declared an international "public enemy number one" and disappeared with a stash of Euros and U.S. currency rumored to be in the tens of millions.

"Thank you for your diligence, Commander," Doris said. "The Doctor is forever in your debt."

Well, well, well, I thought.

Moby snapped off a salute and marched to a hidden path in the undergrowth. Before entering he turned to Toro.

"Vee shall meet again," he said, and vanished into the darkness.

Once inside the house where we were to be quartered, Doris, hands on her hips again, took a good long look at me and Toro and totally ignored Ivan. Her eyes rested for the longest time on Toro and her expression told me she was filing something away in her brain, for what reason I couldn't fathom at the time. She handed each of us a hollowed coconut filled with an effervescent fruit liqueur that tasted like a thoroughbred and kicked like a mule. I felt a little dizzy as she showed us the rooms we would stay in for the night and I noticed Ivan slurring along like a catatonic robot trying to walk under water. We ended up in a small, cozy sitting room decorated like the home of an early twentieth century country squire. There were floor lamps with tasseled satin lampshades, hand carved teak furniture, and multi-colored braided throw rugs. You would have thought you were in a plantation outside of Boston except for the moldy reek of jungle humidity. In the center stood a low coffee table laden with freshly cut tropical fruits. A rattan fan turning overhead completed the picture, stirring the air just enough to make it tolerable.

"So, what is the purpose of your visit?"

I was about to answer Doris' question when Ivan snapped out of his present traumatic stress disorder and blurted out, "I came to tell you I love you!"

He stood up and moved toward her

"I've always loved you.," he stepped. "I will always love you!" Another step. "Can't you see I came all this way because I love you?" Hands extended and head tilted to one side. A human question mark.

Doris turned to me and Toro.

"Ivan has been plagued by certain conditions as long as I have known him. With me he displayed a borderline personality, paranoia, and the immediately apparent condition you have just witnessed."

"Obsessive Love Disorder," I said.

Doris smiled. "Bravo, bravo man."

"You piece of shit!" Ivan attempted to lunge at me but his next step brought his shin directly into contact with the coffee table and he fell face first into the mango and papaya slices. Instead of getting up he remained face down in the fruit platter licking his lips.

"Sweet," he said.

Doris lifted her arm and spoke into her glittered bracelet.

"Housekeeping to Bungalow 'A' for a spill." She placed one glitter boot foot on Ivan the Limp and casually shoved him off the table. "Also a trash pick up. Thank you."

She sat, crossed her legs, and lit a Cuban cigar so fragrant I was tempted to ask for one. Next to me I could hear Toro's breath coming with unnatural frequency. I need not have worried because she laughed and produced a box full of Bolivar Belicosos. Soon we were all lit up from every possible angle.

"You were about to explain your presence here," Doris said. She pointed at the now completely unconscious Ivan on the floor. "We receive infrequent desultory visitors to our small island. The few that have spent some hours among us have been scared off by the guards, or Moby, or the peculiarities of our inhabitants. In your case, I'm quite certain it is no accident."

I decided to throw reality to the wind and dive right into my fiction.

"My name is Charlton Bronson..."

"The actor?" She leaned closer and stared.

Toro burst out laughing. He waved his cigar in a big circle as he elongated the next words.

"DOOOOOOCTOR Cha-arlton Bronson."

Doris shrugged, leaned back, and took a long pull on her Bolivar.

"Does that disappoint you?" I said.

"Yes and no." She gently stubbed out her cigar and wrapped it to finish later. "Yes I'm disappointed you're not the actor."

"And the 'no' part?"

"The no part." She glided toward the exit. "No, I'm happy you're here. Dr. Marvelous has been expecting you."

As she walked out the door, Doris told us to get some sleep. In a few hours we would be having breakfast with the Doctor and his day begins at dawn. Toro and I sat silently for a while. Finally he shook and shivered like he had a sudden chill.

"Did you see the way she looked at me?"

"Are you having a fantasy experience?" I said. "No more mixing alcohol and Bolivars for you."

Toro had a pained look on his face.

"No, my friend. It was creepy, how she looked at me. Like she was dissecting me, and not in a pleasurable way."

"Well, Senor, there is something strange and foul that's been haunting us since we came ashore. And that last bit about him knowing I was coming injects far too many uncertainties into this operation."

I stared deep into Toro's eyes.

"You don't think I told anybody about this?" he said. "I would be cutting my steadiest source of revenue. Cutting my own throat." He wiped a torrent of perspiration from his forehead with his sleeve.

I believed him. Toro Del Oro is a fearless human. In all the years I'd worked with him and through all the crazy dicey situations, I had never seen him sweat.

We lifted Ivan and deposited him in his room. Toro complained about having left his toothbrush in the dinghy then closed his door. I heard him moving something heavy in front of it and pulling on it to make sure it was secure. I sat on my bed with my communication device and, having nothing more to go on than a weird feeling possibly brought on by whatever was in that coconut, sent my first scheduled encrypted message simply as "All going well."

I always sleep soundly when I'm on a mission as long as my senses detect a reasonable distance from danger; although there have been times I've stayed awake for four or five days straight without any chemical help; just pure Armageddon adrenaline. As weird as the day had been I had the feeling that Dr. Marvelous was looking forward to meeting me, possibly Toro, and maybe even his former Grad. Ass., and that no harm would come to any of us, at least for this night. At moments like this it's almost like my brain, knowing the presence of peace, prepares for the approaching necessity for extreme acuity and adaptability by stretching out on a comfort cloud for a solid few hours; re-balancing and recharging. Besides, the bed was comfortable, the mosquito netting was diaphanous, and the air conditioner in the window was cranking out a cool lullaby. But as my head hit the pillow my resting process was interrupted by the professional black ops part of my brain that clicked on one belated but obvious question: Where the hell do they get the power to run air conditioners, electric lights, ceiling fans, wall outlets. Other questions came racing forward about the population of the island; the sources of food, medicines, ammunition? Peculiar inhabitants? A large yawn convinced me of the low probability or priority of obtaining answers at that moment and that it was best to wait for the day. We'll see.

FIVE

I was awakened by Toro leaning over me, toothbrush in mouth, garbling something about "Bo-Be. Outside." Then I heard the bullhorn.

"You vill be dressed and present yourselves on ze front porch in five minutes or ve vill be forced to come in and get you. Ze Doctor is vaiting. This is your first and last varning."

"Where'd you get the toothbrush?"

Toro realized he still had the instrument in his mouth and pulled it out.

"I sneaked out in the middle of the night. My teeth must be clean, especially after mangoes and Bolivars. But listen."

He put his lips close to my ear as if he feared we were under some sort of surveillance.

"There are guards posted all over the place. I was surprised they didn't hide my boat. It was dragged up the beach and tied to a tree and maybe they forgot about it. Who knows? I cut the rope so it looked like it snapped and I took it down the shore about a half mile. It's well hidden because nobody messes with my dinghy. On my way back I smoothed out my footprints in the sand. Wait!"

He ran across the hall to his room and returned with a small vial filled with sea water and what looked like a shred of cotton candy floating in it. I immediately recognized it as a highly poisonous, insidiously small species of jellyfish.

"It might come in handy," Toro said. His face shook with a poorly suppressed guffaw as Moby began a final thirty second countdown that ended abruptly at "5, 4, 3, 2……"

"Halt!"

Go Doris! I thought as I dressed quickly and joined Toro who was waiting outside my door.

"One funny thing," he said. "I have a compass app on my phone and it keeps spinning like a crazy clock. GPS doesn't work either. I followed the stars to the shore so I had no real problem but still, it was strange."

I took a quick look at my communicator. It seemed fine but there was still no response to my transmission. If it didn't come soon I would have to try other less reliable methods. For now, I focused on the pending meeting and getting into character. Toro and I pulled Ivan from his room and maneuvered him out the front door. He kept muttering "I'm OK. I'm OK," as if he was trying to convince himself. I, for one, was not convinced but completely unconcerned as I had written him off as being any help long before his performance in the sitting room.

Outside, Doris stood in what I now considered her signature pose: hands on hips, legs firmly planted, with a blank expression on her face. However the glitter show was replaced by a more conventional tropical outfit of khaki shorts and blouse, topped with a wide-brimmed khaki hat. Moby stood behind her swinging his bullhorn and unsuccessfully suppressing a scowl aimed directly at Toro. He looked fresh and dapper in his crisply pressed S.S. uniform and raised the bullhorn to his lips but stopped when Doris' jacked up her right hand without turning around to look at him.

"Good morning," she said. "Follow us and be careful where you step."

That seemed like an odd request as the way ahead was clear and well worn. Suddenly a dozen small animals charged across our path and disappeared into the brush on the other side. Ivan was finally stirred out of his lethargy as he jumped three feet into the air screaming "Rats! Rats! I hate Rats! There's rats!" Granted, they were the size of smallish rats, but for the few seconds they were visible I could swear they looked like tiny pigs. As we emerged into a clearing we were greeted by miniature bleating animals that lowered their horns as if to attack then scattered as we moved closer. Toro looked at me wide eyed and whispered, "Baby goats?" Yes, they were goats. But too small even for newborns.

We finally came upon a long cinder block building lifted several feet off the ground by concrete pylons. Carved into a polished piece of mahogany above the lintel were the words:

"Never let your sense of morals prevent you from doing what is right." - Isaac Asimov

Two giants dressed in full length black robes and carrying AK47s guarded the entrance. They must have been eight feet tall and their torsos seemed to be rippling even as they stood still; everything about them was out of proportion; especially their heads which were far too small for their bodies; like the stunted stems of swollen over-ripe bananas. They moved awkwardly aside as we mounted the steps and Moby turned the wheel on a steel door not unlike a water-tight hatch on a submarine. He swung up his bullhorn and before Doris could stop him yelled "Schnell!" He smiled and seemed so pleased with himself that he hardly noticed our complete obliviousness to his barking. We sauntered inside followed by the two guards who seemed to duck with their ankles to clear the lintel and positioned themselves on either side of the door as Moby re-secured the hatch.

Inside we paused in a reception area with similar décor to the sitting room at the house except that the rattan fan was pushing around cool, air-conditioned, mildew-free air.

"Wait here," Doris said.

"All day," Toro said: eyes closed, a broad smile, and hands lifted in thanks to the gods of artificially created temperate zones. He removed his linen jacket revealing the holstered Bowie knife under his left arm pit and Moby immediately jumped in front of him, put the bullhorn in his face, and blasted out "No weapons are allowed in the compound!"

Toro clutched at his holster but Moby was too quick.

"You vill get it back after ze Doctor dismisses you."

Toro's eyes flashed venom which only caused Moby to smirk harder as he admired the blade and stuck it in his belt.

"If you get it back," he said.

"Where did she go?" Ivan popped into consciousness. "Where is she? I have to talk to her." He jerked his head around the room. "But what will I say? How can I convince her? This is the most important moment of my life." He spun around faster and faster until he started to get dizzy, lost his balance, and again fell face first onto a coffee table, fruitless this time. At that moment Doris returned, placed her army-booted foot on Ivan's rump, and shoved him onto the floor. He slowly turned onto his back and stared up at Doris, her hair lightly billowing from the whoosh of the ceiling fan.

"Is this heaven?"

"No," she said. "It's Iowa."

Even Moby had to laugh at that one. Toro and I helped Ivan get on his feet. As his eyes revealed a wobbly but successful journey back to reality he put his hands to the sides of his head and was about to panic when Doris turned away.

"All of you come with me."

She led us into an adjoining room where a table was laid out with fruits, nuts, and a chafing pan with hot scrambled eggs and foot-long, six inch wide strips of bacon. Toro picked up a piece and glanced at me sideways, then shoved it in his mouth.

"Excellente. Is this from a pig or an elephant?

I tilted my head towards Doris and he stopped chewing.

"I realize you all must be hungry. Please indulge in some of our island specialties, all freshly harvested and prepared this morning." She waved her hand over the food like a model at a car show. "Unfortunately the Doctor will not be joining us but will meet you all afterward in his office. Bon appetit."

We wiped out most of the food. Even Ivan roused himself sufficiently from his googly-eyed concentration on Doris to consume large quantities of fruit and bacon, but only after Doris gently cajoled him.

"Eat!" She glared at him with twisted lips and bared teeth. Toro paused in his noisy consumption long enough to chuckle but quickly lost his jolly demeanor when Doris turned and smiled at him sweetly.

"Food is the engine of a man's strength," she said. "El hombre hermoso."

Toro looked at me with his eyes bugged out. I just shrugged, trying to appear calm and nonchalant while my mind was churning with anticipation and rehearsing different pathways and possibilities for getting inside of Doctor Marvelous.

All of us, including the two guards, were led down a hallway that stretched out the length of the building. Everything was glossy white and the floor was paved with spotless uniformly light gray tile. The first door on the left was open and we were led inside a large room lined with bookshelves bolted firmly to dark paneled walls. It could have been mistaken for a library at Harvard except for the clusters of beakers and displays of small animal skeletons scattered about the room. A man and a woman, both shorter than Moby, stood in front of a desk on which were neatly stacked notebooks, several cans of colored toy modeling compound, a brown briefcase, and a scattering of red, orange, and green gummy candies. The man was young but balding. What hair remained around the sides was thick and brown and drooped past his shoulders. His eyes were closed and the overhead lights glinted off his pate as he moved his head back and forth with a swishing motion. The woman, who had short curly hair and wore a floor length white frock over combat boots, spoke first.

"I am Doctor Cho," she said. "I am a plant geneticist and am responsible for the vegetables, fruits, nuts, and roots that feed our human and animal inhabitants. So, also, the repast you have just enjoyed." She smiled mechanically and pointed a finger with a psychedelically painted five inch fingernail straight at the bespectacled eyes of her companion who stood with a slouch so pronounced that his chest hovered a few inches farther back than the heels of his running shoes. He wore a short white lab coat festooned with pockets loaded with pencils, various sized dentist's mirrors, thin screwdriver-like devices with wires protruding from their visible end, and what appeared to be some sort of viscid dried fruit sticks that had welded one pocket shut. His trousers could best be described as Cossack bloomers that were tucked into high-top canvas sneakers..

"This is Doctor Kykshinski." she continued. "He is responsible for all power generation, electronic devices, video, music, and security systems on the island."

His eyes remained closed as his arms lifted up to conduct an invisible orchestra. I pointed at Moby's bullhorn. "That, too?" I said.

Moby made a move to grab a blackjack hanging from his belt but stopped when Doris snapped her hand up to his face.

"Commander Moby is the master of all *physical* security and is in complete control of all of his accouterments. Dr. Kykshinski's main contribution here is keeping this island powered and invisible. Isn't that right?" Doris turned to the man and raised her voice. "The celebrated Dr. K?"

At this he snapped out of his reverie and removed two small wireless earbuds. He smiled and raised one eyebrow.

"I must apologize. I sensed your presence but," he pointed at his ear, "Tchaikovsky."

Dr. Cho leaned into his face.

"Tchaikovsky? I thought today's selection was Frank Zappa."

"What's the difference?" said Dr. K.

SIX

At that moment a side door slapped open and, after a short dramatic pause, a tall, thin, wild-haired man emerged into the room wearing a black robe covered in crescent moons with a pointed wizard's hat to match. Doris, Moby, Cho, Kykshinski, and the guards snapped to attention. Ivan looked more bewildered than ever. Toro twirled at a nonexistent handlebar mustache and blurted out with a flourish, "The Wizard will see you now!"

I sized up the figure that ignored all of them as he glided to the center of the room. *Quite possibly off his rocker,* I thought. If so, my mission was over. I was conflicted as to whether that was a good thing or not. (We'll see.)

"Greetings Earthlings," he said. "So glad you could come. Now all of you leave except the guards and," he turned to me. "You."

As the others marched out I took a long look at Cho and Kykshinski. Her name and face carried only a vague recollection but something about Dr. K stirred a dim, uneasy memory deep in my frontal cortex. I turned back to find Dr. Marvelous peeling away his hat, robe, and fright wig to reveal a brightly colored floral tee shirt, cut-off jeans, and a brush cut head of hair. He smiled a crooked smile.

"Please excuse my ludicrous subterfuge but I wanted to meet my visitors' expectations of what a mad scientist looks like. Were you impressed?"

"It was interesting," I said.

He quickly lost his smile.

"I don't care," he said. "I want to know why you're here."

Here goes, I thought. *Break a leg.*

"I am an Oxford graduate with a degree in genetics. I've read all of your published papers as well as news stories about your experiments and," now I paused, "your extra-curricular challenges."

"That crap follows you forever," he said and picked up some of the modeling clay from his desk. "But I asked you why you're here."

He began to shape the clay while he talked and before he finished speaking he had fashioned a tiny giraffe. Watching his hands work almost threw me off my script. I decided to put him a little off balance.

"Doris said you were expecting me."

It worked, somewhat. He stopped playing with the clay and put one hand up to his nose, fingering the still visible monkey bone scar.

"I keep a very short list of possible collaborators who meet three criteria and whom I am always expecting, or at least hoping, to appear here at any time. The first is that they be scientifically advanced enough to be labeled 'genius'. The second is that they are fed up with the materialism of those who hold the real power in this world. I admit this is fantasy thinking bordering on psychosis. However, Dr. Cho's and Dr. Kykshinski's names were on that list, as was yours. You see they are here and now, you. Perhaps some psychoses are fruitful, do you agree?"

Kykshinski! I remembered suddenly: Ukrainian nuclear physicist and force field virtuoso who disappeared a few years ago along with some reactor hardware and fissionable material.

"They just showed up here one day?" I said.

He smirked his signature smirk. "I don't care to describe their individual journeys or the method of their acquisition. It doesn't matter, as yours doesn't matter. You're here. Finem fabula."

'End of story'. It seemed a darkly appropriate expression if you're someone who believes the end is all that counts. I shook off my internal philosophical digression and crossed my arms to get that confident look.

"As I said I've studied all your work and I believe you are onto something; something huge that your earlier work only hinted at. The more I investigated, the more excited I became. I resolved to find you and offer you my services; to become a part of whatever future-changing work you're doing."

He kissed the giraffe and placed it gently on a shelf I hadn't noticed before that was filled with other small clay animals exquisitely shaped and appearing almost alive.

"So why did you stop?"

Ok. For a moment I was stumped. He picked up a small comb and began trying to tame his eyebrows.

"You published your results of a mildly interesting but technically brilliant study concerning the herd instinct. You were for a time, as they say, the toast of the academy. Then you never published again."

"I dropped out."

"You disappeared."

"Doesn't make me a bad person," I said. He laughed: a loud, short, high-pitched 'Ha!' He put the comb down, apparently giving up domesticating the wild bushes over his eyes, and folded his arms. For an instant I got the feeling he was mocking me.

"That is the final criteria that got you on my list. Criteria Three: you vanished, utterly. Why?"

It was time for the plot twist, Act One.

"I quickly became bored with the direction of my investigations when I was constantly approached by large corporations and Universities whose only interest was turning research into profits. I wanted to accomplish something no-one had ever done before; something much more fulfilling and positive and perhaps even world-changing."

"So you only care about having a fundamental impact on humanity: a selfless individual." He stopped and pushed himself right in my face. "Or a selfish individual, yes?"

I stared right back at him.

"I was already famous. I wanted more. I had ideas that I needed to flesh out and expand upon without interference, some of it based on your work. I set up shop at a remote location in Scotland. Stayed off the grid: no telephone, no internet, solar panels and a windmill for electricity and peat moss for heat. I had clandestinely obtained the DNA of two mammals with widely divergent characteristics and worked for months experimenting with different clusters of gene arrangements until I experienced a breakthrough. By combining certain genetic elements of rhinoceros and Shetland pony I produced the worlds first genuine Unicorn."

I paused, waiting for his reaction. His nose was still only inches from mine when he lifted one eyebrow and the opposite corner of his mouth.

"Oh, really," he said. "I've never heard of such a thing. I imagine, if it were true, the entire world would know about it by now."

"Never got the chance. When the villagers heard about what was going on they came at night with gasoline cans and torches led by the local preacher waving a Bible and cursing me for blasphemy and trying to play God. Burned my quarters to the ground along with all my papers, vials of genetic material, and the unfortunate unicorn. I only survived by hiding in the cistern, although I came near to boiling to death. Been bouncing around the planet and staying off the grid ever since and," another dramatic pause. "Looking for you."

He looked away from me and swung slowly side to side, his eyes turned up to the ceiling until he seemed to come to a decision and turned to the guards.

"You are dismissed," he said. "But first."

He waved his hand at me.

"You have been wondering about my guards."

I looked up at their heads almost touching the ceiling.

"Yes. Almost everyone else here seems to be a midget, a dwarf, or," I paused. "A Moby."

"Stand down," he said to the guards. Their bodies seemed to snap in half. It was either the most impossible contortion ever accomplished or else the punch line of a parlor trick. When they flipped off their robes I realized it was the latter, for underneath each cloth had been two four-foot individuals, one standing on the other's shoulders.

Deuces wild, I thought. Their faces remained soldierly stoic but a slight twinkling in their eyes revealed their appreciation of the joke as they marched out and closed the door behind them.

"Yes," Dr. Marvelous said. "They are very good for scaring off the rare intruder. And true, everyone on this island including your friend Toro and except for myself, Doris, and you, are under four feet tall. Oh, and Ivan." He smirked. "Don't you want to ask why?"

He could barely contain a giggle as he waved his hand in the air.

"It doesn't matter. I will show you," he said.

He led me into a room filled with scientific instruments including conventional and electron microscopes, various delicate hand tools, laser contraptions, and, of all things, a microwave oven. In the center of the room, prominently placed on a marble column, was an enclosed glass vat with a viscous white material slowly being churned by a steel blade in the center. Embossed in gold letters accented by multi-colored precious stones was one word: MOBY. Dr. Marvelous was about to exit the room through another door when I stopped him.

"What is this?" I said, pointing to the vat.

"What does it say on it?" he smiled.

"Obviously it says Moby."

"That is what it is."

Every time I believed I had gotten a handle on his cut of humor he threw a new shuffle into the deck.

"Do you know why Commander Moby is here?" he said.

I was supposed to be a reclusive and inglorious scientist so I had to play dumb.

"I assume he has some kind of military or security experience. At least that's the act he's putting on."

"It's not an act. Moby is a tough, vain, disciplinarian and one of the most wanted men on the planet. A brutal, merciless, genocidal slave dealer with delusions of grandeur and quite proud to be so. Also he was, strangely enough, at one time, the leader of a famous acapella group."

"Why would you have someone like that here? He sounds dangerous to have around."

Dr. Marvelous lightly stroked the vat and blew dust off the gold letters.

"No, he is not dangerous, to us. In a way we are his greatest hope. I will explain in a minute. Suffice it to say that in spite of our self-sufficiency we still have need of items that cost money in the larger world. We can use no credit cards, bank transfers or other payment methods that might be traceable. We make all our purchases strictly with cash and Moby has a trove of it worth many millions, all illegally obtained of course."

I had suspected as much but I acted shocked anyway.

"Whatever work you're doing here is being financed by some kind of monster? How can you do that? I always thought integrity was the most attractive of your talents."

He smirked.

"There is a large cache of moral ambiguity in our situation. However, once you have seen and understood what we are doing here, I am confident you will agree there is no better way to cleanse filthy money than to use it for the greatest good."

He hugged the vat.

"Thank you, dearest Moby."

I morphed myself from shocked and indignant into exigent and impatient.

"You still haven't told me what that is."

He clasped his hands behind his back and began to pace back and forth as he spoke.

"Commander Moby is not here out of the goodness of his heart, that being a physical and spiritual impossibility. His most fervent ambition is to replicate himself and has been deeply frustrated all of his life by his inability to do so. We have convinced him that here, with our advanced work in genetics, we can successfully multiply and distribute his DNA to an infinite number of ova either through artificial insemination or in vitro fertilization."

"That's insane."

He paused his movement.

"Quite," he said. "Commander Moby believes he is the progenitor of a new master race. That is his quid pro quo: we mass produce his DNA, he turns over his cash."

Staring at the swirling, creamy liquid in the vat I started to feel breakfast creeping up my throat. Dr. Marvelous held out both hands in supplication to the container.

"This," he feigned wiping a tear from his eye, "is the master race."

I couldn't believe that he appeared to be getting emotional over one of the most evil deals I had ever heard of. He then removed the cover from the cylinder and fished some of the thick white waste matter out with the palm of his hand.

"Try some," he said. He saw the look of disgust on my face so he shoved the entire lump in his mouth and smiled.

"I can't do this," I found myself saying out loud.

He ignored me, carefully replaced the cover, continued licking his hand, and smirked.

"It's just whipped cream. You should be able to smell it from there. It's made fresh every morning and is very deliciously fragrant."

I don't often feel confused and fooled at the same time, but this strange man had pulled off a pure bluff. I continued my act by holding my head in my hands and uttering, "What?"

"We are not monsters. Quite the contrary as you will soon see. This is strictly a show for Moby who comes in here at least once a day to talk to it, as he believes it actually contains his quantumly multiplying sperm and the little fellows can hear him. He has no knowledge that his daily donation of effluent is placed in a safe container that is then zapped extravagantly in the microwave and the ashes sprinkled into one of our sewage disposals. You look a little out of sorts. Perhaps we can continue our tour another time."

That woke me up. I immediately snapped back into character.

"No, I'm very relieved and even more excited now to see what kind of work you're doing that could be worth all this bullshit."

For the first time he laughed out loud.

"Bullshit is wonderful fertilizer," he said. "Follow me and you will see."

SEVEN

When I passed through the next door I was surprised to see that the interior of the building held a series of open air courtyards separated by bamboo fences through which you could get nothing more than a sense of the area beyond. My eyes were momentarily clouded over from the heat. When they cleared I was standing before a twelve foot high green plant. Its leaves were dripping from the humidity but stood firm and thick, perfectly angled toward the sun. I looked around and the entire space was filled with a variety of similarly out-sized flora: tomatoes big as basketballs, asparagus clumps thick as baobabs, and a watermelon large enough for a small apartment.

"This curtilage harbors at least two of each major fruit and vegetable family, genetically modified to take the greatest advantage of this particular environment. You can see the result with your own eyes."

Continuing my act I rubbed my eyes in feigned disbelief.

"Incredible," I said. *Are they edible?* I thought.

Dr. Marvelous stroked one of the smooth green appendages. "You are thinking 'Are they edible?' Yes?"

Before I could respond he broke off a small piece of a leaf and held it to the sunlight, then dipped it into his open mouth where it gently and pleasantly crunched between his teeth.

"Not only are plants like these edible, they are so packed with nutrients that one 400 square foot plot like this can feed most of our island family year-round. But come," he said as he walked through a bamboo archway into the next space. I plucked a bite-sized piece off the same plant; sniffed it; licked it; chewed and swallowed it. *Kale,* I thought. I chewed another chunk and uttered out loud three words I never thought I would ever say in life: "Damned good kale."

When I walked through the next door Dr. Marvelous was standing in front of a black curtain that blocked the view beyond. I could only hear the sound of something dragging through the dirt but sensed a lumbering and enormous presence. From somewhere unseen the doctor produced a sparkling magician's cane.

"This," he waved the cane toward the curtain as he yanked it open. "Is 'Babe'."

Right there, behind the black screen, my entire field of vision was filled with a huge pinkish-white object sporting a foot long curly tail.

"Now that," I blurted out, "Is a butt!"

Dr. Marvelous turned to look. He shook his head in mild disgust.

"Babe," he called out. "Turn around and greet our guest."

Slowly, almost noiselessly, with the gentle drama of a ballerina, the beast reversed its direction and I was confronted with two triangular ears wider than a high-roller's blackjack table and a pink, truck-tire-sized snout. The two clear and lively eyes danced at the Doctor then turned to me and with a smooth pursing of leathery lips made the following sound:

"Oi-ooooink."

"It's as big as a rhinoceros," I said. "Where, on earth, did you get that?"

"She is only tangentially a denizen of this planet, and mostly given that she is here now. Before she was created none like her ever existed."

"Created?"

"Yes," he petted her nose which lined up perfectly with his. "Babe is the first of her kind and the mother of all elephantine swine on this island."

"If she's that big I'd like to see the male."

He smirked. "In the words that half the humans who have ever lived longed to hear, dating back to our cave ancestors and well before the myths of the Amazons: Males are not necessary."

He patted Babe on her chest, apparently a signal that she was dismissed, and she snorted at me, turned, and ambled over to a pile of partially chewed greenery.

"Babe is designed to be extremely fertile. She is inseminated monthly and produces a new brood of anywhere up to a dozen infants every 5 months and, you will be pleased to know, she produces males and females which grow rapidly to enormous size. They provide our people with higher quality and denser protein than could ever be conjured in a lab while consuming half the plant matter of a normal sized pig. They, along with the plants you viewed in the other room, are the givers of the nutritional bounty that keeps all of us healthy, strong, and mentally sharp."

Unlimited bacon and ribs, I thought. *No country for vegan men.*

He took me along a catwalk that skirted one wall of the yard toward another opening in another bamboo fence.

"Of course we are working on developing other sources of protein such as similarly modified cows. But these things take time and right now, are not my area of concentration."

I wondered what that area might be. After all, that's what I was here to discover. The next enclosure seemed to be deserted. The floor was thickly carpeted with dozens of varieties of lush green bushes, most of them about four feet tall. The humid air seemed to hover over the plants like it was afraid to touch them for fear of being devoured. Still, the leaves of all the plants were heavy and shiny with moisture and motionless in the confined, windless space. For once Doctor Marvelous was silent as he leaned on the railing observing the scene. Then I detected a motion in the upper branches that belied some sort of activity below. The doctor put his finger to his lips, quietly reached into his pocket, and pulled out a handful of gummy candies. He flung them out over the vegetation and a hand shot out of the greenery and snared a few of them. Then the owner of the hand, apparently delighted, began to jump up and down and sprinted on all fours to the edge of the catwalk where we were standing. It reared up laboriously on its short back legs and proceeded to bare its teeth in a song of grunts, clicks, and joyous howls.

"Greetings Garth," the Doctor said as he reached in his pocket, leaned over the railing, and held an orange, squishy sugar lump before the creature who softly plucked the treat with an amazingly precise index finger and opposing thumb. Placing it squarely on its tongue the apparition started chewing when its eyes fixed on me like I had just appeared out of thin air. I don't know if it could read expressions but my mouth hung open and I could feel my eyes bulging. Balanced awkwardly on two short hind legs was a vision from a 1930s Hollywood adventure movie that had scared me to death as a kid. In spite of the short height and tiny features, I found myself mindlessly staring at the miniature image of what had so unnerved me as a child: King Kong.

For a moment I was unhinged but managed to regain control of my mind when a voice like a low jazz flute solo brought me back to reality.

"He's waiting to see if you have candy. He thinks all white men bring candy."

A tiny, dark, woman with a netted bee-keeper's hat that shrouded her features sashayed down the catwalk.

"Doctor M," she laughed. "You should share your goodies with your friend. Let him offer a tidbit or you may destroy Garth's entire fantasy world." She turned to me and smiled. "I am Phillipa. Who are you who stares at my baby like he is some kind of monster?"

Before I could get a word out her 'baby' leaped onto the railing and hugged the woman who, at around three feet ten inches was only an inch taller than he was. His arms, however, were each long enough to wrap completely around her shoulders. I was afraid he might crush her but she touched her nose to his and he lightly leaped back to the ground, grinning from hairy ear to hairy ear.

"Now shoo!" Phillipa said. "You've had enough sugar. Do you want to be the worlds first diabetic gorilla?"

Garth made some grunting noises that sounded like a laugh and disappeared into the vegetation. Phillipa turned to me and removed her hat. Behind the dark netting and framed by the silkiest, blackest, funkiest dreadlocks I'd ever seen was a face so alluring that it simultaneously froze and melted my helpless eyeballs. She was one of the younger people I had seen on the island so far and one of the shortest; a perfectly proportioned miniature super model so sweetly transcendent that her mere presence seemed to envelope me in a fragrant cool fog. I guessed her age at about 29 and from the tattoos on her shoulders and chest an AC-DC fan.

"Well?" she said. When I moved my jaws and no words came out she repeated her previous question. "Who are you?"

Dr. Marvelous cut me off before I could answer.

"Dr. Bronson and two of his friends made a surprise visit to our island early this morning."

"You mean the muscular funny man and the pale nervous ghost who sniffs behind Doris? You came with them?"

The presence of everyday conversation was helping me re-balance and I managed to move like a sane person again.

"I wouldn't exactly describe them that way but yes, we arrived on the 3 a.m. dinghy."

She crossed her arms and looked sideways at me.

"Another funny man. Your being taller only stretches out your jokes. I like your dwarf friend better."

Dr. Marvelous spoke up. "Dr. Bronson is a genetic researcher who might be of value to our cause."

I didn't hear him. I was enjoying the repartee with this charged up woman.

"Now you," I said.

"Who me? I'm the monster trainer here. What do you think?"

Dr. Marvelous moved to stand between me and Phillipa in an attempt to recapture the moment.

"Phillipa is originally from the Andaman Islands. She was working toward her doctorate in evolutionary science..."

"When I got involved in trying to save mountain gorillas instead of studying them into oblivion. I find hands-on work far more satisfying. Do you agree?"

I had a lot more questions for Phillipa but a device buzzed in her pocket that she turned off and shrugged.

"Excuse me, now. It's time for choir practice. Maybe we'll see you at the concert."

When her pocket started buzzing again she ran down the catwalk and disappeared. I listened until her footfalls faded, closing a portal to wonderland. Snapping back to reality I turned to find Garth standing next to me. Call me crazy but I swear he shrugged and then passed silently into the darkening brush.

"A mountain Gorilla?" I said. "It must be a baby to be so small."

It took a moment for Dr. Marvelous to react to my question as he seemed preoccupied, his face turned to the next door along the walkway. Slowly turning back to me his lips formed a strange crescent half way between a smirk and a smile.

"Yes. Garth is the size of a baby gorilla, but he is a young adult and will grow no larger. One of the simpler genetic adjustments I have developed in my research. But you must not be fooled by his size. If you were to attempt to wrestle with him he could easily break you in half."

He paused to pop the last gummy into his mouth.

"A 200 pound male ape-child with all the power of a 400 pound gorilla. Difficult to accomplish but magnificent in its simplicity. If you know the code."

My eyes searched the underbrush hoping to get another look at Garth Kong but the only movement was the gentle waving of the greenery in the sudden cool breeze. At that moment I realized the sun was getting low on the horizon and I had learned very little about anything that would be interesting or valuable to my clients. I decided to take a risk and draw a new hand.

"I admit I am incredibly impressed and humbled by your accomplishments: a monster pig, the shrunken ape, and a botanical revolution unlike anything ever seen before. And it's laudable that you've created a communal safe haven for dwarfs, midgets, and pygmies. Your work here is beyond 'marvelous' and I hope in my heart that I can be a part of it. But I must admit I don't understand the need to hide what you've shown me from the rest of the world."

"I could say the same about your unicorn."

He winked at me and signaled me to follow him. We exited the courtyards by a door at the far end of the catwalk that led to a small, chilled anteroom that contained several lockers and a plaque that read:

"Science gathers knowledge faster than society gathers wisdom." – Isaac Asimov

that was mounted above another of those submarine doors on the opposite wall.

"This room is a buffer." He leaned against a wall and searched his pockets in vain for another gummy. "It is critical that the temperature in the next room is kept constant and the air as clean as possible. This door here leads into that room and is automatically locked. It is programmed to be impenetrable until the air in this room stabilizes to be equal in every way to what is on the other side."

He stuck a finger in his mouth to dislodge a candy which he had apparently saved for later between his molars and his cheeks. Noisily and breathlessly he chewed and swallowed.

"Um," he said. "Sweet."

He took two full body Kevlar suits out of one of the lockers and handed one to me. He had his on in a practiced flash and as I struggled with mine he waited with one hand on the pressurized door.

"Aren't you dying to know what is on the other side? It might help you understand."

"Of course," I said as a red light above the door turned to green. Dr. Marvelous stood directly in front of me, tilted his head forward, and stared into my eyes.

"If you follow me into this room, you will see something that can truly be called earth shaking. Something that will fundamentally alter life on this planet. Forever."

I fought the urge to turn up the sycophant volume. Instead, I played it close to the vest.

"That sounds more like what I expected to find here. That's why I came."

He looked down at the floor then back into my face. His crazy eyebrows, squished together under a surgical mask, cast a shadow penetrated only by spiked reflections of the overhead lights at the center of his pupils, like a cartoon robot with lasers for eyeballs.

"If you enter that room with me..." his breathing came harder and he paused, pulling his head back a few inches from my nose.

"First," he continued. "I must ask you." He turned and moved a couple of paces toward the wall and remained with his back to me.

"This morning you attempted to communicate with someone using a non-conventional device that our security system did not recognize."

So maybe my message got through, I thought.

"Still, we blocked it successfully."

Ok, maybe it didn't. He turned away from the wall and faced me again.

"This island is protected and rendered imperceptible to electronic, thermal, and photo/video instrumentation by a locally generated field invented by Dr. Kykshinski that acts like an invisible Faraday cage. Ships at sea never come close as their navigation systems are corrupted as far away as ten miles. The system is also capable, among other things, of reading and decrypting all forms of communication waves."

He took a step towards me.

"Your message was indecipherable. What was it and with whom were you attempting to communicate?"

I wasn't totally surprised at this development since I had not received the prearranged acknowledgment from my clients; my device seemed to be seriously malfunctioning; and something weird was happening with Toro's phone. I revved up my acting chops and threw a minor twist into the plot.

"Oh no! I told my friends I would be out at sea alone for a few days and would let them know I was all right. They must be worried sick."

For a moment he seemed embarrassed but snapped out of it quickly.

"Communication is forbidden. We will discuss an exception if it becomes necessary."

"Necessary? I don't understand."

He threw up his hands in frustration and returned to his nose-to-nose position, now breathing quite heavily.

"I cannot take any chances. We are too close to ...." he opened his eyes wide. "Do you still wish to see what is in the next room?"

The time had come to roll the dice.

"Yes," I said.

"If you enter that room with me," he spoke softly and gripped my shoulders lightly with both hands. "You will never leave this island."

That's what you think, I thought. I figured that what lay beyond that pressurized door was the payoff for this bizarre adventure; the golden ticket; the million dollar answer; the ultimate jackpot. I paused for a few seconds to appear to be thinking hard about this grave and final decision. Then I smiled slowly while raising my index finger to the bush at the bridge of his nose.

"Let's do it," I said.

EIGHT

Inside the door was a small entryway with a glass pane through which was visible another dimly lit room; small and crowded with tables. Black shades covered two heavily barred windows on the far wall so it was hard to see any detail until Dr. Marvelous turned off the light above our heads and my eyes adjusted. His reflection and mine disappeared from the glass and I counted about 15 petri dishes perched on electric warming plates and evenly spaced on the tables. He ordered me to touch nothing and we moved into this room with no light, no sound, and the faint vinegar odor of ultra-controlled air. The first dish I came upon employed a magnifying cover that enabled visual inspection of what appeared to my geneticist's eye to be a fertilized human egg. All the other dishes appeared identical. My heart started pounding. I was able to maintain control, however, and put on my best scientific poker voice.

"Where did you get these?" I said.

He waved both arms in the air.

"We have multiple sources; laboratories around the world, all perfectly legitimate. The most trusted and committed members of our community travel off the island when necessary to acquire them and bring them back here."

"Moby's people?"

"Not on your life. I did say 'trusted', didn't I?"

"But Moby's money."

He put his hand to his brow and sighed.

"This is not some Hollywood horror movie experiment conducted by evil scientists wanting to take over or destroy the world. In truth, if successful, our work here will set humanity free."

"And so," I said, "since by coming into this room I have dedicated myself and my talents to the success of your work, then please tell me. What is your work?"

He bent to inspect one of the dishes and frowned.

"Everyone on this island believes that our aim here is of cosmic importance."

"And what do they believe this cosmic aim to be?"

"They all understand that if we succeed, their sacrifices will halt the extinction process and they will have contributed to ultimate preservation."

"Is that true?"

He smirked. "Of course. I do not and will not lie to them. We are dealing with advanced genetics here and they are committed to our goal and our need for secrecy."

"Ultimate preservation."

"As I said."

He moved along the tables inspecting the contents of each dish. I stood in place trying to conjure the perfect tone for my next question. The wheel was spinning; the winning number about to be revealed; and I didn't want to blow it now.

In my best flat, objective tone I said, "Preservation of what?"

He stopped to inspect a digital gauge on the wall that displayed air temperature and humidity. Suddenly he spun around and pointed at me, his face taut, eyebrows crunched together, his squeaky voice elevated to a nearly inaudible squeal.

"This is your last chance. Are you in or out?"

"As I said," I said.

His eyes softened, the arm dropped, and he took a few steps toward me.

"Preservation of what? You ask. Why," he waved his arms over the petri dishes, "the entire human race, of course."

With both hands hovering over the dishes he closed his eyes, lifted his head, and spoke; his voice a smooth, tilted, sing-song mixture of 1960's R&B and Gregorian chant.

"What you see before you, we hope, are the seeds of a new humanity. In a few days time we need to sample and inspect the fluid from each of these zygotes to determine if our intervention has succeeded and we can proceed to the next step."

His cadence soared as he opened his eyes. "It is scientifically and morally critical that we do this before they reach the embryonic stage so that if we need to destroy them," he paused pretending to adjust his mask so I wouldn't notice he was hyperventilating. I could almost see his heart beating in his bony chest. He cleared his throat.

"So that if we have to destroy them they are still nothing more than eggs."

I understood from that statement that this was not his first attempt; that there had been many failures before. I was moved by the sadness in his eyes. When he spoke again his voice was raspy, like a canary with a sore throat.

"Once the cells start dividing we have to move quickly to inspect the recombined duplicates in order to make a proper decision whether to allow the process to continue or not. If you are willing," he paused, lowering his tone, "If you are able, your assistance in this procedure would speed things up to a more satisfactory and comfortable degree, even possibly enabling corrective intervention."

His eyes appeared old and worn above his mask, like his tank was nearly empty of something vital and deep. He motioned toward the door and we tip-toed out.

Back in his office he sat behind his desk and rested his head on a hard brown leather satchel that was worn around the edges. I strolled calmly around the room checking out the displays and the books that lined the walls. Inside I was gently boiling with anticipation. I was certain he was about to deal me the royal flush so when he lifted his head I was ready. He was about to open the satchel when something made him stop. Instead, he put his hands in the pockets of his white coat, searched around for a moment, and smiled weakly in celebration of finding one more gummy hidden in the pocket seams.

"It's been a long day," he said. "I must rest now. Tomorrow I will show you my notebooks. The more you internalize what I have done; the more you understand my methodology; then you will be prepared to work quickly when the time comes. You can also familiarize yourself with my equipment although I am sure you have used such instruments before."

"I'd like to get started tonight, if possible." I liked the island and the food but, so far, had seen nothing to justify staying longer without narrowing the probability of substantial net winnings for my clients. My inability to communicate with my base of operations disturbed me as well. Besides, Toro was itching to get away from Doris and her as yet inexplicable designs on him.

Dr. Marvelous stretched his arms in a huge, inflated yawn and in one motion shrank back down to normal while popping the last gummy in his mouth.

"The island council is gathering tonight and I must be there. Your initial forays into my work will require my guidance and I'm already so exhausted that I can only hope to stay awake long enough to cast my vote at the meeting."

"What are you voting on?"

I realized after the words came out that it was rather presumptuous of me to ask, especially since I didn't really care. It was my way of hiding my annoyance.

"Doris will see that you are provided a royal repast. I must lie down for a few minutes now and will see you in the morning."

He stood and placed the leather satchel on a shelf behind his desk then turned and called for the guards. I started to follow them out.

"Wait," he said. "To answer your question, we are voting tonight on what to do with you and your friends."

"What to do with us?" I said. I had a few choice words on the edge of my vocal chords but thankfully I was spared the possibility of showing my hand when he waved his at the guards and they politely nudged me toward the door.

"Good night," Dr. Marvelous said as the door closed.

NINE

"We've got to get out of here."

I held my hand up then waved it around the room. I suspected there might be some listening devices around and in any case, it was best not to take chances. He immediately understood and softly transitioned to small talk about the food and the accommodations while we feasted on another excellent meal. Afterward we savored the sweetest Bolivar Belicosos, settling our full bellies in the disturbingly quaint sitting room of our bungalow. My friend Toro is as intrepid as they come. Despite his sometimes over-clocked bravado and, at times, his thunderous silliness, there is no-one else in the world I would rather have at my side in a difficult, dangerous situation. Something in this state of affairs seemed to have shaken him a bit. I figured he wanted to escape that night but for me that was out of the question and I did my best, in my own way, to help him focus.

"I'm not sure what to think of all this yet. I admit that some people might be a little apprehensive. It's a gamble, and some people just aren't gamblers."

"El comico!" Toro sputtered as he gagged on and swatted away a serious puff of gray tobacco smoke.

Just then Ivan shuffled by in the hallway, hands deep in his pockets, and wearing the mask of abject failure I'd seen squished on his visage after every one of his interactions with the love of his life. He hadn't noticed us and we heard him whimpering as he dragged his limp body into his room and closed the door.

"Got to find her. Got to make her listen. Got to find a way."

Toro and I looked at each other and beams of stifled laughter met in the middle of the room. He pointed his finger at me.

"El comico."

Then he pointed at the empty hallway.

"El comemierda."

"Si," I smiled. "The comedian and the clueless idiot."

"Shit eater!" Toro said a little too loudly. I paused to listen but heard nothing coming from Ivan's direction.

"I was being kind," I said, "let's get down to business."

We simultaneously stood up and walked outside. We thought we would be avoiding any spy surprises that might be hidden in the bungalow but as we descended the stairs a young dwarf popped out of the trail wearing a wireless headset and jerking some stilted hip-hop moves, all the while fixing his eyes on our movements. He continued to dance, trying to act distracted as he followed us. I quickly got tired of his amateurish performance.

"Something we can do for you?" I shouted in his face. I was only trying to make sure he heard me over whatever was crackling in his headset but his facial features began to melt and he froze in the midst of an acutely angular move. He attempted but failed to move his lips so his garbled response was not so much a word as it was a disgorgement. Toro rolled his eyes, leaned forward, and said, "Boo!" with such quiet menace that the watcher leaped backward several feet, turned, and ran; this time without the frenetic gyro-technics.

We found a secluded place to talk and, given what we had gathered from the day, set about bouncing possibilities off each other.

"We can't leave yet. I spent half the day with bushy brows and so far it's a blind bet and he's got the hole card. Lots of stuff intriguing to me, personally, but nothing of interest to my clients. Not yet. Give it a few more days. There's something really deep going on here. I sense that he's feeling some kind of pressure to produce results and so I will likely be working directly on the big project tomorrow. We'll see."

"You don't understand. Do you see the way that Doris la Loca looks at me? Like somebody standing at a buffet filled with all her favorite dishes spread out in front of her, trying to make up her mind. Mmmmmm," he rubbed his hands, "what should I devour first?"

"Maybe she just likes you."

"She called me an interesting specimen."

We proceeded to give each other detailed accounts of of our after breakfast escapades.

Doris had dumped Ivan off on Moby who was content not to have to be near Toro. She took Toro by the hand, complimented him on his strength, and gave him an insider's tour of the facilities.

"You won't believe it," he said, "but they have a small nuclear power plant that's enough to run the whole island as well as some kind of invisible magnetic dome that keeps them hidden from all electronic surveillance."

"And keeps all our communications from getting out."

"Mierde," he said.

I told Toro about the giant vegetables, the humongous pig, the dwarf mountain gorilla and the petri dishes of human eggs. His eyebrows slowly rose up as I talked.

"Carajo. Damn," he said as he took a final puff then crushed his cigar into the ground.

I was glad he understood the possible monumental ramifications. What I didn't want was for him to sense my own mixed feelings of excitement, apprehension, and dread, so I quickly moved on and told him about the Moby vat. The clouds hovered over his face for a moment then vaporized in an explosive laugh. Finally he regained control and told me how he spent his day with Doris who rubbed his head, squeezed his biceps, and constantly spoke in lilting tones while leaning within inches of his nose. Finally he mentioned a concert taking place the following night. I thought of Phillipa and her choir practice. Toro had other ideas.

"What are you grinning at?" Toro said. "Apparently Moby, the Sturmfuhrer is also Moby, the choir director."

"I think he won a Grammy award once," I said.

Toro spat on the ground. "Different Moby. Not this 'Choir Boy'. Muchacho del coro demente! Tomorrow night is their monthly concert. Everybody on the island attends."

"Just our luck," I said, smiling.

Toro grinned. "Nuestro suerte, de hecho."

"Indeed."

By the time we retired to our rooms we had worked out several skeletal scenarios that, considering indeterminable future variations, would provide us with a fluid basis for working out or, if necessary, winging a final flight plan. Someone had freshened up the place and left each of us a clean change of clothing for the next day along with a note about leaving our "habiliment" on the bed to be washed along with the sheets and pillowcases. For a brief moment I considered how this might not be a bad place to light for a few months. There was something about the people and their quiet, seemingly harmonious existence; something like a melody plucking out on my synapses that was unfamiliar and 180 degrees at odds with my appetite for engaging with improbability. On the other hand my desire to pierce the kernel of the enigmatic Doctor and explore the secret depths where he was meddling played like a crescendo of major chords in my risk-attuned ear. So I rationalized that since I was being paid for information, then perhaps I needed to stay until I got it. In the meantime why not enjoy myself? I would be playing with house money. I decided to rest my analytical psyche and reconsider the angles in the morning, but it was becoming more critical by the hour that I communicate with my base. Before slipping under the mosquito netting I tried again but my device was pulling nothing. I resolved to request a communication exception the next day and fell asleep dreaming up a convincing sob story about my poor, bewildered and frightened family, wondering where on earth I could be.

TEN

We were awakened the next morning to another sumptuous breakfast in the sitting room. Ivan had managed to stir himself early and sat resplendent in his crisply pressed khaki shorts and polo shirt while he wolfed down pounds of sausage and eggs. His hair was immaculately greased into a swirling point above his forehead and I could tell he was ready to launch an all out assault on Doris' heart. The three of us had been supplied with identical accouterments but Toro remained in his linen suit because he refused to walk around like, as he said just loud enough to be heard on the mainland, "some B-movie bwana". But I surmised his interim plan was to make himself as unappetizing as possible. I didn't mind the outfit but decided to personalize my getup by rolling up the sleeves past my shoulders exposing my rather ordinary biceps adorned with the most extraordinary tattoos: on my left arm a roulette wheel over black dice showing seven, all arranged to resemble a high roller flower; on my right arm five aces and a large pile of thousand dollar chips.

Ivan stared at the images and, apparently feeling his wild side, blurted out, "You must be a gambler."

"You bet," said Toro and waited for a reaction, but aside from the joke being somewhat above the boy's intellectual limits, Ivan's concentration was now focused on trying to wrap a piece of bacon around a slice of papaya. Toro looked at me and shook his head.

"Vacio humano," he said.

"Un vacío de múltiples maneras," I said.

Breakfast ended with the sound of a bullhorn on the front steps.

"Step outside. Now! I hope you enjoyed your last meal sppplIffft..." Moby's barking ended abruptly when someone apparently pulled the bullhorn away from his mouth. When we came out Doris was holding the offending device while Moby walked in rapid circles behind her, waving his arms and chattering to himself. The broadcast somehow penetrated Ivan's perpetual fog and he was the first one out the door, his torso showing signs of a developing panic quake.

"Last meal? Last meal? I'm innocent, I tell you! It was them," he pointed at us,"They did it."

Doris, as usual, placed her hands on her hips but added a sideways glare at Moby and a head down, eyes up stare at Ivan. Toro slid over behind me for protection as she turned away from Ivan and smiled at us.

I raised my hand. "Guilty."

She didn't blink. "From now on you will have your meals in the community mess hall where everyone dines. This is not a punishment but a privilege; a sign of your acceptance into our home."

"Everyone's guilty of something."

It wasn't meant to, but my statement regarding the universal human condition must have pricked a blister in Moby's cold, hard innards and he tore the whip from his belt.

"Insolent swine!"

Before he could cock the handle Doris turned on him and jerked her hand up in a stop signal. Air hissed through Moby's teeth as he peered around Doris's hip.

"To me you are uninvited, unwelcome, unwanted interlopers, and I promise I will hound you until you beg to leave. Especially that gestank drekskerl behind you."

I could feel Toro tense behind me. Doris calmly turned and bowed ever-so-slightly to Moby.

"If you please, Commander. Would you escort Dr. Bronson to the laboratory? His importance to our project requires accompaniment by the highest authority. I will entertain the others."

I was impressed. There appeared to be much more to Doris than the masculine pose and poker-faced cover. Despite her fearless confrontations with the psychotic Moby she had no trouble at all stroking his self-importance without betraying an ounce of grovel. Moby rose the full length of his four foot height, whipped off a superior salute, and turned crisply on his boot heels.

"Dr. Bronson," he snapped and motioned for me to follow. I turned back to check on Toro. I needn't have worried. I could tell by the knit of his brow and the hint of a smile that his mind was concocting a plan to allow him to survive a day with Doris. Behind him Ivan was thinking too, except his cognition manifested itself with arrhythmic fisticuffs to the sides of his head. I surmised that lunch debriefing would be uniquely entertaining and forged ahead to catch up with Moby.

I joined Dr. Marvelous already in progress. He hurried me into the "Moby Room" and sat me down in front of a stack of notebooks.

"I apologize for the haste but there is much work to be done today."

He reached up on a shelf and snapped the locks shut on that same brown briefcase he'd had in his office. I noted it had industrial strength combination locks and the faded brown leather appeared worn in spots that belied an inner skin of a hard substance, probably steel. He popped a gummy in his mouth, leaned over me, and opened the first notebook.

"These are my notes starting from the very beginning: experimental DNA manipulation with goats, chickens and rabbits." He smiled and leaned back. "So much for my 'extra-curricular challenges'."

"I was referring to the rumors about you and Doris."

"Ha! Rumor has at best a tangential relation to veracity. The perception engendered by the babbling of a simple jealous unfortunate resulted in a public cliff dive into utter fantasy. Truth is indeed stranger than fiction but the entertainment value exuded by salacious gossip lies far north of the appeal of genuinely earth shaking achievements, even when conceptually simple enough for complexity averse intellects."

"Feel better now?"

He stood with his hands in his lab coat pockets, his head tilted, searching for the right words.

"I do suppose Doris loves me, but in a way that would be impossible to explain, especially to Ivan. It's somewhat tragic as the boy began with an excellent mind and great potential but devolved rapidly into addle-brained drivel the moment he sensed Doris' apathy. But enough of this tomfoolery. Gummy?"

He handed me a soft green candy the size of a jelly bean and popped a red one into his mouth. I was taken aback by the juicy, sweet, freshness of the morsel and immediately understood his apparent addiction.

"Made here by a master confectioner from Thailand who no one ever took seriously because he is shorter than a yard stick and in the kitchen needed the accommodation of a ladder just to stir the pots."

He laughed then paused suddenly as if he had walked into a wall; cut off abruptly, inexplicably, and with a sound like a sob. He appeared embarrassed. His voice softened and he gently placed his hand on my shoulder.

"Please peruse this record of my work. You must understand it completely and I am confident you will. I will be sitting over there," he pointed at a workstation with what appeared to be an electron microscope, blinking boxes, and other instruments. A hand carved mahogany sign on the wall read:

"To succeed, planning alone is insufficient. One must improvise as well." Asimov.

"I must begin analyzing samples from the individuals I showed you yesterday. We are approaching a critical juncture. This afternoon you will assist me in this analysis. So, as you read the notes, please do not hesitate to ask questions should they arise."

"What's the critical juncture?"

He hurried out the door. "Please read. I will explain later."

So I did. As I flipped through the pages I found myself engrossed. I couldn't get through it fast enough. I won't get into the details but it began with lists of re-ordered nucleotides and expanded into theoretical combinations breathtaking in their originality. I tried skipping ahead, like when reading a mystery novel so beguiling that you can't stand the suspense and read the last chapter first. It didn't work. I found that if I didn't follow the order as laid out, the later entries made no sense. The handwritten notes were dense and difficult at points but that only pushed me harder. It felt like a cosmic kill game, doubling the stakes with every turn of the page. Then the deal paused. I came to a list of names in groups of six, first names only, and dates, filling three pages in chronological order. It seemed out of place but I found myself reading through it, not really knowing why.

At that moment Dr. Marvelous returned carrying a sealed white container which he gently placed on a table. He seemed not to notice I was there as he carefully connected the optics from his microscope to a port on top of the box and began adjusting it the old-fashioned way, by peering through a dual eyepiece. He stood as if alone as his consciousness entered the box and he utilized dials on the front and sides to shift around and focus on whatever was inside. After a few minutes he slumped down in a chair, his eyebrows arched; his eyes closed. To re-establish my presence and bring him back into the world I cleared my throat.

"Could I have a look?" I said.

He barely moved. "Tell me what you see," he said.

What I saw caused a sensation like slamming the brakes on my heart. I turned to see the Doctor holding a towel over his eyes. "Tell me," he said. He dropped the towel revealing reddened, slightly swollen eyes. "What do you see?"

"I see a damaged human zygote."

He stood, put his hands in his pockets, and looked squarely into my eyes.

"Margaret," he said. "Margaret, who must now be destroyed."

"I don't understand," I said.

"She cannot be allowed to develop further. Allowing her to become what she would become is more painful and insentient even than sending her away now."

Then it hit me.

"Those names in your notes," I said.

"Ah, you've gotten quite far." He searched his pocket and emerged with a gummy, but he only looked at it and slowly put it back. "Failed attempts. All. Margaret is one of many; unfortunately probably not the last. It is highly complex and delicate; creating something...someone new. A gamble, with mighty stakes. Are you willing to gamble in this way."

He didn't know it but he was speaking my language. Still I thought it best to reshuffle

"It's a lot to think about."

"Please do," he said. "I could really use someone who understands the science and possesses the skills to facilitate the work. And the will." He opened the box, removed the petri dish, covered it, and placed it in a small refrigerator. "The will," he said, "and the compassion." With that he picked up the box and moved toward the door. "All must be checked today. Those that have progressed properly will be inspected again tomorrow. We will conduct a ceremony for Margaret during the concert tonight, as well as any others. I look forward to the day we can hold a celebration."

"Wait a minute," I said. "A zygote is not yet a person. Why give them names?"

He smiled. "Respect."

As he left the room my insides told me the game had changed. I felt compelled to push ahead harder but in his notes the data and sequences became denser and more intricate until I reached a series of entries that stopped me cold; not because I couldn't fathom their import, but because I could. I wanted to be sure about what I was seeing so I ran my eyes slowly over the pages repeatedly in an attempt to verify my initial perception. Subtle fore-shocks in my brain began to coalesce into virtual tremors in both hemispheres. Astonishment and clarity grappled toward the surface, battling a never before encountered resistance too entangled to distinguish as either logical or spiritual, or both. My head felt swollen and heavy and about to burst when the office door opened and Doris entered. I must have appeared in a strange state for she looked at me with narrowed eyes and a concerned tilt of her head, but only for the briefest instant. She straightened up and, hands on hips, announced my attendance was required at lunch. I said I needed to speak with Dr.

Marvelous.

"After lunch," she said.

I found myself following her. I was limp, numb, and drained but gradually grateful for the chance to reboot; then to digest and consider the immensity of what I had just learned.

ELEVEN

The mess tent was a large covered patio with open sides that allowed for a sweet cooling breeze that felt surprisingly invigorating. A chattering crowd lined up under a whimsically painted banner with the words:

"THERE IS AS YET INSUFFICIENT DATA FOR A MEANINGFUL ANSWER."

Isaac Asimov, *The Last Question*

The amazingly diminutive people moved along several well-stocked buffet tables behind which was a row of low grills projecting hunger-inducing smells with such magnetic power that I snapped out of my fog. My mind and body were instantly pulled toward the victuals. Before I could get close I felt a tug at my elbow.

"Come with me," Toro said and, without waiting for a response, headed toward a trail marked by a sign announcing "Toilet" in a dozen languages. I lost sight of him around a blind corner but when I turned the bend he leaped from a clump of orange bromeliads and pulled me into the foliage.

"This place is like a bad movie. *Invasion of the Body Snatchers* meets *Terror In Tinytown*. Everybody here is shorter than I am. And nice? Too nice. Crazy nice. Robots in khaki shorts. Descabellado! And Vampira wants to sample my blood."

"We leave tonight."

"Me condenare. Damned if I'll be a part of their experiments. Que?"

"By this evening I will have everything I need. Let Doris have a little la sangre, then you can fake being drowsy, return to our quarters for a nap, and make preparations to carry out our first plan."

An angry glare in his eyes stopped short and he squinted, studying my face.

"You all right?"

He could sense the cold clamp-down attempting to squeeze my inner turmoil. I conjured up a weak smile to put him at ease and his face slowly twisted into that type of grin that says 'Ok, we'll talk later'. He waved his hand as if to brush away a swarm of annoying insects.

"I'll give her some blood. Small price to pay to to get away from La hija de Frankenstein."

We made our way back to the mess tent where we loaded up on grilled shrimp, pork meatballs in mango sauce, and various steamed and grilled vegetables. We sat at an empty table and shared observations about the curious people politely smiling at us as they finished their meals until one of them came over and sat down to chat. Toro appeared annoyed. I wasn't.

"Good food, yes?" said Phillipa.

My brooding immediately morphed into a blissful fantasy state. I didn't even notice Toro strolling away. I don't know if it was her eyes, her smile, her hair, or her fragrance that lit a liquescent glow in my chest. And when she spoke, her clear, crisp, melodic tones played like butterflies in my ears. Dr. Marvelous, his petri dishes, and his whole damned island disappeared in her seductive closeness.

"Yes, very good."

She sat across from me and stretched her hand out to caress an unlit candle between us.

"Do you like to play games?"

Oh man! I thought. I couldn't tell if my heart stopped or if it was beating so fast I could no longer feel it. My expression must have told an obvious story and she laughed; a shockingly raucous outburst; grasped my hand and pulled me from the table.

"Do you play Mah Jong?"

As small as she was I had trouble keeping up with her.

"Can you wager on it?" I said.

"Ha!" A blast of a laugh. "Yes!" A sultry giggle.

We came to a table where the game was being set up. Two tattooed men, one with a Mohawk, were already seated. She pointed to a chair and commanded me to sit.

"I've never played Mah jong," I said.

"Then observe. It's very intricate and nuanced and takes a long time to learn, but no worries. We'll have plenty of time. I will teach you."

Something about her words felt like a soft massage on a piece of my soul that hadn't been touched in a long time. She sat in a chair and tugged at my hand.

"You stand behind me and watch."

Two women pulled chairs up to the table and one of the men started dealing out tiles. Phillipa began to explain the game but I stopped her.

"I'm a fast learner," I said. "But all I need to know right now is how do I bet?"

"Ha!" That raven's call again. The others at the table laughed.

"On me, of course," said intoxicating Phillipa as she smacked her tiles for luck and raised her hand to heaven.

Just then an electric screech yanked me out of the moment.

"Doctor Bronson!" Moby blared through his bullhorn from less than two meters away. "Dr. Marvelous is waiting for you."

I could sense he was about to get even louder when someone pulled the offensive instrument from his lips.

"Dr. Bronson," Doris said quietly. "If you please." She extended her hand, inviting me to follow her. I looked down at Phillipa. She winked.

"Later," she smiled.

As I followed Doris I heard her again.

"I'll place a sure bet for you. You can collect your winnings at the concert tonight. We will dance in celebration." Her opponents laughed and jeered good-naturedly. I felt like I was dancing already, and without any music at all.

TWELVE

Before re-entering the Moby room I prepared myself to confront Doctor Marvelous. I had to know if what I thought I'd discovered in his notes was true. Two reasons: 1. If so, I could justifiably inform my clients that there was nothing here of any value to them; no power to be extracted and amplified; no profit to be multiplied. 2. For me, my churning stomach needed to be either pacified or justified. The nature of what I'd read was too mind-boggling and upside-down to be ignored.

Dr. M sat pensively at his electron microscope. He turned and waved his hand weakly as a form of greeting and resumed his thoughtful pose. I decided to get right to the point.

"Why are you doing this?"

His smile was thin, almost humorless, and he spoke in a quiet, methodical manner antithetical to what he was about to say. I became involuntarily and disturbingly tense as my mind absorbed his slow, lilting words.

"When people choose a path in life, the wise ones realize there is no predicting where that path will lead. The intent for most of us, however, wise or not, begins with the desire to do something important; something to effect positive change; to bring good to many and to individual lives. Something big. Like a ten-year-old standing in front of a mirror with his first electric guitar imagining himself to be one of the Beatles. Or a young girl whose mother is dying of cancer vowing that one day, she will be the person to find a cure. I too was like that. Even at a young age I could see where things were heading and I felt compelled to do something to avert what I perceived as a nearly inevitable catastrophe. Something," he chuckled. "Something big."

"And this is your 'something big'?" I said.

The smile flattened into a straight line. "Ironic, isn't it?"

Irony was far too mild a descriptive for the insane objective of his genetic adventures. Here I feel I should explain that what Dr. Marvelous was working on was a method for recombining the DNA of a typical human with that of a determinant individual genetically programmed by nature with severe and permanent limitations to ultimate ontogenesis; the resulting individual not to exceed a fractional organic constitution half the standard modal stature. In other words, he was attempting to establish a simple and easily applied process to shrink the entire human race into, effectively, a race of midgets. Shorts! Something big, indeed. I pressed him to answer.

"I need to understand why. I don't gamble on unknown quantities."

He popped a gummy and stood up.

"While you were at lunch I managed to check all the other zygotes. If you'll forgive me I must take a rest right now. It drains me, the drama of it. Only Margaret, poor Margaret, matured enough today to again impress upon me the consequences of further failures on my part." He seemed to grow limp for an instant and steadied himself by leaning on the brown satchel on the desk. "You have demonstrated remarkable insight; gleaning in a mere few hours the material construct of this work from my miserable scribblings. I should be more than grateful if you will join me tomorrow in reviewing each step from the beginning. Perhaps your intellect, the endowment blazing behind your eyes, can illumine the flaw in my sequencing."

At that moment I felt empathy for this dispirited, brilliant, gummy-addicted, scientist. I knew my mission was completed but something inside me needed meaningful resolution and I couldn't let him slide out without answering my question. I repeated, "Please answer the question.

Why are you doing this? What's the point?"

"The point is," he straightened up, teeth momentarily clenched. Then he slowly started pacing back and forth, his voice gaining in strength and timber while quickly losing the high tones of exasperation.

"Are you aware that the human population of the Earth exceeded the planet's capacity decades ago?"

"There are those who believe that," I said.

"Believe it," he said. "Food harvests, despite massive application of commercial fertilizers and genetic modification are already inadequate to feed everyone. In addition, such crops as are produced are of diminishing nutritional value. The available farmland is degraded and shrinking. Forests are being destroyed for unceasing construction and to produce energy. The oceans are rising. Deserts are expanding. Access to fresh water is becoming a desperate struggle and is a justification for war. We are on the brink of a mass extinction."

"You're trying to save the planet," I said.

"No!" he said abruptly. "I am trying to save the human race."

He stopped pacing and leaned on the desk.

"As a young boy I was fascinated by science, but my earliest ambition, it might surprise you, was to be a writer: a science fiction writer. I would imagine different futures and write down my ideas until one day, it struck me that all the futures I could foresee were dystopian in one form another and that they all revolved around a catastrophic dissolution of civilization as we know it. It became too depressing so I sought other outlets for my burgeoning imagination."

Here he wildly plucked an imaginary guitar.

"I wanted to be a blues singer. I liked the rawness of it; the defiant head-on confrontation of all the worst possible life events with a low growl, pitched up shriek, and a screaming guitar." He jumped up. "You won't get me! Ha!"

He began to pace again, very slowly.

"Alas, though my father was a musician, I did not inherit his hand/eye/soul coordination. I tried. Lord!" he growled, "I tried. He died when I was ten. I found myself clinging to my mother for solace and sustenance. She was a botanist. A genius at that. Magna Cum Laude of her class at Stanford. Rhodes Scholar. PhD before her twenty-first birthday. Died at thirty-seven; just days after I had been accepted to Harvard at age 15. You see, her love of living things and all that made them tick, that's what I inherited; and when she was gone, I plunged even deeper, pushed even harder, ran with and magnified all she had taught me; reaching to understand everything about what it meant to be human. As my insights increased the demon from my youth began to resurface; the haunted, haunting, vision of ineluctable dystopian descent."

He paused and leaned back on the desk.

"Reality, you see, is far more unforgiving than speculative literature."

Reality was starting to give me a headache.

"So, you believe that shrinking humans to half the size will make a difference?"

"Think," he said. "A meter-sized person would require half the food, produce half the waste, and consume half the energy of the average individual living today." He stood and began pacing quickly, waving his hands and gesturing to punctuate his arguments. "Houses, buildings, transportation: all of it could be significantly attenuated. The depletion of resources could be halted and reversed. Pollution could be more easily managed. Living things on the verge of extinction might still be saved. On and on. All without needing to fight a moral, political, and cultural battle to limit procreation. Don't you see?" He turned, popped a gummy, and leaned into my face. "Humanity would be preserved and prosper. The future of Homo Sapiens secured."

He flopped down into a chair, his arms now limp at his side, his sagging neck barely able to hold up his head. There was something pathetic, noble, and lovely about this odd genius and I found myself weirdly intrigued by his cockamamie notions. I could see the possibility, off-the-wall as it was, but I could also see huge obstacles.

"What makes you think people would accept their offspring being half their size and vulnerable to any larger and stronger individual?" I said.

Without moving he spoke. "I'm no fool. My work here is beyond thankless. It will be ridiculed, denigrated, then tossed on the trash heap." He lifted his head. "But I will have proven the possibility. I will have shown the way. All the information and the description of the process will be there whenever the people are ready for it, although I may not live to see that day." Then his face slowly arched into a grin. "And I, too, have considered the possibility of domination by physically larger specimens. But small stature would be more than compensated for by superior strength, programmed directly into the DNA, comparable to that of a 400 pound mountain gorilla."

He slowly began to chuckle until it built into an almost hysterical laugh. For a moment I was dumbfounded. Then I also began to laugh and joined him in an uncannily boisterous duet. I barely got out the next word.

"Garth?" I said.

He was laughing so hard he could no longer control his lips to speak so he nodded his head, slapped my knee, and sprawled back in the chair.

THIRTEEN

The Doctor excused himself and retired to his office for a nap. Again he seemed overly wan and exhausted as he invited me to continue my review. When I resumed studying the notebooks I found it difficult to concentrate. *What a weird idea,* I thought. Images kept jarring my focus: child-sized baseball players, policemen, exotic dancers; toy-like diplomats seated around a shrunken circle at the United Nations Security Council, babbling like Munchkins in a dozen languages; hotels so small I would have to crawl to get in the front door; bumper cars for automobiles; wide open spaces that were once small parks; small parks now big enough for a full-sized soccer field; tubes of toothpaste lasting for years brushing mini-teeth in mini-mouths; a pizza serving eight people, two slices each. On and on. I tried to get a grip and focus, not very successfully, so I don't know if it was the swirling within and behind my eyes or just dumb luck but on the page before me - page 128, line 33 - I spotted something that halted my tilt-a-whirl mentation. I went back a few pages then ahead some more and kept returning to page 128, line 33. I've never bet on a flaw before but there it was in scribbled black and white: a possible key to Dr. Marvelous' sequencing error. I started to get excited when the door crashed open and Moby strutted into the room. He raised his bullhorn and was about to blast my ears out when I raised my hand and said, "Dinner, right?"

"You think you are so smart," he said. "Dinner, yes. But dinner AND a show. You vill see the results of superior training by superior beings. And you vill enjoy it. Now raus!"

Dr. Marvelous slumped back into the room, greeted Moby, and said to me, "Yes, you mustn't miss the show. You will be impressed and most certainly surprised."

I followed Moby out. Normally I'm not that pliable but my mind was swimming in a current of amino acids and nucleotides, pulled along by an inner debate: should I tell Marvelous my discovery or not? We'll see.

I returned to the bungalow to wait for the dinner bell. (Yes, the dinner bell). Toro was working out the logistics of our escape plan and I felt myself morphing back into the paid operative on a mission. We had decided on creating a diversion to facilitate our escape. It worked out splendidly that everyone on the island would be at the concert. It was a near perfect set-up akin to knowing the order of the cards in a stacked deck. We had concocted an emergency event that would instantly involve all hands: a fire. Toro, minus a few test tubes of blood, rigged a slow burning device that could be ignited before we left for dinner but would not produce the desired effect until after the concert started.

"A cigar," I said. "Brilliant."

"And not just any cigar," Toro smiled, "A Bolivar Belicoso. Though it seems such a waste of a fine smoke."

"You want to get out of here, yes?"

He flourished the cigar like a sword.

"Si! Inmediatamente! Hey," he said, sticking the cigar in his mouth and lifting two clenched fists in the air. "Who am I?"

"Winston Churchill."

"Que Dios me ayude." He lifted his arms again. "Fidel! Are you blind?"

"You don't have a beard."

"I'm not a fat, bald, imperialista either."

The Bolivar was placed on Toro's bed in a ceramic dish with it's band pushed back almost to the shoulder and securely fastened to the mosquito netting. I turned the air conditioner fan to low and positioned the louvers to create a breeze strong enough to "smoke" the cigar but gentle enough to keep it from burning too fast. Toro reached under the bed and I was surprised to see him pull out his gear bag.

"When did you get that?" I said.

"Do you think I went to my dinghy just to get my toothbrush?"

He opened a tube that said "Hair Tonic" and squeezed some of it's contents on the netting and the mattress. The room immediately smelled of gasoline.

"So you're greasing your hair with napalm now?"

Toro grunted, "A little dab will do ya'."

On the way to the community mess hall Toro hid his bag along the path and took care to video the area in case it was difficult to find later in the dark. As we got closer I could hear music playing and began to feel uneasy about the fire.

"In your travels did you notice if there is any firefighting equipment around?"

"Don't worry," Toro said, "The island won't burn up. Every well head has a hand pump and hoses are stashed nearby so fires can be dealt with quickly, but not so quickly as to foil our escape."

Toro moved ahead and walked backward in front of me so he could look into my face. He spoke in a low, calming voice.

"Your mujercita will be ok. The question is," he stopped. "Will you?"

He was right to wonder. The events of this day had really done a number on my emotions. I needed to focus. I assured him that my only goal was to get off this island and complete my mission.

"Have I ever let you down?" I said.

He started moving again and let me catch up beside him.

"Depends on what you mean by down," he laughed. "Sometimes you just screw me up."

FOURTEEN

When we got to the mess the air was filled with the smoke of fired up grills and a cacophony consisting of excited voices, clattering utensils, and musical instruments being tuned. There appeared to be around 120 people there and, guessing that a few were still arriving or not visible for some other reason, for the first time I could get a handle on how many people inhabited this detached micro culture: somewhere in the neighborhood of 150, fairly evenly divided into men, women, and children. The atmosphere was festive enough that even Moby's storm troopers were gun-less and relaxed and everyone buzzed in anticipation of the concert. The person I was really looking for must have been with the rest of the choir "backstage" because I could have picked her out of a full soccer stadium.

"Perfecto," said Toro as we moved toward a table on the periphery that would allow us to keep a low profile. Before we could settle, a tall, sparkling woman in an elegant floral gown, intricately styled hair, and 1940's Hollywood glamour make-up intercepted us and took both our hands.

"Wonderful," she said to her companion, "Our guests of honor are here."

It wasn't until I spotted Ivan creeping around behind her that I realized it was Doris. Toro's eyes could barely stay in their sockets.

"Dios mio. Dolores Del Rio!"

She bowed and kissed his forehead.

"Bienvenido mi Toro. Glad to see you are feeling better."

Her companion, a short fellow with long straight black hair and a beard that reached to his waist line, appeared anxious in a celebratory way.

"Come on," he said, shaking his fists and bouncing from one leg to the other. "We're holding up the show."

We were escorted to the VIP seats directly in front of the stage. Toro frowned and surreptitiously showed me an obscene gesture so I leaned over and said, "Actually, my friend, this might work out better." Before I could elaborate we were served with platters piled high with thick cut grilled pork chops swimming in papaya chutney; barbecued scallops the size of my fist; fresh picked greens with a dragon fruit, coconut dressing; and roasted yams shaped like boats with asparagus spears for masts. I tell you all this because it was an easy deal to go to town on this delicious bounty in preparation for the long night ahead. While we were still chowing down Doris and her companion walked onto the stage and the crowd immediately came to attention.

"Fellow inhabitants of Marvelous Island," her unamplified voice carried to the back row and beyond. "Welcome to our monthly concert."

The crowd applauded politely and she smiled at us which caused Toro to squirm a little in his seat.

"In a moment you will meet the first performer but now," she raised her arms. "Would you all rise and greet our guests of honor: the brilliant Dr. Charlton Bronson and the epic Toro del Oro."

A loud cheer almost took the roof off the building and I could hear melodic voices behind the stage area chanting what sounded like "Hu-Hu-Hu-Hu!" I stood and acknowledged the crowd while Toro waved weakly and immediately slouched back down in his seat.

"And now," Doris said. "Tonight's master of ceremonies: Dr. Kykshinski." She winked at Toro and promenaded off stage.

The long haired, long bearded Kykshinski spread his arms and chuckled.

"I know some of you have not recognized me, but this is my costume and make-up. For later in the show I will amaze you with a sequence of traditional dances from my country."

The applause just inched up to the polite level. Undeterred, Dr. K continued.

"It is an original choreographic medley that I call..." He appeared to be trying to suppress a laugh but managed to blurt out the words: "Some Russian Steppes." He could no longer control himself and doubled over in hysterical laughter. The audience appeared bewildered until someone poked her head out from behind the curtain and gestured that they should laugh. As the artificial guffaws rose to an unnatural level, Toro elbowed me in the side and pointed to the gesturer who was trying to get my attention. I barely got a glimpse of Phillipa as she blew me a kiss and disappeared.

Then the lights went out. In the deep blackness I could hear some shuffling around on the stage then an eerie, amplified voice penetrated the gloom.

"Fear not, my prisoners. With the genius of Dr. K we never lose power."

The audience began to chatter and shout. Some stomped their feet and hooted. We were surrounded by a torrent of human jungle noises as the voice continued.

"As for me……."

A spotlight popped on and the sound of electric instruments blared from the proscenium as the singer growled into a microphone with echo delayed menace.

"I put a spell on you."

The crowd went wild at the sight of Dr. Marvelous in the harsh light wearing his wizard regalia; a prosthetic chimpanzee bone clamped to his nose. The band was unearthly tight and ominous.

"Because you're mine." His voice boomed into the microphone like Dracula singing opera. His arms swirled and flashed in the beam and the audience went absolutely berserk.

"You better stop the things you do." His finger pointing arms swept the crowd. "I ain't lyin'."

The place was filled with such noise and the volume of electric instruments that it took a minute before anyone saw the guard who rushed in toward the stage screaming at the top of his lungs. Dr. Marvelous turned to the band and waved them silent. Now everyone could finally hear the shrieking word: "Fire!"

"Fire!" the guard continued, apoplectic. "The cottages are on fire!"

The house lights came back on and it seemed like a great suction pulled the people instantly out into the darkness. Toro and I stood watching their backs disappear when I felt a hand on my arm. I turned to find Phillipa standing on my seat. She grabbed my collar, pulled me towards her, and pressed her lips to mine for what felt like a glorious, sweet eternity. When she finally released she smiled and giggled.

"Your winnings from Mah Jong, Dr. Bronson."

I couldn't move, I was so wrapped in enchantment.

"You stay here," she said. "We've got this."

For a moment I forgot who I was and why I was there and started after her as she ran. She turned and smiled.

"I'm a brigade captain. And I order you to stay." She started backing out of the building. "So afterwards I'll know where to find you." She turned and disappeared into the blackness.

"Are you insane?" said Toro. "Let's go. Vamos!"

FIFTEEN

As we scurried down the path toward the beach we couldn't see the glow of the fire through the dense vegetation but the clouds and smoke above were illuminated like puffs of sulfurous cotton and bright enough to provide some light for our escape. Toro had no problem retrieving his bag. He didn't realize at first but I took a detour from our planned route away from the beach and toward the cinder block building that served as Dr. M's laboratory. When he finally noticed he yelled out, "Where are you going?"

"I need something out of that lab," I said.

"We don't have that kind of time," he howled.

I signaled for him to be silent as we crept up to the building in case one of Moby's sentries was lurking about. It was unguarded. I paused to pick a flower from a golden chalice vine next to the steps then tried the door which opened easily. Once inside I headed straight to the 'Moby' room. On the way I pulled a piece of paper out of my shirt, placed it on the instrument table with the flower on top. As I continued into the room I heard Toro behind me say "Margaret? Who's Margaret?"

The brown briefcase was sitting on the desk where I had been working. When I picked it up something felt funny about it; it wasn't the weight but the tumbling sound of the contents. I tried the latches but they were locked.

"Are you still an expert at picking locks?" I said to Toro as he scrambled into the room.

"No time for that," he said and reached inside his bag, emerging with a red white and blue striped can.

"Shaving cream?" I said.

"Liquid nitrogen. Do you think Toro del Oro carries only toiletries?" Then he pulled a folding hammer out and clicked the handle straight. "I'm a professional. MacGyver estupendo!""

He quickly sprayed the hinges with the nitrogen than whacked them with the hammer. The metal shattered and the briefcase burst open spilling hundreds of colored objects on the floor.

"Gummies, damn it," I said.

"Is that what you came for? I didn't know you had such a sweet tooth. Now let's get out of here."

At that point I heard a loud click and looked up to see Moby standing in the doorway holding a large hand gun that looked like a cannon in his small hands.

"I knew I vould find you both here. So you thought you could escape by your amateurish diversion; you and your little schosshund."

Toro clenched his fists and moved slowly toward Moby.

"Nobody calls me a dog you vermin from hell."

I had to act quickly. I picked up the can of liquid nitrogen and pulled the cover off the Moby vat.

"Put the gun down. This can contains liquid nitrogen. I spray it in here and your master race becomes a master iceberg."

Moby blinked. Toro charged, head down, and blasted Moby's midsection while chopping the gun out of his hand. The two men crashed into the wall and Moby landed a kick in Toro's most vulnerable spot. As he struggled to get off the floor Moby grabbed the whip hanging from his belt, expertly lashed it in my direction, and smacked the can out of my hand.

"Ha! You have meddled with the wrong ubermensch!"

He kicked Toro who was still writhing on the floor and who flipped over on his back from the impact. Moby twirled the whip once around his head and sent the tip flashing toward my face. I could have been smacked unconscious if it weren't for the fact that I diligently practice all the martial arts that were part of my training which included obscure lessons like self-defense against bull whips. (Honest. It's in the manual.) My timing was perfect as I simultaneously ducked out of the way and, swinging my hand in the same direction as the whip, caught the end and snatched it straight out of Moby's grip; slung it back so I could catch the handle; snapped it on the ground with a loud boom; and whipped it tight around Moby's ankles as he bolted for the door. His head cracked against the floor as he fell facing Toro who suddenly jumped to his feet like he'd just injected a months worth of cortisol, pointed at me, and yelled into Moby's ear at the top of his lungs, "Nobody messes with Indiana Cojones!"

The two of us tied the dazed Moby's wrists and ankles together behind him when Toro noticed his Bowie knife sticking out of Moby's belt. He slid it out and waved it menacingly in Moby's face.

"Now, should I slice you or dice you?"

Moby sputtered, "You can kill me but you vill never destroy me. I vill live forever."

Toro turned toward the frothy vat.

"You mean this?" he said, a sinister twinkle growing in his eye.

Meanwhile I had to think fast. We really needed to get to the dinghy but I had to find Dr. Marvelous' notes to at least have something to show for this mission. I glanced around the room clueless until my eyes fell upon the sign with the Asimov quote. It dawned on me that there were other carved signs around the island and all had quotes from the science fiction writer Isaac Asimov. I stepped to the book cases along the wall. The doctor organized his library alphabetically by author's last name so I quickly found a shelf loaded with standard sized hardcovers of Asimov's "I, Robot", "The God's Themselves", "Nightfall", and a dozen others. On the end was a huge over sized book that looked more like a collector's case. On the spine it read "The Complete Foundation Series – with additional material and notes". I removed the heavy box and inside, among the other contents, was Dr. Marvelous' binder. Jackpot!

My elation was interrupted by Moby screaming. Toro had fetched two things from his bag including duct tape which he was now placing over Moby's mouth. The other was a small vial.

"You see this?" he dangled it in Moby's face. "Do you know what this is?"

Moby's eyes exploded in horror and his muffled voice cried "No! No!"

"Yes," Toro said. "A tiny jellyfish. You recognize the species, right? Deadly, right? Venenoso. Toxico. Si?"

Moby flailed on the floor, angry and helpless as Toro walked over to the vat. The scene was too pathetic to be funny. I laughed anyway. I felt bad because my laughter made Moby thrash so hard he began smashing his head against a cabinet. It was a really nice cabinet, you know? Toro opened the vial and dangled it over the open vat, enjoying this moment of pure torture despite our need to vacate the premises.

"I am become death," he cried, "The destroyer of worlds!" and emptied the contents into the foam.

Moby screamed and convulsed so hard that he gashed his head and blood began to seep out of the duct tape over his mouth. We could still hear his muffled roaring as we hustled down the trail towards the spot where Toro hid his dinghy; him with his bag; me with the Asimov. The sound of excited voices could be heard and seemed to be getting closer.

"I think they're on to us," Toro said as we careened full speed down the path.

Suddenly somebody jumped from the vegetation and tackled me sending the books and binder scattering into the tall grass. The trail side was littered with papers, some being borne into the trees by a growing evening ocean breeze.

"They're here!" yelled Ivan. "Over here!"

He put out a hand and helped me off the ground.

"I'll be her hero now," he said, just as the coconut Toro hurled smashed into the side of his skull and he fell limp to the ground, his lips curled in unconscious, unconscionable joy.

"Let's run," I said.

"What about the papers?"

"Too late, we've got to make it back to the Acro."

Toro led the way. I was grateful for his navigational abilities. The last time I had been this way we were blindfolded. Both of us are pretty fair sprinters and the sound of voices faded as we gamboled on.

"How did this el sapo know where we were?" Toro said.

"He must have followed us from the concert."

"You might be right. He was fuming all morning and I thought he'd explode when Doris kept stroking and stroking and stroking my arm, you know, to fatten up a vein for the liter of blood I gave for your mission."

I laughed. "We're in a bloody business."

"Sangriento Negocio Incorporated! So when do I get mi dinero de sangre?"

"Get us to the Acro and you'll get a fist full of dinero."

"Clint Eastwood! El espagueti western rides again!"

Toro had hidden the dinghy so well we almost couldn't find it. He secured his bag, took off his linen jacket, and started rowing. I took the rudder and swung us out away from the shore to stay out of sight as long as possible. It was getting darker by the minute and I could barely discern the Acro still bobbing at anchor a safe distance out. I was surprised it was still there and wondered why they hadn't towed it in to prevent us from escaping. As for the dinghy they probably assumed it had just broken its mooring and floated out into eternity.

As we circled toward the Acro and came into view of the shore the bank of search lights that must encircle the entire island blasted the water and there we were, right in the middle. We could hear a few voices floating on the breeze when a crazed, ranting, familiar voice blared out from a bull horn loud enough to make waves in the placid water.

"Zey are trying to escape! Launch all boats! Fire at will! Fire at..." The sound cut off abruptly followed by the voice of Doris.

"Hold your fire. Hold the boats."

We could still hear Moby screaming. "Zey are murderers! Mass murderers! Zey have destroyed ze glorious future of humanity and zey must not get avay!"

The next voice on the bullhorn was Dr. Marvelous. "Commander Moby and all within the sound of my voice. Tonight at the concert we were to make a momentous announcement concerning a new, vastly superior multiplication factor for certain amino acids. Moby, you and I will meet later to elaborate. Is that satisfactory commander?"

We couldn't hear his answer but it must have been affirmative as Dr. Marvelous continued on the bull horn. Toro was thrashing like a hydroplane and we were almost to the boat.

"Dr. Bronson. Senor Del Oro. We are sad you have chosen to leave us. Your presence in our community would have been, shall I say, glorious, and you will be missed. I want you to know that I...that we, would welcome you with open arms if you ever decide to come back. I, personally, believe you will not expose us to harm. I trust in your character. If I am wrong, and you broadcast what you know to individuals and groups with the power to destroy us, well...It's been tried before, and, frankly, no-one will believe you."

He paused for a moment.

"It was a joke. Ok. A bad joke. I have a message for Senor Del Oro. Here we go: 'Come back. I'll be waiting.' from 'guess who', and a message for Dr. Bronson: 'You owe me a dance.'"

A shadow tripped across the water and I could just see a tiny figure pirouetting in front of one of the lights.

"Signed," the Doctor said, "The gambler."

We had finally reached the Acro. As Toro lashed the dinghy to the gunwales I took one last look at the now distant lights, the silvery streaks on the water, and the few translucent figures remaining on the sand.

"Good luck, my friends," said Dr. Marvelous. "We'll leave a light on for you."

At that all the spotlights glowed down and off except one, I believe, to give us some light as we fired up the Acro.

"Something is wrong," said Toro.

SIXTEEN

The boat was low in the water. In places it hung below the scuppers and the deck was wet with a two inch puddle at the stern. We splashed on board and I ran to the helm to fire up the engine. Nothing. Not even battery power for the gauges. Toro called from below. The engine was almost totally submerged. He went back on deck to salvage what he could and prepare the dinghy for a long ride: flashlights, hand held flares, parachute flares, floating smoke signals, a case of bottled water, some cans of tuna, and a few large bags of potato chips. Below I fetched a gun and the duffle bag full of cash I had hidden behind the wall paneling. It was a little damp but the bundles inside were completely dry. I secured it inside a doubled up plastic trash bag and joined Toro topside. The light from shore had finally been turned off and Toro was playing with a battery operated lantern, making crazy patterns on the calm sea.

"Do you think your dinghy will make it?" I said.

"Dinghy will be fine. Triple wall inflation lined with Navy Seal quality flotation material. If we get lost at sea, a hundred years from now they will find this ghost ship with nuestros esquelitos holding these between our phalanges." He held up two Bolivar Belicosos he had sequestered in his bag. "Besides, barring any storms we will be in Matanzas in 6 hours."

"All right. I'll take the first leg."

Toro frowned. "Ten hours."

He insisted on doing the rowing so I sat at the rudder trying to get my communicator to work. Time was growing short to abort Plan A and I couldn't raise a signal of any kind: no satellite, no encrypted channel, and definitely no standard cell service.

"You're more likely to contact space aliens here. We're just southwest of the Bermuda triangle," Toro said.

"Do you actually believe that junk?"

"Haven't you ever seen *Death Ship* or *The Triangle*?"

"Sure," I said, "And *Death Ship 2, 3 and 4* and *The Triangle Lives* and *Return of the Triangle* and *Abbott and Costello Meet The Triangle."*

"Dios santo! How did I miss those?" Toro's laughter carried over the waves as he gave another dozen mighty pulls on the oars.

The island was now out of sight and the Acro was barely visible on the horizon when I heard a familiar, disturbing buzz overhead. Toro stopped rowing and looked up into the darkness.

"A drone. Is this part of the plan?"

I dug my gun out of the trash bag and pointed toward the sky.

"This wasn't supposed to happen for another 12 hours. You have a gun in that bag?"

"You going to shoot down a drone with a pistol?" Toro pulled a small semi-automatic out of his bag and listened for the drone sound. I grabbed a flare and fired it in the general direction of the buzzing. When it detonated we caught a glimpse of a black fuselage heading in an odd direction and both of us started firing, hoping to get lucky. No dice. Within minutes we saw a blinding flash to the northeast, too close to be attacking the island, that momentarily illuminated the dead hull of the Acro as it disintegrated. Flaming debris sprayed into the air and floated, still burning, on the swaying surface.

"They blew up your boat," Toro said. "You could have been killed. Demonios! I could have been killed. What kind of friends do you have?"

"Not and never were my friends," I said. I took a long, deep draught of the warm, salty air, threw my communicator into the drink, and pulled out the cigar Toro had given me. "Take note: mission ended via termination of contract."

Toro laughed as he pulled out his own Bolivar Belicoso and lit his and mine with a lighter that resembled a miniature blowtorch.

"Just like Harpo," he said. "Los Hermanos Marx."

We sat for a few minutes, each lost in our own internal hologram, until Toro patted me on the back and took up the oars again.

"You are officially un hombre muerto."

"A dead man. Yes. Drew aces and eights." My mind started percolating some very interesting scenarios.

"Could have its advantages," I said. "Very possibly a winning hand."

Toro laughed and began singing a series of bawdy Cuban ditties so lascivious that, when combined with his facial and tonal expressions, they required no translation. His powerful oar strokes punctuated the rhythm of the songs and pulled us through the calm sea at an impressively inhuman speed. He only paused once, when we finally sighted land, to relight his cigar and watch the sun rise over his home island.

SEVENTEEN

I'm sitting here now in a tavern a few thousand miles from my former residence writing this all down so that someday I can give it to anyone who might care. I'm putting actual pen to actual paper, just like Dr. Marvelous' notebooks, because nobody can hack nor otherwise surreptitiously scrutinize papyri without actually holding it in their hands; that is, after first taking it out of mine. My new bag is packed with new clothes and new essentials I bought so as not to disturb the apartment contents of the "missing and presumed dead" me. They'll find it just as I left it before commencing my final, yes final, mission. As for the bag of cash I figure they'll just have to assume it's floating slowly to the bottom of the Florida Strait along with my carcass. What I've been able to find out through ultra-secret anonymous channels is that for some reason my clients believed I had stiffed them and absconded with the money. They hadn't heard from me in days and the final straw was when their drones could find nothing but open sea at the coordinates I had provided. So they shifted targets in-flight and settled for blowing me and my boat into the next dimension along with an enormous amount in unmarked bills. Frankly, I never realized I was worth that much. Makes me think I've been underpaid all these years. I'll just look at it as fair retroactive compensation.

For now I intend to exist incognito to the point of invisibility so I used a false identity to make arrangements with a very loose banker I know of in Switzerland to hold a good portion of the money. I gave enough to Toro for him to pay off all his extended family's mortgages and bills and to live comfortably for a very long time. He's a good man and we both owe each other our lives several times over after all the insane assignments we have worked together over the years. He doesn't have to worry about my clients since they have no idea he was with me. I trust him implicitly and now out of necessity since he is the only person at this moment, on this planet, who knows I'm not shark food. And, if necessary, he'll have a good idea where to find me.

It's about time for me to vamos now and head down to the marina to take possession of my new used cabin cruiser, paid en la palma de la mano, as Senor Del Oro would say. "The Phillipa" is a fine, fast vessel with upgraded navigation equipment so all I have to do is punch in coordinates and it practically steers itself. I might get in a little fishing if the weather stays good and ruminate on the odds of me actually succeeding in creating an entirely new life. I've been a gambler since I was old enough to count money but this time I am, as they say, betting the farm. There's a small matter of what to do about page 128, line 33 and I'm planning on performing a deep plunge into the intimate intricacies of Mah Jong. Maybe some dancing, too.

We'll see.

The End

ENTRY ONE:
CARLO'S BOAT

Chapter Six: The Rescue

The violence of the waves pitched large chunks of helicopter over the breakers and pulled them back into the rocks repeatedly until the foam was littered with all sizes and twisted, pummeled shapes of jagged metal. Carlo held his phone steady, documenting the scattered remains. As the waves continued to pound, a black figure catapulted into the lagoon, hit the water with a thud, and bounced once before it, too, was sucked back toward the rocks.

"Stay here," Papa shouted as he crawled up on the jetty and hobbled toward the end to get a better look. Carlo jumped into the book-laden boat and, as he struggled to uncoil the rope that held it to the dock he watched as Papa climbed into an old hollowed out canoe and paddled toward the debris. Gellato skimmed forward; a rush of adrenaline charged his ancient muscles and bitter memories drove his old bones, plowing with all the strength he could muster into the bubbling maelstrom. He struggled to keep straight toward the shifting, wave-tossed object, sighting it out of the corner of his eye while he tried to avoid the leaping froth and salty bullets shooting toward his face. *If I try to stop, the waves will crush me,* he thought. Instead he looked for and caught a receding pulse and rode the crest like a surfer, charging past what he now confirmed was a human body, churned and broken. He had no time to discover whether it was alive as his canoe landed on the rocks and shattered, depositing him in a crevice; his torso partly wedged in a hot fissure. He saw the body lifted up and about to be dashed on the stones when he pushed himself loose, wobbled upright, broke its fall, and fell backward onto the rock; his arms wrapped around the motionless chest. He prayed their combined weight would keep them from being immediately sucked out to sea.

What now? he thought as he spat out salt water and gasped for air. The mist obscured everything; it was as if he were buried alive in an angry cloud. As he clutched the limp body he thought of his son; the joy of his life; the pain of his loss; and how hard he had needed to work to overcome the sorrow at his failure. Then he thought of Carlo. "Who will make his sandwiches?" he whispered.

"Papa!" Carlo yelled. He sounded far away. Gellato shielded his face with the dead man's arm just in time to spot an oar emerging from the crashing waves and fog, cutting through the wind like a spear.

"Catch it!" Carlo yelled. It was a good shot, right on target. The oar bounced close enough for Gellato to get a grip on it and feel the weight of an attached rope. He held the oar with both hands with the body between, pressed against his chest. "Pull!" he shouted as they jerked headlong into the water. When he returned to the surface he could see Carlo rowing his boat hard, the rope attached to the rear seat, dragging them into the calmer waters. When they were safe from the undertow Carlo stopped rowing and pulled them toward the boat. He held onto the collar of the inert man's leather jacket as Papa crawled slowly over the gunwale.

"We'd better tow him to the dock," he said to Carlo. "Maybe after I catch my breath I will have the strength to help you lift him."

When they reached the dock Carlo jumped in the water and pushed up while Papa pulled until the leather jacketed figure rested in the bottom of the boat; waterlogged and lolling with the waves. Papa felt a little dizzy and leaned his back on the dock.

"Is he alive?" Carlo said.

"Feel for a pulse." Papa sat up and lifted the man's eyelids while Carlo reached for his wrist. Suddenly the body lurched over on its side like an electric shock had passed through it and a stream of water exploded out of its mouth; then a quick caught gag; then another gush of water; then a series of low moans and staccato breaths. Carlo stared, mouth agape, and Papa pulled his hands away; Carlo could see they were shaking. The man slumped on his back, his face distorted in agony, heaving his shoulders until, suddenly, his eyes popped open. He tried unsuccessfully to lift his head which produced another fit of coughing, this time with smaller projectiles of blood and water that splattered his chin and chest; his eyes frantically moving in all directions in his rigid head. Papa took a deep breath then gently brushed the hair off the man's forehead and placed his fingers on his temples. The breathing slowly became more normal and the coughing less frequent; shallow and dry.

"Carlo," Papa said, and the man twitched; eyes popped wide. "Call your mother. Tell her to get Giovanni and the others down to the inner shore. This man needs to be taken to hospital."

Carlo touched his phone screen. Gellato could hear ringing, then shrieking so loud the boy had to pull the phone away from his ear. Papa snatched the phone.

"Rozita, listen to me."

"You!" she said, then sounded like she was choking for air. Papa knew from long experience that this was his best and possibly only chance and he seized the moment in a loud firm voice.

"We need an ambulance. Fast. Meet us on the inner shore as soon as possible."

As he clicked off he thought he heard the man say something. Carlo leaned his ear toward his face. Papa joined him and both their heads hovered centimeters from the man's lips, blue and cracked from the salt water. A hoarse whisper pushed a few words out of his motionless jaws.

"What did you say?" he said, barely audible.

"Papa called for an ambulance," Carlo began excitedly.

"Carlo!" Gellato motioned him to be quiet and leaned over, speaking softly.

"You will be in good hands soon." Then Papa stopped. It appeared the man was almost smiling and his chest moved slowly up and down as if a laugh was struggling to emerge.

"Where," he said haltingly, with a strange, lips-only grin and ricocheting eyes. "Where am I?"

"You are safe. We will take you to..."

"Where?" - now louder, his pulsing breath pushing the words. "Where am I?"

""You are safe," Papa repeated. "You are in Carlo's boat."

It was unmistakable now. The salty lips parted and the cough became a quiet, then louder, then insane, unstoppable, hysterical laugh; eyes bulging, chest heaving, back arching until he finally wilted and drifted out of consciousness.

Papa arranged the man's arms and legs so he lay as flat and naturally as possible in the bottom and moved to the back to take the rudder.

"Text your mother and tell her what happened. Tell her we are all right but that we have a seriously injured man who needs immediate attention." He opened a liter of water and drank half without pausing as Carlo finished his communication and started pulling on the oars.

"I will never understand people," Gellato said. "The crazy, inexplicable things they do."

"I know that word, Papa," Carlo said. "It was in a book by Hemingway. I looked it up."

"Smart boy. Understanding requires effort, but it is always worth the perspiration. Me? For figuring out the mind of humans, I can no longer afford to excrete such excessive volumes of water. Rather than shrivel up and die in pointless toil, I instead seek to understand the fish; to catch them, and know them. And in the end, perceive their essence as rubbed with garlic and slow roasted, pristine, over a fire."

"Papa, you make me hungry again."

"Yes. There is no deeper understanding than that brought forth by filling an empty stomach."

Carlo always enjoyed sparring with Gellato and his philosophical jokes, but this time, instead of smiling, his eyes peered straight past his grandfather and into the distance. Gellato turned to see what he was looking at and there, through the pounding spray, far in the distance, glittering metallic sparkles spread across the horizon and could be seen dancing in the undulating mist.

"Do you see them?" Carlo said. "What could they be?"

"I don't know," Gellato frowned and squinted. This was something he had never seen before. When he turned back Carlo could see that his face had turned pale and his brow was wrinkled in confusion and concern.

"Papa, are you all right?"

He looked directly into Carlo's eyes.

"Row faster, my boy. Row faster."

ENTRY ONE:
CARLO'S BOAT

Chapter 7: On The Bridge

The Sam Ham Show:
News "Commentator": Sam Ham.
Reporter On The Scene: Mel Visbrein.

SAM: Ok, we are "live!" I know this is unusual for us, to be "live" I mean, but this is an unusual and rapidly developing story calling for unusual measures like us being actually and in real time right on top of things in a "live" way. Our man on the ground, or, I should say on the bridge, is reporting calm seas and a beautiful clear sky. How's the weather out there Mel?

MEL: Calm seas and beautiful clear skies! Proud to be out here with the Seventh fleet and ultra-excited because, at the conclusion of the operation, Admiral Finnegroot is going to let me water ski behind the aircraft carrier.

ADMIRAL BEENEROOT: For the seventh and last time my name is "Beeneroot", And furthermore I said no such thing.

MEL: As you can see, Sam, Admiral Beetlejuice is a little tense right now as we have visual confirmation of some sort of activity in the distance.

SAM: Activity. That sounds dangerous. Can we see it?

MEL: Admiral Vandersnoot will not allow us to point a camera in the direction of our destination for security reasons. But I can describe it to you.

SAM: Tell us! Tell us!

MEL: Calm seas and beautiful clear skies. Perfect conditions for hot dogging; maybe even a serious deepie.

EXECUTIVE OFFICER: Sir, the Captain has requested that you hold it down. We have visual contact with the target area and have commenced battle stations.

MEL: Sam, did you hear that? Battle stations. I'm looking in the direction of the horizon and I see....

SAM: Tell us! Tell us!

MEL: Calm seas and beautiful clear skies. Let me see if I can snag the Admiral. Admiral Rutabaga, Sir, what are we looking at?

CAPTAIN PELKIN, Executive Officer (XO): Mr. Visbrein. The Boatswain's Mate will escort you to a location befitting your level of professionalism and curiosity where you will be free to point your camera wherever you want.

BOATSWAIN'S MATE: The Brig, Captain?

CAPTAIN PELKIN, XO: The Brig, sailor.

MEL: You hear that Sam? The Brig. Must be like the bridge only spelled different and with an insane view. Thank you Admiral Baconbeans. And Sam, the next time I'm "live" I'll be "live" from the bilge.

BOATSWAIN'S MATE: Brig, sir.

SAM: Mel? Mel? Well, folks, Mel will be back with us later. We'll bring you all the action as it happens or even before it happens so stay tuned.

Captain Archibald, Commanding Officer of the Carrier Hollywood, strained to focus on the pale white wall visible through her binoculars. Her upper body was straight and square but the muscles in her arms were relaxed and smooth despite the weight of the massive visioning device gripped firmly in her hands. She could see waves crashing on what appeared to be some kind of reef and random exploding wind shafts launching spectacularly upward; disappearing into the impenetrable cloud. Admiral Beeneroot; wiry, wrinkled, bespectacled, short; stood next to her fumbling with a very large telescopic infrared device.

"I can't make out a damned thing," the Admiral said.

Captain Archibald lowered her optical instrument and shook her head. "Radar charts some cliffs surrounding a lagoon. There is a blip that is most likely a pier of some kind. Otherwise, nothing."

"No boat? Where's the damned boat? No heat signatures? Radioactivity? Communication waves? What the hell is going on?"

"The real-time satellite image is coming up on the screen now, Admiral," the CO said.

A crystal image of the coastline showed mostly green treetops and several roads approaching or following the shore, with a protrusion jutting into the sea that looked like a ball of solid wax that had rolled up the coast and gotten stuck in a depression. Zooming closer showed more detail of the swirling wind currents but little else.

"There it is!" cried the Admiral. "I see it!"

He gestured toward a slightly darker area on the image that was long, thin, and barely visible.

"It's the damned boat! We've got the bastard now!"

"Sir," the CO said. "All indications are that it's a permanent, static structure made of wood. We can't be certain exactly what it is but it's probably not a boat."

"Have you ever seen the shadow of a submarine anchored at shallow depth, Captain? I know what I'm looking at."

The Captain replaced her binoculars in their holder and turned crisply, facing the Admiral.

"It's unidentifiable, Sir, and shows no signs of being anything but an inert object."

"Damn. We need more information. Send a couple of jets in there to recon the area."

"No good, Admiral. The cliffs are too close and the air currents too strong to risk it."

The Admiral removed his hat and flung it to the deck. "What is this, the Bolivian Navy? Send in a chopper then, for God's sake."

Captain Archibald clasped her hands behind her back and never blinked.

"Sonar has detected sunken wreckage of several helicopters, Sir, in addition to fresh debris. The air plumes near the breakwater must be impenetrable."

"Impenetrable?" Admiral Beeneroot yelled. "Impenetrable?" He reached his hand up, grabbing for his nonexistent hat to dramatically thrust it on the floor. Instead he tore away a piece of his own gray hair and howled.

"This is unacceptable," he snapped at the CO. "Prepare a missile for launch." Then he whirled and pointed at the XO. "And you pick up my hat. We'll smoke this fiend out. He'll have to show himself."

Captain Pelkin, Executive Officer, stretched out his massive right hand, attached to an appendage so long the other officers jokingly called it a "yard arm", and leaned slightly to snatch the Admiral's hat from the deck. He ceremoniously brushed the pristine peak and handed it back.

"Admiral," the XO said. "NATO forces are moving in from the land side. It might be a good idea to wait."

Captain Archibald rubbed her forehead, trying to calm a runaway headache, and pointed to the image on the screen. "We don't know what we will be hitting there. Could be civilians or even residences. The area appears accessible from the land side, so I concur with Mr. Pelkin, Sir. Let the infantry exert pressure on the ground and our presence off shore will prevent any attempt at escape. Might present an opportunity for us to capture him if he is foolhardy enough try."

Admiral Beeneroot gingerly replaced his hat on his head; his thin lips and hollow cheeks pulsating in shades of purple and red. He took a deep breath and closed his eyes.

"Captain Archibald," he intoned; slowly; through clenched teeth. "I ordered you to prepare a missile for launch. I'll be damned," he started to shake, "if I will countenance even the slightest possibility of some trench monkeys capturing," hands flying in the air, eyes bulging, voice caroming off the bulkheads like a bullet inside a bell, "the most wanted criminal in history!" Calm and composed again, "Do I make myself clear?"

"Yes, Sir," the CO said. She turned crisply to Captain Pelkin and proclaimed in a loud voice, "Prepare a surface to surface missile for launch, Captain."

Pelkin saluted and turned to speak into a microphone but Captain Archibald grabbed him by the elbow and walked him toward the outer door.

"Captain Pelkin, please deliver the orders personally. We must carry out the Admiral's orders with the utmost alacrity."

As they reached the door, out of ear shot of the Admiral who was cursing under his breath and still trying to work the infrared telescope, she stopped the XO and spoke softly.

"Aim for the center and set it to depth."

Captain Pelkin nodded and winked, then disappeared down a ladder.

ENTRY ONE:
CARLO'S BOAT

Chapter 8: Fire In The Hole

Carlo pulled the oars as hard and as fast as he could but it seemed that every time he looked over his shoulder the cleft in the cliff they were heading for moved farther away. At his feet the injured man's flaccid torso swayed to and fro with the motion of the boat. A low groan signaled that life was still in the body but his breathing was becoming weaker and more sporadic. As they neared the hidden passageway through the cliffs a sound like thunder broke high in the sky, so loud it left deafness in its wake. His eyes jerked upward to the area of the crackling boom but before Carlo could blink something smashed into the center of the lagoon sending a pillar of water into the sky and a huge wave radiating toward the boat.

"Hold on, Papa."

Gellato clutched the rudder just as a monstrous thump kicked the boat into the air followed by an explosion that roiled the waters, shooting blasts of steam in every direction. As the boat splashed down on the crest of a wave, Papa saw that it was filling with water and that Carlo, shaking the lagoon from his hair, managed to pull the oars in as the force of the explosion propelled them toward the cliffs.

"Get in the bottom of the boat and hold tight," Papa yelled as he fought the rudder even though he could not see through the downpour. Another wave lifted and blasted the boat forward. Airborne again, he could now see they were about to be smashed on the pink rocks when a violent cross current sucked them sideways, spinning the boat, pulling it into a swirling vortex until the boat was jetting backwards and all he could see were jagged edges and whirling foam spinning in darkness, an echoing roar as they bounced off the stones, then suddenly sunlight as the boat emerged from the pinkness, shot across the narrow channel to the inner shore and beveled across the beach, coming to rest in a cluster of Saint Augustine grass half way up the escarpment. Papa sat frozen, breath coming in rapid gasps; shoulders and head vibrating as he slowly loosened his white-knuckled grip on what was left of the rudder pole. Carlo carefully maneuvered around the motionless body and hugged his grandfather. Gellato looked into his eyes.

"Carlo," he said, his voice quiet and raspy, "That was some ride, eh?"

The boy jumped up and threw his hands in the air.

"My papa! The master navigator!"

"Carlo!" came a voice from the top of the slope.

"Out of the whirlwind and into the fire," Gellato said.

"Mama!" Carlo cried out. A rush of joy mixed with a pang of sadness as he saw her youthful black hair swirling around her sunken eyes and cheeks. She looked thin and palsied against the steel gray sky but he felt like she was the most joyous sight he had ever seen. She was yelling something else but was drowned out by the blaring siren of an ambulance screeching to a halt on the road behind her. Two uniformed emergency workers rushed beside her and she pointed down the embankment. Their names were Giovanni and Paolo and they gestured wild prayers to the sky as they began to shimmy down the slope. Something happened and both fell flat then tried to scramble back up to the road on their bellies. The boat began to shake and Carlo turned to see Papa standing in the stern facing the inner cliffs that rippled and swayed and began to shed huge chunks of pink stone into the water. Papa turned to Carlo, his jaws smooth and tight; skin flushed; eyes gleaming; wisps of gray hair flapping against his cheeks; clenched fist slowly thumping his chest. The boat began sliding back down toward the water which was now bubbling fiercely from the impacts of many stones and releasing steam as if it were about to boil. He heard his mother scream as Gellato threw his arms in the air.

"He awakens!" he cried.

At that instant the entire cliff side shivered and shook and completely, utterly disintegrated; large and small shards falling like pink and brown hail collapsing straight down into the watery earth, blasting a volley of salty air with a terrible, deafening, roar. Gellato gripped Carlo and dove into the bottom of the boat next to their motionless, oblivious passenger just as a tremendous wave exploded from the shore and erupted up the slope, shooting the little boat to the crest and onto the road. They landed next to the ambulance as the water receded down the incline leaving behind splatters of smoking blanched grass. Giovanni and Paolo, standing stiff like horrified mannequins, snapped into action and hurriedly examined the injured man. Concluding he was still alive they ignored the convulsing earth and expertly loaded him on a stretcher, managing somehow not to drop him, and secured him in the back of the ambulance. Papa sat on the asphalt road behind the boat, silently observing the unfolding spectacle. At his back, despite the din, he heard Rozita sobbing quietly as she hugged Carlo. The ground continued to quake under him and the air was filled with dust, steam, and a roar so thunderous he could feel it in his bones. Rozita and Carlo helped him to his feet as Giovanni gestured for them to get into the ambulance.

"We need to get out of here. Now!" But his voice was blown into the ether by a sudden, sulfurous blast of hot air. As he stared past the three figures clinging to each other on the crest he saw balls of molten rock shooting into the sky and furiously twisting ghosts of boiling water. Hissing vaporous ribbons blew holes in a thickening fog as the water below lurched and crashed and suddenly disappeared; sucked into the splitting earth.

"Look, Carlo," Gellato whispered. "Just like the old ones said." The explosions; mighty, trembling, cracking sounds; shrieking jets of pulverized water and flaming stone pounded around him. His face, glistening with the mist of ages-old water conjured from the depths by an unknowable force, softened into a quiet smile while in his head he heard music; lovely, ancient, ethereal, divine. He didn't notice when Giovanni and Paolo lifted and carried him to the rear of the ambulance. Rozita and Carlo piled in next to the man on the stretcher as Paolo worked on him and Giovanni slammed and secured the rear door. Giovanni pushed the accelerator to the floor and the vehicle careened up the gentle slope inland toward the town, throwing Carlo and Gellato against the door. They stared out at a dark, hulking apparition now visible through the fireworks, shuddering blood red, black and gray, jutting hundreds of meters into the sky, ocean-suffused mud sloughing off its sides; pinnacles of solid stone dappled with cooling lava penetrating through the clouds and smoke like cathedral spires.

The mountain had returned.

Emergency alarms blared into every corner of the aircraft carrier.

"Mayday! Mayday! All ships full speed astern. All hands secure all doors, hatches and ports," Captain Archibald yelled into a microphone.

"What the hell just happened?" Admiral Beeneroot squirmed, still wrestling with his viewing device. The LCD screen above was filled with an image of bubbling white fog.

"All ships, do you see what I see? Emergency full speed astern. Secure what you can then all hands get off the deck. Mayday! Mayday!"

"I demand to know what just happened," the Admiral stammered.

"The missile you ordered hit its target, Sir." Captain Archibald yelled over the roar of the wind battering the bulkhead. She pulled the telescope from the Admiral's grip and pointed out the window toward the horizon. The Admiral stared for an instant at a sight he had never before seen in forty years on the sea. Then his body went limp and he crumpled unconscious onto the deck.

"Mr. Pelkin," the Captain said, "see that the Admiral is securely strapped down then brace yourself." She turned and stared across the distant bow, trying to gauge the speed and height of the wall of water roaring toward the fleet. She watched as some of the forward vessels disappeared under the tsunami and gave one final order.

"All hands brace for collision."

ENTRY ONE: CARLO'S BOAT

Chapter 9: Something Happened

The Sam Ham Show:
News "Commentator": Sam Ham.
Guest 1: Creese Meloncho p.

SAM: Mel? Mel? I think we lost Mel's feed. Could someone get us re-connected? We're missing all the good stuff.

CHIEF ENGINEER: It's not on our end. It will take some time to trace this out.

CREESE: What happened?

CHIEF ENGINEER: Something.

SAM: Something happened? I know something happened. Our audience can see something happened. Whatever it is, we're in the dark. Do we have anything from satellite?

DIRECTOR: Coming up on the monitor now.

SAM: Oh my God! People look at that! It looks like it's...it's...what are we looking at?

CREESE: It's the certifiable location of the criminal Carlo and his boat.

SAM: But what are we looking at? This is no time to be nebulous, Creese.

CREESE: My nebulous is sharper than most people's crystal, Sam. My sources deep in the deep state tell me the Seventh Fleet was dispatched by an undisclosed commander-in-chief to an undisclosed location at an undisclosed time and arrived there totally undislocated, under-commanded, and over-shrouded with complete secrecy.

SAM: Not any more.

CREESE: Look, I'm an amendment guy: first, second, you name it. The people have a right to know. Those ships are after the greatest threat to humanity that's ever existed; probably the biggest radical leftist liberal in history. Why shouldn't the people get to see it "live" in their living rooms?

SAM: Good question, Creese. I'm sure our sponsors feel that way too. But I don't see any ships. Has the Navy developed an ocean-bound stealth technology?

CREESE: What happened?

SAM: Fascinating. We'll come back to that after a commercial break.

CREESE: They were there a minute ago. They've disappeared. You saw them.

SAM: The ships, you mean?

CREESE: Something happened. You saw them. There was a whole fleet there.

SAM: Not any more. At least not that I can see now. Amazing! We'll see if we can find out but first we have a bulletin from our newsroom. Geronimo?

GERALDO: Thanks Sam, and BTW it's GERALDO. So, here we go. Geraldo Nirvana reporting. This network and the rest of the world, including the Sam Ham show, have learned in real time of the swamping of an entire U. S. naval fleet. On this broadcast we watched as all forms of communication vanished in what now appears to be the deadest of smoldering dead spots. Even military satellites, including the secret ones, are only detecting impenetrable fog and cauldrons of tremendous hotness too intense to be the heat signature of warships. Literally measurable billions of people have followed the drama, mostly on this network, the best source of real news on the planet; the drama surrounding the pursuit of the elusive Carlo and the attempt to capture Carlo's boat. Now, people around the world, most of whom get their news right here, stand petrified at the ominous spectacle of a power never before seen on earth. We go now to our host Judge Chlorine Flippo and our featured panel of world religious leaders to get their take on these events, available exclusively on this network.

JUDGE FLIPPO: Can you believe this? What a mockery of everything we believe is real. Mock, mock, mock. That's all these power-mad left wing radicals want to do. Well guess what, you God haters, your time is almost over. We've got your sick hero on the run and it's now only a matter of time.

REVEREND APPLEJACK, FORMATION LEADER, PASTORAL MOTORCYCLE CLUB OF THE ADIRONDACKS: Judge Flippo, you must realize he seems to have escaped, and in the process destroyed an armada worth trillions of dollars. Something cosmic is progressing here and we need to recognize it in order to decide our course.

PASTOR WILHELM, UNITED CHURCH OF PATRIOTS: What drivel, and a waste of precious time. I think it should be obvious to anyone with half a brain, including all of my flock, presently flocking around their screens to hear the truth, as I see it, that this mysterious figure known as Carlo is none other than the anti-Christ. Who else could single handedly sink an entire fleet of nuclear warships and slip away undetected? Beelzebub I tell you! Beelzebub incarnate!

ARCHIE RAMJET, HOUSE OF BUDDHA MONASTERY AND WINERY: There is no devil, only Man.

PASTOR WILHELM: Why the hell is HE here?

JUDGE FLIPPO: Now boys, let's not argue. The world has a dependency for what we promote here and I insist we all recognize the gravitational force of this thing.

REVEREND APPLEJACK: We must stay calm and think. We don't know yet if the fleet is obliterated or just damaged and to what extent. All we can see is what's happening far above the surface. To believe this Carlo is Satan when nothing is really known about him is premature at best. For all we know he is the second coming.

RABBI SCHMOTZER, FIFTH REFORMED TEMPLE OF THE CATSKILLS: To have a second coming you must first have a first coming.

PASTOR WILHELM: How would you know?

ARCHIE RAMJET: There are no comings.

PASTOR WILHELM: Shut up!

JUDGE FLIPPO; Calm down already. We have to go back to Sam now, thank God, with an amazing scoop as always. Sam?

SAM: Judge Flippo a real scoop it is! You can't scoop any better than this. From Washington we have our great patriotic leader "live" from the White House. This IS a treat, the kind that makes my mouth tingle with anticipation. History in the making. Go ahead Mr. President. The world is watching.

PRESIDENT: I want the governments of every nation to understand that this horrible criminal must be captured or destroyed. It's a disgrace what happened to those ships and unlike my predecessor I intend to respond with maximum force like the world has never seen. Any country that refuses to cooperate in finding him will suffer a total attack that will be beautiful and perfect, also such as the world has never seen.

SAM: Do you mean a "brutal" and perfect attack, Mr. President?

PRESIDENT: Yes. A beautiful brutal attack such as the world has never seen.

CREESE: Do you mean you're going to nuke 'em? Finally?

PRESIDENT: I'd say that's pretty final. Nuclear is a beautiful thing.

SAM: Not to appear as if I disagree with you, sir, but might that touch off a nuclear war and, possibly, though I know you've thought this all the way through yourself, but seeing as how some countries might not take too kindly to this level of gentle persuasion, that possibly this could mean the end of civilization a we know it?

CREESE: Yes! Back to the primeval! Survival of the superior!

PRESIDENT: Well I'll tell you this: they won't be laughing at us any more. Now if you'll excuse me I'm due at the first tee.

SAM: Sir? Sir? Well, Creese, what do you think about that?

CREESE: Yes! Yes! Yes! We will kick some righteous, diverse ass! America above everything!

SAM: Dare I say it?...FORE!

CREESE: For what?

SAM: What more needs to be said? Let's kick it back to Judge Flippo. Hello Judge.

JUDGE FLIPPO: Thanks Sam. Can you believe this? What a heroic defense of everything we believe is real. Attack, attack, attack. That's what power is for, and it's about time. And guess what, America haters, your one world rule is almost over. It's only a matter of time now.

SAM: Where'd everybody go?

JUDGE FLIPPO Three of my guests had to step outside for further discussion regarding their trivially clashing points of view. However, Reverend Applejack managed to rise above the fray and is still with us in the studio. What say you to all this, Reverend?

REVEREND APPLEJACK: I say you do not know what you are dealing with. Nobody knows. Nobody knows the day or hour. Nuclear missiles will be ineffective at best.

JUDGE FLIPPO: Ineffective? I guess they don't teach nuclear fission and bomb technology at the seminary.

REVEREND APPLEJACK: I'm afraid not. But I will tell you what they do teach: "What kind of man is this? That even the winds and the waves obey him!"

JUDGE FLIPPO: That's what they teach you? Boo hoo I'm shaking in my boots.

REVEREND APPLEJACK: You will be shaking in more than this if it is true.

JUDGE FLIPPO: If what is true?

REVEREND APPLEJACK: A great power caused the sea to move and then obscured the events of this day with impenetrable clouds.

JUDGE FLIPPO: You are starting to scare me. Can we get the other three back in here? At least they were entertaining.

REVEREND APPLEJACK: "At that time they will see the Son of Man coming in a cloud with power and great glory."

JUDGE FLIPPO: O. K. Reverend. (ROLLING EYES) Thank you for that insight. Why don't we go to commercial right here? Yes? Yes. Thank God.

As night fell, Gellato and Carlo stood among a large group of wide-eyed gawkers, introspective onlookers, and news crews with reporters who spoke slowly, searching for words. There had been no time to evacuate or seal off the area. Hundreds of trembling locals knelt and crossed themselves and silently gave thanks for the miracle of survival. For hours a pink and brown snow had fallen, the progeny of ash, pulverized rock, and steam that slowly scoured the sky until finally, for the first time in Carlo's lifetime, the stars became visible over the spot that was once his beloved lagoon. Silhouetted against the sparkling night stood the towering specter of a legend.

"Gellato," said one of his old angler friends whom he hadn't spoken to in years. "What became of the dead fish you hauled out of the lagoon?"

Gellato glanced at the man then turned back to the mountain.

"He is not dead. They took him to the hospital."

"He's the pilot isn't he? I watched the whole thing on television," the man continued. "What did he say?"

"He asked where he was. When we told him he laughed."

The man did not seem to care that Gellato perfunctorily acknowledged his existence only out of old-fashioned courtesy. Unmoved. he continued his badgering.

"Has he said anything else? He must have spoken to Giovanni and the other whats-his-name. Or to the nurses and doctors at the hospital."

"They tell me he's in a coma. Every once in a while he opens his eyes and laughs like a madman. That is all I know."

Frustrated, the man gave up and turned to walk away. He stopped suddenly and turned back.

"What about the other fellow? That pazzo reporter?"

Gellato thought for a moment. "Is that what he was?"

"Remember, Papa," Carlo said. "I showed you some of his videos."

"Ah, yes. Pazzo he was. I don't know what happened to him. Only the pilot, who must be pazzo too."

Having failed in his quest for insider information, the man walked away to see what he could find out by pestering the news people. Gellato looked down at Carlo who was standing in the angled pose that was his thinking mien.

"Perhaps my books that washed out of the boat might have survived, maybe somewhere near the peak."

"You are a comedian," Gellato said, and patted him on the head. "Tomorrow we'll look for your boat. Maybe the books are still there."

A gasp arose from the crowd as the top of the mountain began to glow bright enough to swallow the celestial bodies immediately overhead. Hundreds of people raised their phones to take pictures or videos. From a distance, deep inside the darkening land, it looked like a giant candy corn: brown at the bottom, pink in the middle, and radiant yellow at the top. The massed sprinkling of LED screens at it's base danced like a necklace of stars dementedly serenaded by a towering, cosmic canticle; the soaring chant of an invincible regenerate choir; the return of something long believed to be lost; imperious, frightening, grounded, but at the same time sloping gently upward, in diaphanous swirling sweetness, holding a candle to the night.

(to be continued)

ENTRY SEVEN:
THE ESSENTIAL HUMANS OF THE WORLD INTERNATIONAL, INC.

First Annual Stockholders Meeting
Transcript of Session One: Keynote Address

EHW PRESIDENT:

Welcome Shareholders!

(loud cheers)

Members of the Board of Directors, Trustees, Members of Upper Management, Unwelcome Guests,

(loud boos and catcalls)

They are here. You know it. I invite these particular guests to identify yourselves as we have nothing to hide and neither should you. No-one? In truth, I fervently hope that by the end of this meeting, you will be convinced of the righteousness of our Corporate Mission Statement and thus will inform your puppet masters that you are human and free and that they can all go to hell.

(wild cheers)

But I digress. Welcome also to all International corporate divisions joining us on line, and welcome all curious and committed friends of all shareholders around the globe. Peace and prosperity be with you as we embark on this journey together.

(cheers, ovation)

A moment ago I referred to our Corporate Mission Statement which is: "To ensure justice for every person, in every way, everywhere on this earth we share." To any of you who are new to, or unfamiliar with, our Organizing Principle I shall state that now, and those of you who have taken it to heart, please feel free to say it along with me:

I AM AN ESSENTIAL WORKER.

I HAVE ALWAYS BEEN AN ESSENTIAL WORKER.

I WILL ALWAYS BE AN ESSENTIAL WORKER.

(loud cheers, standing ovation)

All right let's get down to business. In a moment I will outline the basic workings of our corporation but first I wish to point out that the Board of

Directors you see on this stage consists of thirteen members. Six of them are distinguished benefactors including economists, philanthropists, financiers, retired business owners, and labor leaders. You should recognize most if not all of the other seven; after all, they are your colleagues and friends and YOU elected them.

(cheers, ovation)

I also stress that we ARE a corporation; an INTERNATIONAL corporation; and therefore we are governed by national and international rules for conducting corporate business. Why do we choose to organize ourselves in this manner? Why aren't we a labor union or some other form of organized labor? Why a corporation? As one justification: in America, as most of you are aware, according to the United States Supreme Court, corporations are people. Corporations have the right to use their economic power without restriction. Workers cannot. Corporations can create monopolies and hold society hostage – after all it's a free market. Workers cannot. Corporations can organize themselves any way they see fit to "maximize profit" for their shareholders. Workers cannot. Whereas if you wish to organize to protect your human and economic rights as a worker – that's not allowed. Corporations can structure their compensation to concentrate wealth among the few at the top and to hell with everyone else. Workers WILL NOT.

(loud cheers and applause)

THEY can wield their economic power in any way they wish because corporations are people...

(long pause)

... and you're not...I am not...WE are not, as long as we are defined as workers. Workers are tools, resources, raw materials, nothing more, with the same rights as all other inanimate objects: none.

That's why this is not an organization of workers. We are a corporation with products, resources, and raw materials to sell. I will explain in a moment. First, one piece of necessary business: let me say that any of you who work for a corporation that forced you to sign what is called a "non-compete" agreement – such immoral and possibly illegal agreements do not apply here. Our corporation is not a competitor. We are not selling cars, steel, crude oil, corn, appliances, toys, or hamburgers. We do not operate fast food restaurants, big box stores, banks, or gas stations. Not yet. More on that later. However if you have signed such an agreement, I repeat, it does not apply here. You are not an employee or in any way employed by this corporation. You are a shareholder, and you have the right to own shares in any corporation you choose. You can even own shares in your company's competitors. You can own shares in every big box company on the planet. You can own shares in every bank in the world. You can own shares of every politician in your government...

(pauses)

Yes, you know it.

That is why we are not an organization of workers; we are a corporation. But what exactly do we sell, you ask?

Economists often conjure their theories in a vacuum with little relation to what happens in the real world. Humanity, morality, and justice cannot be part of the equation; they cannot be quantified and they are messy and uncontrollable. You, as an individual, ARE present in the equations, but only as production equipment and consumption equipment; the former to be squeezed for every drop of profit, the latter to be manipulated to engorge on product to maximize that profit; all with no consequences other than lucre or loss; bonuses for the squeezers and manipulators, dividends and increased share value for the shareholders; the trading of blood for fat.

So what are we selling? Certainly not workers; certainly not human beings; certainly not YOU. You are shareholders after all. Corporations build their finances with products, not people; by selling shares, not shareholders. Our products are the following: on the tangible, quantifiable level we sell intelligence and strength; brain power and muscle power; the ability to efficiently and effectively carry out all aspects of administration and production. On the intangible level we sell integrity, loyalty, originality, creativity, unity. No, our product is not human beings. Our product is all the incredible productive and righteous power that human beings possess...and that, my friends, is the key. Possession. Who owns your skills and temperament? YOU own them. Who owns your knowledge and experience? YOU own them. These are the products you sell; NOT your body and most assuredly NOT your soul.

(wild cheering)

Our corporate wares consist of YOUR individual human products, to the power of millions. It is all the things that make you essential, for you, I repeat, are and always have been, essential. You know it.

(cheers and applause)

But how do we come up with a value for these products? We are Capitalists, and we understand the basics of how markets work. Overprice and no-one buys your product. Under price and you have a deficit, a loss, and your business goes down the drain. Somewhere in the middle is a happy medium: a value that covers the costs enough to provide a decent profit for the products of your minds and hands. A happy medium where the consumers of your products receive a fair value for their money and will buy from you again. A happy medium where all members of the corporation are compensated fairly according to their contributions toward those surplus funds we call profit. A happy medium where leadership and effective management still beget the highest rewards but on a realistic, moderate scale, and not an obscene and unbalanced proportion. Am I making sense?

(cheers and applause)

We are Capitalists. We should respect and admire our fellow shareholders who, by sweat or skill, increase the value for all of us. We should cherish and then compensate those who put in long and often tortuous hours to ensure the smooth operation of this machine...I'm sorry...person we call our corporation. We should expect to pay those with the talent and drive to rise to the top. So, too, should they expect that compensation to be within the bounds of decency; compensation that richly rewards their contributions but never at the expense of fair recompense for those sweating at a different level, for we are all important to the corporation's success. We are all contributors to the bottom line. We are all, all of us, essential.

(cheers and applause)

Now how do we intend to sell our product? You all have jobs or careers already. You are all presently employees of corporations. How is this all supposed to work? Right now, our efforts to bring in new shareholders are moving ahead rapidly, but concentrated in a few key, target industries. For now. Our heaviest marketing effort is focused on bringing in shareholders from the financial industry. Once the number of shareholders employed by a particular financial institution reaches a certain threshold we will begin the process of negotiating with that corporate institution for the use of your skills, knowledge, etc.. Ah, you say, doesn't that make us the equivalent of a labor union? Negotiating wages, salaries, work rules and benefits? It would be, if we were a labor organization. But we are a corporation. And just like a company will negotiate and sign a contract for supplies, energy, or any number of necessary commodities and services; so must they negotiate with us for the production elements you provide.

Sounds crazy, doesn't it? Most companies would most likely just fire all of you and promote other more loyal and pliant individuals from within or entice skilled individuals away from other companies with promises of more money and possible advancement. And yet...perhaps not. What I have described to you is merely the first step in a long term plan which will be carried out industry by industry, company by company, country by country. The financial world is just the launch pad. We shall negotiate fair compensation for the skills provided by you, our shareholders. If the individual entities refuse our offers then...our shareholders will be pulled from that company.

(gasps and uneasy crowd sounds)

I can definitely smell the coffee brewing. Perhaps we should seize this moment to take a break.

(uneasy crowd sounds including increasingly vocal objections)

And perhaps not. Alright. I know I've rattled your cages. Is that irony?

(nervous laughter from the crowd)

Those of you who are presently employed in the financial industry are justifiably shocked and dismayed. It would be insane for you to give up your job, your career, your opportunity for advancement by following the demented tautology of an obviously fermented philosophy; better to bury yourself and your loved ones in the ground like mushrooms, ready to be plucked and consumed amid the truffle souffle at the banquet of your obscenely rich bosses. Do you think I am funny?

(stunned silence)

I always wanted to be a poet. Now you see why I went to business school. You know it.

(growing laughter)

But would it not truly be insane if the souffle were to be your ultimate fate? It does not have to be that way. Maybe, just maybe, the companies you work for will have an epiphany. As you pack up your things and walk toward the door they will try to hide their descent into justifiable panic. Over half their work force is headed to the street. Good Lord! How will they conduct business? Maybe as their sobs echo through empty halls and cubicles they will come to the realization; the knowledge; that epiphany I spoke of; that with those fading footsteps go the skills and creativity and knowledge essential for running a profitable business. ESSENTIAL! Do you hear me? ESSENTIAL!

(growing cheers and applause)

Remember, this is step one. We may, of course, successfully negotiate an agreement and then there will be no need for further action. But if they let you walk out the door, we are ready this day to implement step two. As of one week ago we have completed all the legal activities necessary to open a new corporate division. And those of you exiting your former working life, if it comes to that, will proceed directly into your new life; your new home; bringing all that makes you valuable to bear on the success of the newly chartered EHW International Bank!

(gasps, cheers and applause)

But we are getting ahead of ourselves. I urge all of our financial industry shareholders attending here and at our global meetings to go to the seminars over the next two days that will explain our plans in great detail. And I stress again that our strategy stretches across all industries. When we are ready to offer a contract to a big box store, so will we be prepared at that time to open up our own chain of big box stores, if necessary. The same goes for factories, hospitals, universities, you name it. One step at a time. One step at a time.

Before I close I will provide a brief answer to the big question I suspect is swirling around in your heads right now. "What's in it for me?"

(laughter)

Not bad for an amateur mind reader, eh? First, I remind you that you are shareholders, and as shareholders you will share in this corporations profits. Second, the direct compensation for the use of your skills, what is commonly referred to as your paycheck, will be paid to the corporation and then offered to you through the corporation as a series of options. You can receive a paycheck as you always have, only bigger of course. Or, you can take your compensation in the form of company stock. Yes, you'll be right up there with hundreds of CEOs around the world being paid in ways that significantly lower your income taxes. You will have a choice of several mixtures of direct pay, deferred pay, stocks, and other investments; all designed to take maximum advantage of the tax laws. You may study the details in our online annual report and have all your questions answered at tomorrows half-day session entitled:

Audience shouts: "What's in it for me?"

You know it.

The more complex answers to that question are covered, as I said, in the on-line annual report which includes a frequently asked questions section, chat functions, and a toll-free number for you to get clarification if you should need it. Hard copies were provided in your attendee's packet. Now, the simplest and most profound answer to the question "What's in it for me?" is, as follows. As a shareholder in this corporation, you will be part of an organization committed to the advancement and well-being of all shareholders, AND stake holders, AND society at large. I know that sounds heavy, but the burden is lightened by the unity of our people and our principles; by our sheer numbers as we continue to grow across the entire planet. There is strength in numbers and as we increase; as we add to those numbers; as we support and uplift each other; as we do our due diligence to choose the best and proper path in our corporate decisions; as we share the burdens and responsibilities of not just corporate shareholders but citizens of humanity; we will find it is possible, preferable, in fact imperative, to powerfully commit to, and live our lives by, the Mission Statement of this, your organization: "To ensure justice for every person, in every way, everywhere on this earth we share."

(cheers and applause)

We have much work to do. We have transcended the threshold of a long, difficult, remarkable journey. We have acted boldly, intelligently, morally, and decisively; a decision that requires all of us to move forward together; for it is only together, unified in purpose, that we can approach that goal: Justice. Justice for all. It is only together that we can overcome the barriers that will be put in our path. And there will be barriers and backlash; subversion and setbacks; darkness and defeats. We must be ready. We must learn. We must adapt and adjust. We may be slowed by these unnatural impediments, but we must not waver. Our objective is simple, reasonable, universal: a fair and equitable distribution of the wealth we help create. A fair and equitable reward according to our contributions. The possibility of a good life for all and a share not in the wealth of nations, but in the wealth of all humanity.

Thank you for your kind attention.

(standing ovation, loud, sustained cheers and applause)

I will be here after lunch for a Q&A session. We will have microphones set up or you can text your questions. Once again, peace and prosperity be with you, my fellow share holders.

THE END

ENTRY ONE:
CARLO'S BOAT

EPILOGUE

"All right, I was sleeping in the boathouse. So what? Nobody uses it any more."

"It's private property."

Sergeant Pierce handed the woman a plastic bottle of vitamin water. She chugged it and immediately gagged on it.

"It's warm."

"Power's been out since the storm. Just came back on about an hour ago."

"What storm?" she said. Margot ran her fingers through her long, tangled hair. She was pale ashy, thin, and ragged beyond her 28 years; leaning one elbow on the Sergeants desk like she was posing for a photo spread in Modern Derelict Magazine.

"How long of a bender were you on?" Pierce said.

"Only a chump would expect me to remember that. Haven't you ever drunk a bit too much?"

"We found three empty bottles on the floor of the boathouse along with some of your other," he hesitated, "possessions."

"Yeah? Only three? The others must have fallen through the holes. That place is rotten. Got to watch where you step. Smells like dead fish too."

"Then why were you living there?"

"That's a dumb question."

An officer named Tatum entered the small office with a paper bag in his hand.

"Red Cross was out of sandwiches but they had some hard rolls," the

Officer said. "Unfortunately no butter."

He walked out as the Sergeant pushed a roll across the desk to Margot. She frowned at it.

"No butter, huh?" she said.

"No butter."

She picked it up and took a guarded bite; then a bigger bite; then demolished the rest in a matter of seconds. The Sergeant slid her another one.

"So tell me what happened this morning."

Her mouth was so full her nostrils flared with the effort to breath.

"Nothing," she said.

Sergeant Pierce smiled to himself. After the flooding and rescue efforts of the last few days he was happy for some comic relief. He picked up a few hand written papers from his desk and pointed at them.

"It says here you were picked up at approximately eight a.m. for suspicion of looting."

"And vagrancy. But I'm not a vagrant. I have a home."

"The boathouse?"

"Home is where the heart is." For a brief instant she almost laughed then grabbed her head in pain.

"You all right?" the Sergeant said.

"I do tolerably well considering." Her face in a wince, she slouched back in her chair and crossed her legs. Through the worn spots in her jeans Pierce could see discolored skin and what appeared to be scabs.

"Somebody been beating you?" he said.

She smirked. "God's been punching me."

"Tatum," he called out. "Why wasn't this woman taken to the hospital?"

The hulking young officer stuck his head in the door.

"No squad cars or ambulances available right now, Sarge. Most of the EMS vehicles are in four feet of water in the parking garage under the hospital."

"I don't need an ambulance," Margot said. "I can take care of myself."

Pierce ordered Tatum to get an ambulance as soon as one was available and turned back to Margot.

"Where were we?" he said.

"Suspicion of looting. At least that's where they say I was. I have no idea what you were up to."

He resisted the urge to laugh out loud but kept his professional composure; just barely.

"This report says you were found pounding on the door of the Beachbanger Mini-Mart, screaming something unintelligible, and just about to throw an object through a window when you were apprehended."

"I was yelling HELP! HELP! Can't get any more intelligible than that. If anybody's listening."

"Why were you yelling HELP?"

"I told those boys who cuffed me and shoved me in the car that there was a crazy man following me and they needed to cuff HIM and shove HIM in the car. But as I said, apparently they weren't listening."

"They must have been listening. It's in their report."

"Lot of good it did."

"This man who was following you, is he the man who beat you?"

"Damn it, nobody beat me. At least not that I can remember. But if somebody did beat me I can tell you for sure it wasn't him. I was just about sober when I first saw him and one look was enough to sober me up completely, and quickly."

She began to gently wring her hands and slowly shake her head.

"I wake up falling off that busted up cot, such as it is, and try to stand up. There's a couple of inches of water on the floor and I can't tell if I'm weaving or the house is waving. I get myself over to the broken window to get some fresh air and maybe wake up a little better when I see this gigantic fish half in and half out of the water on the shore."

"Was it a beached whale?"

"Roll your eyes if you want to. I've seen the whales we get around here and this was no whale. This one was bigger and had a long fin on top. Not like any whale I've ever seen." She wrung her hands faster as she spoke and started bouncing her crossed leg. "He was huge and blue-black and then he puked up some squirmy glob on the sand. I couldn't be sure if what I was seeing was what I was seeing so I dumped out my bag to find my phone so I could take a picture. I know if you can take a snapshot of something then it's not an hallucination. I know that from long experience. So I turn the phone on and I'm amazed there's still some life in it. I point it through the broken glass and the fish is gone, the fish and the puke, and I can't believe it. I start turning the phone sideways and up ways thinking I'm maybe aiming it wrong when this horror movie face fills the screen. I must have pushed my finger on the button a dozen times out of fright but for all that I maybe only got one picture before the battery died."

She paused, out of breath, looking up at the Sergeant, then leaned to look past him and sniffed the air.

"Is that coffee I smell?"

Pierce had slowly been drawn into her story and at first appeared surprised by her question. He recovered quickly, walked out the office door, and returned with two small steaming cups.

"The return of civilization," he said, and slid a cup across the table. She bent over it and frowned.

"No milk? What kind of civilization is that?"

"Got sugar if you want it."

"That's all right," she drained the eight ounces in one toss and tapped the cup on the desktop. "What I want is more coffee. In a bigger cup. And another one of those rolls."

Pierce went out and came back with another small cup and handed it to Margot who curled her lip and groaned.

"Sorry, that's all we have, and fresh out of rolls," he said. "Now you've told me a very interesting story but what does any of it have to do with you trying to break into the mini mart?"

"I know you don't believe me. If I had my phone I'd show you. This guy, he..."

Pierce held up his hand.

"Tatum. Was there a phone among this lady's effects?"

Tatum; tall, hefty, linebacker shoulders, angled sideways to fit through the doorway, appeared holding a device.

"This it? We put it on charge as soon as the power came on so it's working now."

"Why did you do that?" Pierce said. "That's private property."

"Just trying to be nice," Tatum smiled.

"Leave him alone, 'Sarge', and you give me that here," Margot said. She took the phone from Tatum, thanked him, called up the photo of the man she had seen and handed it to Pierce. His eyebrows shot half way up his forehead.

"Jesus," he said.

"Doesn't do him justice," Margot said, "and fortunately can't photograph the smell; like a fish market that's been doused with bleach at midday in full sunlight on the hottest day of the year. He told me he was puked up by that big fish I saw after he'd spent three days in its belly. For a second I wanted to help him but then I thought, I know that story, and I wasn't in the mood for any kind of sermon."

"You believed him?"

"Well, I couldn't be sure. I didn't have all my faculties about me. I'd just regained consciousness from a very long jag. But his story fit what I thought I'd seen from the window. Like I said, I felt sorry for him, that is until he limped toward the door. I didn't want him coming in but the door is nothing but a couple of rotted planks with busted hinges and I couldn't stop him. Tried to run but I tripped on a raised floorboard and landed at his feet looking up into his slimy beard and freaked out eyes. Almost got clunked by some thing he had hanging from his wrist."

Pierce couldn't stop staring at the image on the phone screen. Beneath the fish guts and seaweed there was something familiar. He knew this man.

"Hey!" Margot slapped the desk, getting Pierce's attention. "Are you going to ask me more questions or can I leave now?"

"Yes," Pierce looked up. "I mean no, you can't leave yet. I still don't get what this has to do with your attempted looting of that mini-mart."

"Looting! I was running for my life."

"Did he threaten you?"

"Not physically, but maybe in an existential way."

Pierce tilted his head and raised one eyebrow. "Existential?"

"Yeah. You can look it up if you need to. I've got a Webster's on my phone."

"I know what it means," he looked down again at the picture on the screen. He had a feeling he couldn't shake and it was starting to really bother him. He looked up again.

"Could you please clarify what was threatening about him? You may be charged with criminal behavior and I'm trying to understand exactly what happened."

"I can't tell you exactly what happened. All I know is after I stood up he grabbed me by the shoulders and started talking. Damn, his breath smelled like a dead man's must smell after laying in the grave a few days."

"Dead men don't breath," Pierce said. "So what did he say that got you so shook up?"

She slapped the desktop and mimicked a silent laugh. "Dead men don't breath. A good one Sarge. We should be a comedy team."

"What did he say?"

"Ok. All serious now. I can't remember exactly what he said because I was in no condition to take notes. Besides, I don't usually carry a pencil and a notebook. Not these days anyhow."

With this she began laughing hysterically, slapping the desktop again, almost spilling her coffee.

"Sorry," she said. "Just reminded myself of my favorite cartoon ever. I don't remember the cartoonist but you'll love this. There's two bums sitting on the ground leaning against the wall in an alley, both with paper bags of booze in their hands. One of them says *'It all began the day I discovered the ultimate meaning of life. By the time I found a pencil I'd forgotten it.'"* She laughed and slapped again.

"Very funny," Pierce said, with a wry smile.

"Wait. You haven't heard the punch line. The other bum points his finger at him and says *'You too?'"*

Suppressing a laugh with great difficulty, Pierce could not prevent a broad, twinkling smile.

"Ok. Got it. So can you tell me what you remember about what he said?"

"I'm paraphrasing here, but it was something like *'Help me. Take me to the authorities.'"*

"And that scared you?"

"There's more. Then he lets go of my shoulders and, I remember this exactly, looks deep into my eyes with his bugging yellow eyeballs and says '*We don't have much time.*' Kind of shook me inside a little. Creeped me out totally, actually. He's saying one last word when I shove him to get by and start walking toward the street and I turn around and he's walking behind me, following me, repeating that same last word over and over again until I finally get extremely spooked and start running, if you can call it that, until I'm out of his sight. Like, I still hear that word in my head as I come to the mini mart and start banging on the door but, of course, nobody's there. I panic because I need a place to hide and I look back and there he is in the distance, his mouth still moving, and I pick up a metal piece of something floating in the gutter and take a swing at the window. I'm kind of loopy by this point and I miss it entirely; whack the brick window frame and that makes my whole body vibrate; painfully I might add. That's when your boys show up and I don't know whether to be relieved or run. So I make an executive decision and turn to scat and plow right into the damned window. They take advantage of my momentary giddiness to come after me, cuff me, and wrestle me toward the squad car. All the while I'm trying to tell them about the guy. I look around and he's gone. They must have thought I was hysterical because by that time, truthfully, I was."

"So you had no intention of looting the place?"

"No. Actually I had an uncharacteristically lucid moment where I thought I'd have the opportunity to do something I've always wanted to do. Like in the movies when someone's being chased and they go in the front door of a building and immediately out the back, and then the chasers don't know if you're hiding inside or if you did, in fact, escape. Always wanted to do that and I figured aquaman would be completely confused and I would finally get away. Although, honestly, I can't say for sure that I wouldn't have grabbed a couple of candy bars and some chips on my way through."

"But you didn't. And you didn't break the window either. I can only conclude that the result of this investigation is that no crime was committed."

"So I can go now?"

He was looking still at the face in the phone, trying to imagine it without the streaky gunk, wild hair, and foul detritus, when Tatum entered and announced the ambulance had arrived to take the suspect to the hospital.

"I don't need to go to the hospital. I told you before."

"Officer Tatum, could you please bring in the arrest report. This lady is no longer a suspect." He turned back to Margot. "It's protocol that someone in your condition must be examined by a physician before you can be released. Besides, they have real food at the hospital," he smiled, "such as it is."

When Tatum returned with the paperwork Sergeant Pierce checked it over then placed it in front of Margot.

"Could you sign this please Ms.," he paused and reached for the papers to re-check her full name. Margot held them close to her chest.

"Showers," she said, "Margot Showers. And no jokes. Believe me, I've heard them all a million times."

She signed the papers and handed them back to Pierce who handed them to Tatum.

"Could I have my phone back now?" she said. "I've got family pictures and stuff on it, you know. Things remembered."

Her face was hard and stoic but she couldn't hide her glistening eyes. Pierce looked at the screen one last time when something clicked in his mind.

"Officer," he said. "Who is this? I know I've seen him before. I just can't place him."

Tatum stared at the image and shrugged. "I don't know. Maybe looks a little like some guy I've seen on TV. Maybe a reality show."

Pierce knit his brows, stared harder, then shook his head. *Can't be,* he thought, as he handed the phone to Margot.

"Do you need a wheelchair?" he said absently.

"No thanks, I can walk."

As Tatum led her out Pierce sat frozen in his seat. After a moment of deep, troubling thought, he sprang up and hurried outside. The Emergency Crew was about to help Margot into their vehicle when she spied Pierce coming out the door.

"Forget your manners, Sarge?" she grimaced.

"Yes, forgive me," he said. "I wish you luck."

"Luck is a residue," she flashed a brief smile. "And that's where it ends."

"Ms. Showers. You never told me the word he kept repeating that finally set you off."

She paused, put a hand out to stop the tech from closing the door and tilted her head slightly. In her gut she had a flash of long buried emotions; involuntary, nascent, calico: something akin to pity, sadness, community, fear, and hope. She lifted her hand, index finger raised toward the sky, her mouth slightly bowed upward into hollow cheeks.

"Repent," she said softly. "Repent."

THE END

BONUS FEATURES

The following excerpts are from two works in progress:

Cerberus Rizzo and the Lusus Naturae is the first novel in a series revolving around a group of individuals with exceptional but peculiar talents, battling to reverse the enslavement of the human race to and by technology and its masters.

Bill Bayo is the story of one man who becomes a famous artist completely by accident as the result of a prank. With the help and support of his family and friends, he becomes determined to use his accidental gift to help people hear the cries of human joy and suffering; feel them in their souls; know them as their own; and never turn their hearts away.

These novels may be serialized for subscribers to my web site before actual publication. Go to iamchooch.com and keep checking back for new information.

BONUS FEATURE ONE

EXCERPT FROM
Cerberus Rizzo and the Lusus Naturae

BOOK ONE: The Antique shop

I.

It was a good day, so far; excellent in fact. Sunny and warm. It had been a very profitable July and the owners were pleased. Even in this scarred neighborhood with its dense, creaking houses, leaning on each other like rigor mortised corpses stacked upright, the children came out in droves with their coin chips and spoke, almost yelled, into the ordering sensor. “Chocolate in a dish with sprinkles.” “A vanilla cone.” “Pistachio cookie sandwich.” Gleeful laughter followed as the products emerged freshly made into the distribution receptacle. When all were satisfied, the ice cream bot moved on and sped up when it sensed it was clear of its customers. Smoothly, silently, perfectly, it passed out of the jumble of brown and gray structures onto a quiet country road, headed for the next housing cluster on a two-lane blacktop that skirted a sunken lake. The children who stood in the street battling to lick up their treats before they melted could still hear the goofy jingle that played constantly from the vehicle. “Here’s the Happy Ice Cream Bot. You can really eat a lot! Come-up-to the Happy Ice Cream Bot. Eat and eat and eat a lot.” They started to sing along. Then the song disappeared so abruptly that they paused in the unexpected silence and stared down the road. It always lingered a lot longer, the jingle, fading slowly, and never seeming to actually end. "Ah, it's just the wind's changed," they finally concluded, and returned at once to their feast.

Cerberus Rizzo never chose to be poor and it's not that he didn't want to work. "Hell," he would say to anyone who questioned his apparent indolence, "my old man busted his butt at the wire mill for 37 years, lost his job and his pension when they laid off 90 percent of the workforce and replaced them with ne'er-do-well hunks of plastic and metal with a couple of programmers and a mechanic to keep them updated and greased. He died right before they came and boarded up our house. What person in their right mind would choose that?" Since that day, fatherless and homeless, he bounced around from one shack to another until he'd worn out his welcome with the few friends that still lived in town. He applied for and got a free ride to plumber's school because the government said there would be great demand for skilled trades people and service technicians. They were correct, except that now there were too many plumbers and carpenters and roofers and not enough work for half of them. It didn't really matter to him. His true calling was elsewhere.

These days he slept under the railroad trestle listening to the heavy rumble of loaded freight cars and wondering who the hell had the money to buy any of that stuff. In spite of the noise he found it peaceful under the cross ties. The cops stayed away from that part of town and he was shielded from the surveillance drones that couldn't come too close because of the high voltage catenary dangling over the train tracks. It really messed with their guidance systems and scrambled any microwaves that might be trying to infiltrate the air space; no flight control possible. The magnetic halo the overhead wires generated was a blessing in another way: he was able to build a device from junked computer parts that allowed him to suck voltage from the air if he was near any source of power. The 13,000 volts from the catenary generated enough to run a small electric hot plate as well as powering and recharging his electronics. The device could even work with a relatively weak source like house wiring if the power wasn't turned off yet. *Tesla,* he thought, *Tesla would be damn proud.*

You might think it was dangerous with no law enforcement there, human or otherwise, but he had taken care of that, too. He found and dismantled a crashed drone, gutted it's video camera, inserted it's laser light behind the lens and wired it to a battery. The resulting beam was strong enough to burn holes in cardboard; very effective on corneas even at a distance of 100 yards. "I am," he thought out loud, "what people used to call 'mechanically inclined'." But that was just a practical necessity of living off the grid as much as possible. His real business was invisible, under the radar, and unstoppable. "Like an earthquake," he would say to himself. "Like an earthquake."

This day he was waiting for a ride to his first plumbing job in weeks. Unlike most of his miserably scant calls this one had not come from one of his tradesman apps but directly, via voice message. "We are in need of your services," the voice said, followed by a client's name and address. *Who leaves voice messages?* he thought. He was pondering the intrigue in that and the soft, almost bland male voice on the other end when he spied a lumbering apparition that almost made him burst out laughing: an ancient, pre-computer Cadillac Fleetwood the likes of which could only usually be seen in movies from the 1960s, with two-tone black and silver paint, twin fighter jet fins on the back, and a front hood long enough to swallow whole most of the current I-Drive guided vinyl vehicles. He watched as the driver pulled to the curb and his window came down in a herky-jerky motion that belied a hand crank. *Holy shit,* he thought.

"You be calling for a ride?" the driver said with a Jamaican accent. He had a thin, raddled face encircled by a short gray beard and a full head of white dreadlocks. His eyes were lackluster and serious but his thin lips curved up almost to his nose in a smile that rippled his wrinkles all the way to his hair line.

"I be did," Cerberus said mockingly. "How do I be getting into this thing?"

"Ha!" the man laughed. "You be pulling the handle like you be pulling my leg. Right there."

Cerberus feigned surprise when he pulled the chrome bar and the door popped open. He tossed in his knapsack, sat on a cracked and faded gray leather bench seat and marveled at the space. *Bigger than most peoples' bedrooms,* he thought.

"Close the damn door," the driver shouted and turned around to stare at his passenger. "The hatch don't be closing itself on this boat."

"Sorry. I be used to more modern t'ings."

"Damn those t'ings." The driver's eyes glared for a moment then softened with an almost mischievous twinkle. The wan smile returned with all the creases. "And be careful who you be mocking, my brother." He turned to the front, spun the wheel, and guided the car onto the deserted morning street.

Cerberus looked at the shriveled driver I.D. taped precariously to the back of the front seat headrest. The picture was old but recognizable and underneath was the name Bell Weather. Out the window he saw buildings and empty lots he did not recognize.

"Do you know where we're going Mr. Weather?"

"I picked up your call didn't I? And the name be Bellweather. Not Mr. Bell or Mr. Weather. Bellweather. One word. That be enough."

"Funny sort of a name."

Bellweather emitted a low chuckle. "Who says such a thing? Coming from a man called Cerberus which be the Greek name for the Hound of Hades." He stared at Cerberus from the rear view mirror. "You be the Devil Dog."

"My father had a strange sense of humor."

"I like your father alright, though I know he be dead."

Cerberus was about to power up his hand held device to check the GPS when that last statement made him pause.

"How did you know that?"

Bellweather looked at him in the mirror and began to whistle. The inference of forbidden knowledge crackled in Cerbrus' electric tutelary undermind jolting him forward in his seat.

"Tell me. How did you know?"

"There be things easy to know these days. You hiding from somebody?"

Cerberus sat back. It was nothing. A couple of random facts that somehow leaked into the ether. He picked up his tablet and accessed the GPS. Something was wrong. He rebooted and tried again.

"You looking for GPS you be wasting your time."

Cerberus pressed a couple of more icons: nothing, no access at all. *So,* he thought, *maybe there's more here than just a simple pick up.* He looked out the window and still could not place where they were.

"Where are you taking me? You with the Security Force or just a freelancer?"

Bellweather chuckled. "I be taking you to the address you entered with your request."

"How are you going to find it without GPS?"

Bellweather reached for something next to him on the seat and held up a large softcover book with yellowed edges and stains on the cover.

"This be called a map. And I am not a bounty hunter or anything like that." He looked at Cerberus in the mirror. "You are safe with me. Safer than just about anywhere. Invisible to the trackers. This car is....." He seemed to be searching for a word. When he found it he smiled. "This car be a rolling Faraday Cage, only much better."

This guy is really strange, thought Cerberus. *Probably one of those 'matrix' paranoids with nothing really worth hiding. Just likes to play the game.* He powered down his device, leaned back into the plush leather, and stared out the window.

They finally entered more recognizable territory and glided past the factory where his father once worked. The large parking lot was almost empty. He remembered how it used to be full, twenty four hours a day, seven days a week. The sound of machinery still penetrated the tightly sealed windows but it was dulled and toneless and held no welcome. He couldn't help staring, eyes gently dancing, quietly smiling until they had passed. Just ahead were neighborhoods with houses missing pieces of siding and apartment buildings with crumbling stairs and rusted window air conditioners; idle men and women sitting on porches and covered stoops trying to cool off in the unholy July heat; and beautifully preserved all-plastic electric cars that nobody could afford to charge any longer, now collecting dust by the curb. Finally they approached a gated entrance to a private road. He showed his identification to a camera on a pole.

"Who are you visiting?" came a voice from a speaker. He couldn't tell if it was real or robo, but it didn't matter.

"Xaviera Bannisteros."

"Press your left index finger on the pad below the camera and state your name and business."

He wiped his finger on his leg and pressed it in the middle of a small black cross.

"Cerberus Rizzo. Plumber."

The gate lifted and they passed through. In a transition not unlike going from black and white to color, they entered a street lined with well-kept houses sporting golf course green lawns and expensive shrubbery. Bellweather slowed down to read the numbers on the houses then parked on the street next to a driveway with a shiny, late-model Self-Controlled All-Drive. *Nice SCAD,* Cerberus thought as he noted the rental company identification plate on the bumper and the out-of-state license plate. He grabbed his knapsack.

"How much for the ride?"

"You pay me when I take you back."

"What makes you think you'll get the call?"

Bellweather smiled. "You pay me when I take you back. Happy plumbing."

"Suit yourself," said Cerberus and headed for the front door.

II.

"Hold your horses!"

He could hear someone scrambling inside. A woman wrapped in a green bathrobe opened the door. Her silver hair was puffy and thin around her smooth, glossy face. Cerberus glanced at her elbows. *Old as dirt* he thought. *Dad always said check out the elbows.*

She pushed back her over-sized red-sparkle Cat-Eye glasses and examined him up and down from his sneakers to his straight black hair and Elvis Presley sideburns.

"You don't look like a plumber," she said. "Come in."

Cerberus shrugged like a half-hearted apology and stepped into the foggy odor of freshly brewed coffee and toaster oven pastries.

"I'm sorry. You surprised me," the woman said. "I'm supposed to be aged-out so I keep up the pretense by not knowing what day it is."

"You don't look aged-out," Cerberus said.

"You're a bold little creep aren't you? Would you like some coffee?"

"Yes Ms. Bannisteros. I would like it very much."

"Coffee!" she called out. A gurgling sound immediately commenced from a room toward the back of the house that he assumed was the kitchen. She waved her hands in the air and shouted, "Come on. I don't have all day. And what would you say if I told you now that I'm not Ms. Bannisteros at all but the housekeeper?"

"You're not the housekeeper," he said, and showed her the profile he had searched-up on his phone.

"Damn the internet! Damn all the internets there ever was!" she grunted.

Cerberus smiled. "And go to work."

She put her right hand on her hip and stared into his eyes. He could feel the turning of a drill bit somewhere in his frontal lobe, like she was looking for something and knew exactly where it was. Finally, he shook off the odd feeling and continued.

"If you would be so kind as to show me where the problem is."

"Say what you really mean."

He couldn't help but laugh out loud, though he turned his head so he didn't blast her head-on.

"Show me the problem so I can fix it and get the hell out of here."

"Ha!" She clapped her hands. "I must say it's refreshing to talk to someone who doesn't sound like the spawn of an algorithm. It's right here under the sink. You can get started right away. I'm sure you have many appointments. You'll have to excuse me while I take care of some business."

"Actually unless I get another call you're it for today. So time is not of the essence."

"Essence is all there is to time." She motioned to a glass-top table outside on a balcony. "Sit and drink your coffee, then. There's freshly zapped previously frozen cinnamon rolls in the dispenser. They're not the worst. I know the baker." Her smile glowed for a moment then cooled off rapidly as she waved her hand like she was swatting at smoke.

"I'll be on line for a while. Take your time or you might be finished before I am."

III.

Jake Parsons adjusted his ear buds and stared at the small, miniature Mars Rover-wheeled machines gyrating across the floor as if they were programmed to follow the music in his ears.

"You keep a knockin' but you can't come in – woooooo!"

He was tall, slow moving, and with muscles that sagged from age and disuse. At one time he was Foreman of Janitors in the factory with 40 men and women to manage over three shifts a day, seven days a week. His title was now Chief Maintenance Engineer and he supervised a small army of robotic floor vacuums, dust blowers, dust suckers, sensor drones, and particulate-level-triggered exhaust fans. The only other human in his bailiwick was Wilson Pavlitch, a bearded, gangling, ex-motorcycle head who had once been dubbed a mechanical genius of the first order by one of his professors at Harvard.

"Hey Wilson."

At the moment, Wilson was wandering around between the assembly lines getting a huge kick out of the floor bots calmly navigating around his feet as he set them down in unpredictable patterns. The man pretended not to hear. He was singing an ancient Phil Ochs tune while inserting his own updated lyrics.

"I ain't a-mopping anymore."

Jake threw his arms in the air and started toward him. Just then an alarm sounded. Wilson stopped singing and watched Jake dancing around the bots as they danced around him. Finally Wilson put up his hand.

"Go back to your throne," he snapped, "and out of your misery, King of Rock and Roll."

"Number seven..."

"Has a clogged grease injector. I'm getting there." He started to walk down the line of machines and turned back toward Jake with narrowed eyes and a pro wrestler rasp. "I knew it before it happened. You can sense the tonal change in the input line."

"You're such a bullshitter."

Wilson pulled a small device out of his pocket.

"Oh look. The sucker's off. Battery must have died," he said as he stuck his foot out and almost succeeded in diverting a bot into a wall. "They're the bullshitters. You want to know the secret to beating them? The secret is: if you can't re-program them out of existence, ignore them until they run out of power. Just make sure you've cut off the physical switch to the charging stations. You, know: pull the plug. They'll know what the problem is but be powerless to do anything about it other than sound an alarm somewhere upstairs. Then they'll just wait until one of us comes to the rescue as their batteries drain out their last ions. We're a lot alike, us and them. The forces of nature dictate our moves without us even realizing it. We don't have any control over what happens in this world we have now and neither do they. The main difference is they can't be embarrassed."

Jake pushed a button on the alarm panel to silence the annoying screech.

"I don't need a lecture. Just deal with it."

He sat back in his chair and turned the volume up.

"Come back tomorrow night and try it again."

IV.

He fired up his tablet and sat enjoying the fresh coffee. *Better than I remember,* he thought. The frozen pastries were supreme quality with strawberry filling that may have actually been real. The air on the balcony was warm but fresh and breezy. He stretched out this unexpected breakfast for nearly a half hour. The plumbing problem took about two minutes to fix. After checking for leaks and clogs he turned off the water under the sink and removed the drain sensor, wiped it clean and blew on it a couple of times then re-installed it. The alarm on the kitchen control panel stopped blinking.

"All fixed?" Xaviera entered dressed in a blue pinstriped suit while skimming through a stack of mail; more paper mail than he had seen since his childhood. She tossed the envelopes spreadeagled on the counter and grimaced, as if the weight of it cut down to her bones.

Curious, he thought, and secretly snapped a picture as he moved his finger around his tablet's screen.

"Pipes are fine. Malfunctioning sensor as usual."

She glanced at the control panel and waved her hand in front of the screen.

"Bless the seen and the unseen," she said and turned to Cerberus. "Technology will be the death of us all."

"So some people say."

"Yes, some people." She handed him a payment module. "How much do I owe you?"

Out on the street he saw another Cadillac parked by the curb, this one a solid silver with a textured black roof.

"I know you see me," yelled Bellweather. "What you be waiting for?"

Cerberus threw his gear in the back seat and this time sat in the front.

"How many of these arks do you own? And how did you know I was ready?"

Bellweather laughed. "Why? It looks different to you? I'll explain at the next stop." He laughed. "We know everything. These things be the easiest kind of hacks. You ought to know."

Cerberus paused, thinking this byplay was getting a bit too intrusive.

"What next stop?"

Bellweather pushed on the accelerator and the Cadillac smoothly punched up to near 80 miles an hour. "I have a stop to make before I return you to your charming abode," he said. "Maybe get something for the innards, too."

Cerberus wondered if, at the first physically possible opportunity, he should bolt from the vehicle. Then flashing neurons started to rattle in his head. *Something interesting is afoot.* He awakened his tablet, settled into the cushy leather seat and brought up the picture he had taken of the pile of envelopes. There were around twenty of them, all identical: same canceled stamp, same marketing graphics, same gonzo return address, same "Current Resident" addressee, but each with a different destination; bound for someone else, somewhere else. *Bizarre,* he thought, and started running possible scenarios through some of the game writing tools on his tablet.

They drove through neighborhoods of unimaginable squalor; buildings with entire walls missing, plastic scrap-covered plywood hovels, and overturned trash container condos, all occupied by dusty, thin, desperate humans of all ages and colors – out of money, out of work, and not a bot to piss on. Bellweather pulled into an abandoned gas station with a handwritten sign announcing "B-Man's House of Antiques".

"You come in with me for a few," he said.

"A few what?"

Bellweather pointed at the mildewed exterior. "Open your mind, my brother. Bellweather knows you be liking this place."

"Oh, it's a beauty, alright."

"Watch this." Bellweather pulled a device out of his pocket that looked like an ancient television remote control and pressed a button. The paint on the Cadillac morphed into a sunburst yellow. Cerberus stared at the vehicle then examined the remote which contained only the typical channel and volume controls.

"The trick is not in the device," Bellweather smiled, "but in the paint-like coating. A special formula described in only one singular book from the distant past, never understood and never translated." He pulled a metallic tarp over the Cadillac and motioned for Cerberus to follow him. Cerberus thought about running but something was squirming beneath the surface and he needed to play it out a little more. He followed Bellweather inside.

The front room was filled with relics from better times: old lamps, small appliances, and sports equipment covered in dust and in various stages of dilapidation. They passed into a second room, dark and empty except for a desk with a computer and a lamp glowing over a large open book. Bellweather faced Cerberus and spoke softly.

"He be here."

Cerberus looked around. *He's not talking to me,* he thought. Silently two figures emerged from the shadows. One was a tall, thin, bald-headed Asian woman. The other was a white, muscular, scar-covered apparition from an old "Road Warrior" movie: orange six-inch Mohawk brush standing straight up in the center of his head and multiple metal objects stuck through his cheeks, lips, and nose.

"You," the Road Warrior said.

Cerberus leaped for the door but it slammed shut before he could reach it.

"Don't be so fearful," the Asian woman said.

"What do you want from me?"

"Only what you are willing to give," the Road Warrior said. He spoke with a soft, curious, hard to place but oddly familiar accent.

"I don't have anything to give. I'm just a poor plumber trying to survive."

"No you're not," the Asian woman said. Her accent was even stranger;

halting, guttural, brutal poetry.

"Be at peace, my Brother," Bellweather said. "These be my compatriots: Enkhtuya and Bash. We just want to talk to you."

Cerberus laughed and mimicked Bellweather. "So, my Brother, you be one of them."

"No," said Bash, the Road Warrior. "You be one of us."

Cerberus conjured some inner chanting to calm himself. The pierced and coppiced apparition moved a step closer and stared into Cerberus' eyes. Enkhtuya, the Asian woman, motioned to Bellweather.

"Show him," she said.

Bellweather moved over to the desk. "Come here, Devil Dog. You may find this interesting."

He pointed at the open book. Cerberus backed toward the desk while watching the two phantasms. His mind flipped rapidly through his options for escape and found them disappointingly limited.

"Turn around and look," Bellweather said.

Cerberus glanced at the computer. The screen was dark and he noted the reflection of the rest of the room and the two strangers watching him. But all this brain activity involuntarily froze when he saw the open pages of the book. Slowly his consciousness reconstituted as he put his hand on the strange writing and felt the delicate roughness of ink on a page. He looked up at Bellweather who was smiling, his arms folded. The other two were behind him, having moved closer to the desk, but Cerberus was no longer afraid of them. A wave of endorphins washed over the pleasure centers in his brain and his eyes gleamed as he stared at the pages.

"This is a beautiful copy," he said.

"Beautiful. yes," Bellweather said, "better than perfect. This one be printed from a deep scan reproducing all markings in every layer of the pages. Even the ones you can't see. They say the original has been destroyed."

"But why?" Cerberus said. He turned a few pages and his heart fluttered at the hand-made drawings and peculiar script. "No one has ever deciphered it."

"Yes, why? And who knows the answer?" Bash smiled and twirled in place, ending with a snap of his fingers.

"Devil dog look," Bellweather said. "Turn back to the first leaf. Never seen anything like this. It be beautiful and powerful, even if you can't read it."

Cerberus eyes ran rapidly over the page. He did feel something odd; not fear or apprehension or even curiosity, but an unexpected movement in his scalp muscles. Bellweather pointed at the cryptic, elegant script.

"Because it is a mystery, above all, except for the name of the man who possessed it last, they call it by his name. But there is no title page. All these words, these symbols," he flipped the pages, "taken together, they be the real title. It be boiled down to this."

Bellweather leaned close to Cerberus face and spoke slowly.

"This is How The World Works."

Cerberus felt a wave come over him somewhere between utter incredulity and cosmic fascination.

"You can read the Voynich Manuscript?"

"He can read more than that," Enkhtuya said. "We will show you. Come."

V

Jake poked at his touch screen, hunting down the various bots and preparing for the change of shift. Three were unaccounted for which meant a possible malfunction in their trackers and the need to physically locate them. He finished the last few bites of a sandwich he had been nursing for two hours to kill time and blew the horn for Wilson. As he suspected, Wilson came wobbling out from between two machines rubbing his eyes and stumbling slightly as he walked toward Jake.

"What the hell is it now? Almost quitting time, dammit."

"Numbers 12, 18, and 44 are missing,"Jake said. "We need to find them before the next shift comes in."

Wilson's eyes suddenly went wide. He lifted his head and sniffed the air. "Hey Jake. You smell that?"

A loud crash was followed by broken glass firing down from the overhead windows. A second crash behind the two men erupted in a screech of metal on concrete. Down the length of the building Wilson could see the machines gyrating out of control, flashing and smashing like a mad movie projector about to explode.

"Jake, What the hell just happened?"

Jake didn't answer. He was kneeling on the floor holding onto a triangular glass shard that pierced the base of his neck. Wilson rushed over and examined the entry point.

"It's all right, Jake. We should pull that thing out. You'll bleed a little but it doesn't look like it hit anything like a jugular vein."

Jake's breath came in short bursts and sweat rolled into the wound as Wilson slowly removed the glass. He ran to the first aid station to get some gauze and was just about to pull the emergency alarm when the alarm went off on its own. Someone was banging frantically on the glass window of the second floor control office, his face contorted in an unhearable scream. All the machines on the floor began to spew smoke and sparks as one by one, in a rapid cacophonous super-heated dance, they either imploded or erupted, hurling ripped metal and plastic shrieking through the smoke.

By now Jake was flat on the floor semi-conscious. Wilson quickly taped a wad of gauze on the cut and started dragging him towards the exit when he looked out over the machine floor.

"Oh my God."

They cleared the emergency exit door just in time. A blast of heat and smoke chased them into the empty parking lot as glass, metal, and plastic rained on them until they reached the shelter of a maintenance shed. Wilson checked to see if his work mate was still breathing then reached for his company cell phone. No service. In the distance he heard a blaring horde of sirens approaching.

VI.

Cerberus turned the pages of the book as Bellweather recited the hidden meanings of the enigmatic drawings and writings.

"You see this page here?" Bellweather smiled. "This be the formula for that Cadillac paint job. On the next page is the method for controlling the color and texture using different frequencies of electron flow. The writer suggested using magnets but we be more advanced here." He held up the remote control. "This once was a TV remote. It's now a simple device to project electric current through the air. The channel buttons adjust the frequency and the volume buttons adjust the signal strength."

"You built that?" Cerberus stared at the gray dreadlocks and scraggly beard.

"I built it." Enkhtuya said, her face devoid of even a hint of emotion. "And mixed the coloring material with exact precision. All according to Bellweather's reading of the scripture."

"My skill at building things be woefully below average," Bellweather laughed.

"So you can read the Voynich Manuscript, something the greatest code breakers in the world have failed to do, but you can't re-wire a simple remote."

"Bellweather doesn't need that type of skill. His gift is far more unique and useful." Bash spoke up. "He can read and translate any language into any other language: dead languages, hieroglyphics, cuneiform, even computer code."

"Even encrypted computer code," Enkhtuya said.

Cerberus paused and let her words coalesce in his brain. He had a feeling there was purpose behind it that required further investigation. He looked at Bellweather.

"Can you write Etruscan?"

"You are being funny. No, my brother. I cannot write. I can decode but I cannot encode. Etruscan be easy to read."

"Seems like a flawed and truncated super power to me."

"But an elegant one," Enkhtuya said. "And incomprehensibly utile."

Cerberus turned to her and took a detailed physical inventory: tall and straight, pleasantly thin, bald skull shaded by a hint of yellow stubble, protruding eyes, pallid skin, dense pink lips precisely level above a fluid dimpled chin.

"What's your superpower?" he said.

"We are much more interested in yours," she spoke through lips so tight the words almost hissed. Bash threw his hands in the air and jumped in.

"Enkhtuya builds impossible things. If you must know. As a child she built a pattern of dominoes that once set in motion felled and reset itself in a perpetual sequence that ran continuously until a 5.7 Richter Scale quake hit her home town. Six months later."

"Impressive," Cerberus said. "But pointless."

Bash smiled. His upper front teeth were filed into points; his lower lip distended, pierced, and calloused.

"Have you ever played RattleFake?"

Cerberus' thoughts paused then started to swirl in uncontrollable loops. RattleFake was a game involving a virtual city; buildings filled with rooms harboring the most ludicrously complex and difficult traps. The machines and devices cranking out obstacles were mysterious, nearly unbreakable constructs that twisted a player's intellect around crazy, seemingly impossible yet utterly logical and brilliant stories; products of a mind that transcended genius into the realm of the otherworldly. It was the ultimate challenge and his favorite game. He stared hard at Enkhtuya.

"You're *Fung Q,*" he said.

For the first time her lips bowed into a smile neither delicate nor proud, simply acknowledging her identity as the architect of an intricate and original world, unparalleled in the vast universe of cyber play. She tipped her head towards him. "The last time we met you were one move away from entering the snake's true lair, *Propinquus Rex*."

His mind slowed to absorb all he had seen and heard in the last few moments. *So she knows my game name,* he thought. *Lots of gamers do.* But it rumbled deep in his spirit that somehow she had put his face to the persona. The three of them stood silently until he resurfaced his inner disguise and turned to Bash.

"And you?"

"*Ballanchine*," Bash said.

Cerberus made a monumental effort not to let his face show the turmoil and uncertainty squeezing his emotions. *What did they want? Where was this going? What was The Ballanchine doing here?"*

"What are you doing here?" Cerberus asked.

Ballanchine was the underground name for one of the most effective, feared, and vicious network security scanners ever created by the gods of cyber hell; a bane and terror to even the most hotshot hackers, including Cerberus in his early days. An enigmatic, cerebral bounty hunter whose presence was only retroactively detectable from the pulverized systems and disappeared code monkeys he left in his wake. Then one day, after years of making life difficult and often deadly for the most theoretically invincible super-hack criminals and anarchists, he fell off the face of the internet.

Bash crossed his arms then pointed a long, steely finger at Cerberus. "The ice cream truck. That was you."

"Oh," Cerberus chuckled. "What makes you think that?"

"This would take too long to explain right now," Enkhtuya's voice began to rise.

"We watched it happen," chimed in Bellweather.

"Wow. You must all like ice cream," Cerberus said. "Now I know everything I need to know about you."

Enkhtuya rolled her eyes. "You are arrogant. However, arrogance provides no mystery. Be aware you are not as incognito as you might think."

"We detected the attack as soon as it began," Bash said, pumping his hips. "I assure you we were not the only ones."

Cerberus scratched his head then held his hands with palms out. "Come on. You're joking right? I'm just a simple homeless plumber."

Bash smiled a saw-toothed grin. "We have something to show you."

"A leaky toilet?"

"You are too funny, my brother," Bellweather laughed. He put his arm around Cerberus' shoulder, guided him toward a darkened doorway, and flipped on the lights. It was a small room with a low ceiling. A charred exhaust fan in the outer wall drifted loosely with the breeze, casting a random motion shadow on a desk that held a small monitor, tilted at a crazy angle toward a pyramid of black melted plastic.

"So that's what I smelled when I came in here," Cerberus sniffed. "Thought maybe you had burned your lunch."

"When you infiltrated the Happy Ice Cream Bot command system," Bash said, "our sensory infrastructure immediately displayed your incomprehensible and nearly invisible penetrating code. This time it was visible, for a moment. A mistake on your part? Unfortunately it was passing too quickly for Bellweather to read so we attempted to stream it into memory and this," he pointed at the plastic heap, "was the result."

Cerberus pumped his fists. "Now THAT is impressive."

Enkhtuya gritted her teeth and waved her arms in frustration. "The time for jokes is over." Her head shook as she shrieked and banged the wall with her fist. Bash seized her shoulders and held her until she calmed down. Then he turned to Cerberus.

"Perhaps you don't mean to be cruel. But a cruel streak would not be surprising considering what you have created."

For a moment Cerberus felt guilt as Enkhtuya's face held tight and red, staring him down as if he were a murderer. He was readying a vague, insincere apology when Bash broke a piece of twisted baked plastic off the pile on the table and swept it overhead in a lilting arc.

"How did you do this?"

What's the point of acting stupid, Cerberus thought. He perceived them as his equals but could not yet grasp a meaning behind their conterminous existence, this place, or this day. There was something they wanted from him. *But what? Why?* He made up his mind to get to the kernel.

"I overclock the processor to the point of fusion. Sparks fly. Things ignite. Rapid interstitial disintegration resulting in more heat. Marshmallows in a hot frying pan," he shrugged. "The usual stuff."

"We can all see what you did, my brother," Bellweather said. "The *Balanchine* asks not *what* but *how*?"

Cerberus shrugged. "This would take too long to explain right now."

Enkhtuya snarled and moved toward Cerberus with clenched fists. "I've had about enough of your insolence."

Bash moved to block her way. She whirled and landed a soft kick behind his knee that made him instantly collapse to the floor. Bellweather grabbed her from behind and just as she was about to plaster his stomach with flying elbows, Bash snapped back upright and held out his hand.

"Enough," he said softly. "Intimidation begets resistance." He turned to Cerberus. "What we seek is knowledge; input and output; for our journey is fraught and twisted, laden with cyber mines, traps, and fatal false pathways."

Cerberus waved his fingers in front of his eyes. "Clear as mud."

Enkhtuya snarled like a mountain lion. "Your 'fool' act fools none of us."

"Enkhtuya *Fung Q* be still," Bellweather said. "We know who he be and he knows we must know. For it be no accident we brought him here, and he knows that too. Isn't that the truth, Devil Dog?"

For a moment nobody moved. Cerberus used the pause to rapidly analyze the situation as well as several alternative approaches to ending what, to him, was an increasingly bothersome and wasteful visit. He settled on a simple but subtle strategy.

"What the hell do you want?" he said.

(END OF EXCERPT)

BONUS FEATURE TWO

EXCERPT FROM
Bill Bayo

Chapter One

When Bill Bayo died he was not considered an artist in the traditional sense. He was not a painter, a sculptor, an actor, a filmmaker, a photographer, a playwright, a poet, or a writer of any kind. He couldn't even be called a performance artist. No one thing seemed to quite fit. He did, however, have a secret, which shocked and amazed people around the entire world when it became known after his death. Some folks thought it showed his true genius. Others thought it proved he was, as they had said all along, a fake. Still others didn't give a hoot since they had never heard of Bill Bayo or his creations. How did this all happen?

Bill Bayo was born sometime in the spring of 1936 on an isolated farm in Montana. No-one knows the exact date since he was, apparently, birthed at home, and never registered with the government or even with a church. We know little about his parents except that they disappeared from the farm and never appeared again. A kindly Postal Carrier attempting to deliver a package found the small farmhouse deserted one day with the door wide open. Inside he could hear the screeching cries of an infant boy. Against all his training he entered the house and found baby Bill Bayo in his crib, covered in his own poop, and howling in a most pitiful way. The Postal Carrier, whose name was Wallace Oid, cleaned him up in the stream that flowed next to the house. (You see, the water pump inside the house was broken.) He wrapped Bill Bayo in an old table cloth because he could find no diapers or anything else made of cloth in the house, put him in his Postal sack and carried him to his Postal Truck. For the entire twenty minute ride to his house the child was silent, his eyes closed, but he turned his head in the direction of even the slightest sound.

At first, Mother Oid was shocked when Postal Carrier Oid pulled Bill Bayo from the sack, but she immediately fetched a diaper from the closet and wrapped it around his tiny bottom. She cradled him in her arms and sang to him softly. He opened his eyes and she thought she saw the beginning of a smile. He twitched his arms to her singing but his eyes stared blankly toward her mouth. He closed his eyes again as she started feeding him from the baby bottle she had been warming on the stove.

"Set up the crib," she said quietly to Postal Carrier Oid.

Before he finished the bottle Bill Bayo was asleep and she gently placed him in the crib that they had used for all three of their children. The crib was decorated with colorful shapes she had knitted and wind chimes she had made and tied to the railings. The slightest movement would cause the chimes to tinkle and Mother Oid would know the baby was all right.

Postal Carrier Oid walked outside to the back porch, sat down in his favorite oak double-rocker, and contemplated the darkening late autumn sky. The Oid house was situated at the farthest end of town at the top of the last steep hill that guarded the entry way to the shadowy forest, the looming mountains, and a near-total wilderness. The front of the house had a covered porch facing twenty feet of cut prairie grass and weeds that passed, just barely, for a lawn. The back yard was a different story. Two fifty foot bluffs to the left and right formed a funnel to a steep, fenced in drop-off about one hundred yards from the back porch. Thirty miles away, like a huge purple dimple on the face of heaven, stood the four thousand foot crag known to the locals as Pearldrop Mountain. It might have been considered an imposing presence were it not for its curly-cue pinnacle that the townsfolk likened to a pinched and stretched out marshmallow.

Mother Oid quietly slipped out the back door and nestled beside her husband.

"Wallace," Mother Oid said, "What must we do?"

"Mother," said Postal Carrier Oid, "the first thing we need to do is pray."

The Oids adopted Bill Bayo. They had three girls of their own: Marla (1 year old), Carla (2 years old), and Darla (4 years old). The girls were excited to finally have a baby brother and Bill Bayo grew up in a household filled with the quiet loving kindness of Wallace and Mother Oid, and the chaotic exuberance of his 3 big sisters.

The Oid's small house was on the fringes of a town with an interesting history. Eight-Cent-Nickel Montana consisted of one copper mine, one high school, fifteen churches, a Post Office, and about 1,800 full-time residents.

You might wonder how a town came to be named after a somewhat similar gag from a Marx Brothers movie, but the name predated Groucho and his brothers by 40 or more years. The name goes back to a time in the 1880s when the town was called Plateau. (It was originally named Plateau even though it was in a river valley, no one knows why). A snake oil salesman came to town and convinced townsfolk that the U.S. Government had created the 8 cent nickel.

"You can use one nickel to buy something for three cents and get the same nickel back as change!" he told them.

He then used one nickel to buy enough goods to fill his cart until it was almost too heavy for his mule to pull. The people were amazed. He left town to the cheers of the populace and was never seen or heard from again. All went well until the merchants in the town realized they were no longer making any money and stopped giving a nickel change for a 3 cent purchase. All commerce came to a standstill until later that year when men building the Great Northern Railroad came through and some railroad workers told the people that no such thing had happened; that a nickel was a nickel and that was that. This caused quite a bit of embarrassment to the hoodwinked citizens. Even worse was the humiliation that, from that point on, all the other towns in the county referred to Plateau as Eight-Cent-Nickel.

Things came to a head in 1925 when the latest contraption, a Public Address System, was installed in the town baseball field. At the county high school championship game the Plateau Copperheads played the Flathead Lumberjacks. When the Lumberjacks won the game in dramatic fashion in the bottom of the ninth the P.A. announcer got so excited he screamed out "Flathead defeats Eight-Cent-Nickel!!" over and over again. The townsfolk became so irate they burned down the announcer's booth with the announcer still inside. He barely escaped with his life and was chased down Main Street in his smoking clothes, looking for all the world like a flailing locomotive pulling a horde of screaming rail cars.

The next day, the publisher of the county newspaper, the *Post and Dispatch*, printed this front page headline in four inch tall bold letters: "FLATHEAD DEFEATS EIGHT-CENT-NICKEL". (He was quite upset, his brother having been the announcer at the game.) This was too much for the citizens of Plateau. But, unfortunately, it was just the beginning. The publisher had also sent the story out over the news wire and within days newsreel companies and newspapers from around the world had come to tell the story with graphic photographs and newsreel footage of the still smoldering announcer's booth. Suddenly Eight-Cent-Nickel was known all over the country. It got so bad that the Post Office started delivering mail addressed to Eight-Cent-Nickel. The townsfolk called an emergency meeting and threatened to secede from the U. S. of A., or at least from Montana, until a local tavern owner pointed out that his business had nearly tripled because of all the publicity and the tourists that had started showing up. He suggested they officially change the town's name to Eight-Cent-Nickel and take advantage of the new tourism industry. At first they wanted to kill him until he pulled a wad of dollar bills out of his pocket to show them how much money was to be made. They quickly put aside their embarrassment and embraced the idea with an almost unseemly passion. Suddenly a cottage industry sprang up in every household. They produced postcards, trinkets, embroidered pillows and bed spreads, souvenir hats and shirts, and hand-carved wooden nickels – all proclaiming in one way or another "I've been to Eight-Cent-Nickel, Montana!" They even started holding weekly re-enactments of the burning of the announcer's booth.

This was the weirdness that Bill Bayo grew up with. Postal Carrier Oid went to work every day with a quiet smile and a hearty "Thanks for the pancakes, Mother!" On snowy winter mornings he would put on his skis and slalom down the hill to the bus stop. Other times he would put on his roller skates, hang his shoes around his neck, and do "S" patterns to the bottom. Mother Oid field-marshaled the household, schooled the children at home, and doled out chores, chastisement, and hugs as the situation demanded. The girls caromed around the house like the world was an amusement park and the house their personal roller coaster. Bill Bayo helped with the cleaning, tended the garden, and thanked God every day for whatever the package was that Postal Carrier Oid had tried to deliver that miracle morning of his true birth.

Other children in the town thought the Oids a strange bunch and would taunt and harass them whenever they saw them – especially Bill Bayo. (Everyone in the town knew the story of how he was found).

Once, when Bill Bayo was eight years old, Postal Carrier Oid took the whole family to the county fair, held that year in Eight-Cent-Nickel. The air was filled with the sounds of hundreds of voices, calliope music, and squeaky rattling carnival rides. The smells of cotton candy, sausage and peppers, cooking lard, and animal poop, came and went at random, like whiffs of spray from a waterfall. Older couples walked slowly, arm-in-arm, among the booths of carnival games and local vendors selling their wares. Children ran around dodging the older folks and the few young men left in the town, all in uniform, trying to make the most of their last days before going off to the world war.

While the Oid children waited in line to get on the Ferris Wheel a group of town urchins encircled them and began cursing and screaming at them in a most cruel and indecent way. A torrent of awful language streamed from the mouths of the shameless punks, led by the loudest and most shameless mouth of all: a tall, gangling teenager named Horace Greeley Barnes, known to his friends as "Heck" in tribute to his colorful vocabulary. The Oid girls gave back as good as they got, minus the more trashy epithets, when suddenly, Bill Bayo clenched his fists and stepped forward to protect his sisters.

Bill Bayo was small for his age. He possessed a pile of mixed stringy/curly brown hair that sat on the top of his head like a two-day old salad. He gritted his teeth and moved towards the bullies, making a bee-line toward the leader of the pack. When he reached the bellowing Heck he began to kick wildly and managed to land direct hits on both of the cretin's shins before Heck grabbed him by the shoulders.

"You little jerk!" Heck screamed.

He turned Bill Bayo around and with one foot purposely pushed him directly under the churning carnival ride. In a split second that felt like an eternity his three sisters managed to pull him back before he could be smashed by one of the flying gondolas. They then proceeded to beat the living daylights out of any child within their reach. Postal Carrier Oid and Mother Oid arrived just in time to stop them from seriously injuring just about every smart-mouthed kid in Eight-Cent-Nickel. Postal Carrier Oid grabbed Heck Barnes by the scruff of the neck and lifted him squirming into the air. Heck snarled as his cohorts scattered. Postal Carrier Oid was not a big man but he had stout, sinewy arms and shoulders, honed in a childhood of chopping wood and helping his father plow the rocky earth on the family farm. He had no problem dangling the boy a foot off the ground until his struggling subsided. When he finally put Heck down the boy slithered off to the laughter of the crowd that had gathered to watch. Bill Bayo could hear him swearing under his breath eternal revenge for this humiliation as his voice faded into the distance.

The Oids left the fair right after that. Postal Carrier Oid took them all to get ice cream since their good time had been spoiled. However, the girls were not sad in the least. In fact they were still flush with the great victorious pummeling they had meted out to the deserving street rats of the town. Bill Bayo sat quietly as they recounted with verve every punch and Indian rope burn they had inflicted. When they had all finished their ice cream he stood up so abruptly that everyone was caught by surprise.

He took each of his sisters by the arm and pulled them over to Postal Carrier and Mother Oid. He pushed them all as close together as he could into a corner of the ice cream parlor, closed his eyes and wrapped his arms as far around them as he could reach. They stood like that for a good while until Mother Oid said, "Let's go home."

The Oids and the rest of the inhabitants of Eight-Cent-Nickel went about their lives as normally as possible until, with great joy, relief, and sadness, the young men all returned from the war in their various states of life and death. The end of the war was marked with a grand parade down Main Street which culminated with the Town Manager presenting the young victors with keys to the city. He surprised everybody when he announced that Main Street, Eight-Cent-Nickel, would be the first road in the county to be paved with asphalt, (it had previously been paved with tar and sand) perhaps as early as the spring, and would thenceforth be known as "The Avenue of Heroes" in honor of the returning veterans. The gathered citizens cheered and threw their hats in the air in tribute and in anticipation of the boom times that they believed must surely be coming. But that winter the copper mine shut down after having graciously handed over all it had of value to the ungrateful and unsentimental mine owners, and by Spring half the town was out of work. Soon some folks began to migrate away and the population teetered on the brink of implosion. Houses were being boarded up so fast that the lumber mill couldn't keep up with the demand for planks. Things got so bad that a morbid joke circulated around the county – that maybe Eight-Cent-Nickel should change its name to Two-Cent-Nickel. Most people did not laugh. They did not know, could never have guessed, that within a few years, a bizarre event would once again bring prosperity.

Chapter Two

When Bill Bayo was 16 years old he got it into his head that he might want to go to college. The nearest university to Eight-Cent-Nickel was the University of Montana in Missoula. His oldest sister, Darla Oid, had graduated from UM with a degree in Nursing and had raved about her experience there. So Postal Carrier Oid loaded Bill Bayo into his car one day and made the 5 hour drive to visit the school. It was a beautiful spring day and the two of them walked around the entire campus and then into one of the classroom buildings. It happened to be the College of Art. It smelled like oil paint, old pipe smoke, and freshly brewed coffee. The place was buzzing with people moving back and forth, up and down the main hallway, talking softly with many an “Ooooh!” and “Aaaah!’.

“What’s going on?” Bill Bayo asked.

Postal Carrier Oid read a sign on the wall and said, “Looks like some kind of Art contest. Modern art it says.” He walked to the first painting inside the door. “Here’s one that’s just a white canvas with a black stripe down the side. I’ve never seen art like that before. I like pictures of mountains and rivers, the outdoors you know.” But Bill Bayo wasn’t listening. He was tuning in to conversations up and down the hall:

“Wonderful!”

“Marvelous!”

“Look at the texture, the flow, reminds me of….water.”

“You call that art? A three-year old could do something like that.”

“What emotion! What depth! It really captures the essence of…..”

“Looks like somebody spilled some cans of paint on a canvas.”

“Unique.”

“Creative.”

“OOOOh!”

“Aaaaah!”

Bill Bayo had an idea. He found out that the students bought their art supplies at the book store so Postal Carrier Oid took him there and paid for a roll of tape and an empty picture frame Bill Bayo had picked out. It was a rough-hewn square about ten inches per side made of fragrant fresh cut pine. They went back to the building with the art exhibit. Everyone had gone into the cafeteria for coffee and cake so the hall was quiet. Bill Bayo located a spot on the lower wall that was empty save for an electrical outlet. He carefully placed the frame over it with the outlet offset several inches to the right and toward the bottom of the frame. Then he nudged it into a slight angle and taped it firmly to the wall.

“Interesting,” said Postal Carrier Oid. “What does it mean?”

“That’s what we’re going to find out,” said Bill Bayo.

He heard a woman’s voice inside the cafeteria saying, “I’d like to thank you all for coming and hope you enjoyed the art as much as you enjoyed these wonderful cakes and coffee. We’ll go back outside for a final viewing then have the final judging back here in the cafeteria at three o’clock. Remember to write down the names of your favorite pieces as well as the artist’s ‘secret name’. Now go to it art lovers!”

Bill Bayo asked Postal Carrier Oid for a pencil (he always carried several in the front pocket of his shirt) and quickly wrote the word “Frame” on the wall below his “artwork.” Underneath that he wrote “Bill Bayo.” He finished just in time. The empty hallway quickly re-absorbed the herd of chattering coffee-and-cake-bloated experts in the subtleties of fine modern art. Bill Bayo and Postal Carrier Oid slipped into the cafeteria, sat in the back, and waited.

At three o'clock the art lovers returned to the cafeteria and, after cleaning out the remaining doughnuts and cupcakes, sat to hear the Dean of the Art School announce the winners of "best in show." The Dean was a tall, wispy lady with a figure consisting of bony warped right angles crowned by over-hennaed tufts of steel wool. When she came to the number one selection her face took on a twisted, confused look.

"The winner of Montana University Art Department's Spring Modern Art Show 'Best in Show' is..........'Frame'?" Here her voice went up several pitches and her eyebrows lifted until they were lost in her hairline. "Bill Bayo?"

The crowd clapped politely.

"Is he here?" she said, scanning the room with wide bulging eyes.

Bill Bayo put his hand on Postal Carrier Oid's shoulder and motioned for him to be still.

"Would anyone like to comment on this selection?" the Dean said. "I must say I am not familiar with the student or his work."

A man with a bald head and a monocle stood up and said, "I have never seen a more stark and bold representation of Modern Man's utter surrender to science and technology. The artist is telling us that all our gadgets have constrained our imaginations to the point where our best expression of our selves is an emptiness we fill with televisions, toasters, and telephones; any confounded device whose root, whose substance, whose very soul and spirit, is a hole in the wall. Brilliant. Absolutely brilliant."

"Are we talking about that frame somebody stuck on the wall out there over the outlet?" came a woman's voice, hardly concealing her disgust. "I thought it was a joke."

A man stood up sporting a handle-bar mustache, "I'd like to know who voted for that ridiculous thing. I think whoever hung that there is either insane or too lazy to learn how to create real art."

Another woman stood up, so short that her orange beret was the only thing visible above the people seated around her. "Philistine! I think it showed the most incredible imagination. I also think this artist has a marvelous eye for both composition and the absurdity of our plastic lives. The choice of a rough pine frame tilted at an imperfect angle brings us back to nature and the way humans were meant to live, while the outlet within it carries nothing but empty electrons. A masterpiece!"

Suddenly the room was filled with people trying to talk over each other. "A new voice!" "A travesty!" "You're all wrong. It's a celebration of the wonders of science!" "Bogus." "Absurd!" "You people are all idiots!"

Bill Bayo heard every word from every corner of the room and his skin tingled from his head to his toes. He and Postal Carrier Oid slipped out of the room unnoticed. Neither said anything until they had gotten in their car and started driving home.

"So what do you think of the school?" asked Postal Carrier Oid.

"I don't think I want to go to college now," said Bill Bayo.

Postal Carrier Oid turned on the radio to hear the weather. The skies had darkened and he couldn't tell if what was coming was rain or snow, or if it was just some passing clouds. "If you say so," he said.

On the way home they stopped at the Bayo Farm. Postal Carrier Oid had started bringing Bill Bayo there for visits when he was still in diapers. The whole family came up twice a year to clean the house and spend a few days relaxing in the solitude. Bill Bayo would sometimes go into the little farm house and stand stock still in the middle, listening to the tiny sounds of the wind and the woods. Other times he and Postal Carrier Oid would walk around the perimeter of the land which was about fifty acres. Thirty acres were rich flat pasture land. The other twenty fell away on the west side in a gentle slope down to a small valley where three streams met to form a larger one that miles away emptied into the river that ran through town. On this trip, Bill Bayo just sat on a flat rock and listened to the stream that rippled by the house.

"What are you thinking, Bill?" said Postal Carrier Oid.

"I'm thinking," Bill Bayo said, "I'm thinking I need to get a job."

Postal Carrier Oid sat down on the rock next to him. "You don't need to get a job on my account. We're doing ok." He started throwing pebbles into the stream which made Bill Bayo smile at the skipping and plunking noises.

"I know," he said. "But it's time I started pulling my own weight."

"You do enough around the house and in the garden to pull your weight and then some," said Postal Carrier Oid.

"Well," Bill Bayo said, "I won't slack off that. But there's something I want to do and I'll have to save up a little money to do it."

Bill Bayo got a full time job at "Mr. Mickey's Musical Instruments and Answering Service" right on the Main Street/Avenue of Heroes bus line in

Eight-Cent-Nickel. He was hired to answer the phone. The answering service consisted of one phone set up behind the counter. Since "Mickey's" only had one answering service client, a semi-retired Doctor, there wasn't much for Bill Bayo to do. He would sit and listen to the occasional customer trying out a banjo or guitar, but mostly he sat by the phone thinking.

Sometimes he hummed to himself one of the hymns he learned as a member of the choir at the First Eight-Cent-Nickel Holy Baptist Church of Jesus. As a child he had been plucked out of the congregation one Sunday morning when half the usual singers were home with tonsillitis. Reverend Makepiece had often felt compelled to request the Oids to tone down his singing from the pews since, until he was six years old, his strident off-key renditions would throw off the oh-so-polished harmonies of the choir. Although he knew by heart all the words in the hymnals he seemed to be following an organist that existed only in his head. On this particular day the Reverend decided that, rather than restraining the boy's enthusiasm, he might as well take advantage of it and stick him in front of the choir where his loudness might at least make up for some of the missing voices. Once Bill Bayo was situated in front of Sister Makepiece, the Reverend's wife who directed the choir from behind the church organ, an extraordinary thing happened. To the surprise of all, Bill Bayo not only sang in perfect pitch, but his voice soared with the spirit of a true anointing. During the final series of hymns several ladies fainted from the glorious renditions and grown men were seen pretending to blow their noses to hide the tears bubbling down their faces. From that day on Bill Bayo became a fixture in the choir and Reverend Makepiece came to believe that his voice carrying out into the street was the reason his little church began to burst at the seams with new believers. Now at Mr. Mickey's he would hum softly to himself and try to make sense of the ideas flowering in his head.

One day when the wind was kicking up outside and the transom over the entrance was open, he became aware of what sounded like a woe-be-gone symphony. All the stringed instruments were lined up on the wall or hanging from the ceiling and the breeze played them with soft haunting strokes. He was alone in the shop so he reached back and picked a trumpet off the shelf and began to play. At first he had no idea what he was doing but he blew into the mouthpiece and pumped the valves until slowly he began to form an atonal melody to go with the background sounds. Within a half hour he mastered enough of the instrument's technique to blow loud enough to be heard on the street. A crowd began to gather outside listening to this music that sounded like it came from another planet. Inside they could see Bill Bayo standing behind the counter swinging the trumpet back and forth, up and down as he played.

"The boy's insane," said an old farmer in bib jeans and a straw hat.

"He's the most!" squealed a young woman with a ponytail that practically reached the ground.

At this point the phone rang and Bill Bayo had to stop playing to answer it. It was Mr. Mickey.

"What in God's Name is going on over there? I'm in the Barber Shop across the street and I look out and there's a near riot in front of my store!"

The crowd had grown and arguments became heated around the relative merits of Bill Bayo's performance. A red-faced Mr. Mickey came running across the street still wearing an apron and neck strips from his half-finished haircut and forced his way through the crowd into the store.

"Bill Bayo!" he yelled, "you're....." He was about to say "fired" when something stopped him. It was the strangest sight; something he hadn't seen since his Grand Opening many years before. His store was filled with customers. He ran behind the counter where the cash register was and smiled over at Bill Bayo. Some young people had gathered around him and were talking over each other with great excitement. Bill Bayo turned his head toward the sound of the cash register ringing and ringing and he smiled. Mr. Mickey paused for an instant, staring at the oddly blank look in Bill Bayo's eyes. Quickly he turned back to the customer across the counter who was handing him a stack of bills for a saxophone. He heard Bill Bayo speak quietly to the eager teenagers who had gathered around him.

"It was something in the wind," he said, and didn't say anything more.

Mr. Mickey had the best day in his thirty-two years in business. He thanked Bill Bayo and told him he didn't have to answer the phone anymore; that he could just play any instrument in the store any time he felt like it. He even gave him a raise and then started paying him a commission. Bill Bayo stayed on at the store for another two months. When Bill Bayo decided to quit, Mr. Mickey hated to see him go. He had played just about every instrument in the store and whatever instrument he played Mr. Mickey sold out of within days. But Bill Bayo had saved enough money to carry out the first phase of a plan that, right now, made little sense in his own mind but that he believed would give him a purpose for the rest of his life. In his heart he felt no fear, just equal portions of uncertainty and wonder. There was a path laid out before him with everything hidden but the first steps. In time, he prayed, all would be revealed. For now, he quietly enjoyed the mystery in his soul; a murmur of endless chuckles pirouetting to the music of a wordless, inscrutable joke.

Chapter Three

Not long after starting at Mr. Mickey's, Bill Bayo had asked Postal Carrier Oid to be on the lookout for a particular item he would almost certainly find along his Postal route.

"If you say so," said Postal Carrier Oid.

Now that Bill Bayo was ready to make his first move, Postal Carrier Oid drove him to what he had found. It was an abandoned house on a dead end street near the old copper mine. There were only a few houses left on the street and they too were deserted. The empty lots where other houses had stood were now overgrown with weeds and the landscaping consisted mostly of demolition debris and rotting automobiles. Behind the houses was a man-made stream bed that had once carried water to the sluices inside the old copper mine. It flowed most heavily in the spring and summer, bulging with the melting snows from the mountains. On this late spring day the waters rushed headlong toward the mine entrance, slapping against the concrete sides and, at places, gurgling over the edge into stagnant, weed-choked pools. Bill Bayo got out of the car and stood in front of the house for a long time.

"This is it," he said.

"OK," said Postal Carrier Oid, "I'll call Artie."

Artie Fuller was the realtor commissioned by the town Chamber of Commerce to dispose of "abandoned properties, eye-sores, and sundry useless structures." Postal Carrier Oid, who knew most of the people in the town, arranged a meeting between Artie and Bill Bayo. In less than an hour the deal was made, the dirt cheap price paid in full, and the papers signed. Bill Bayo was now the proud owner of the most condemnable of condemned houses in Eight-Cent-Nickel – a one and a half story "Victorian Cottage" styled house at 22 Sluicegate Road.

"He sure about this?" Artie had asked Postal Carrier Oid. "Someone buying a shack like this can't be right in the head."

"Oh he's more right in the head than anybody I know," said Postal

Carrier Oid, "Though that might not be saying much."

Bill Bayo immediately got to work. He hired Ernie Benzini, a young, reclusive, out-of-work carpenter with a pick-up truck, who drove him to the local lumber yard. He handed the owner of the lumber yard the rest of the cash he had saved and a list of items to be loaded into the truck: bags of concrete mix, galvanized steel poles, and various fastening hardware. He handed him another list of items to be cut at the lumber mill next door: extra-wide, extra-thick, extra-long, oak planks – as wide and long as they could make them.

The next day the mill delivered the order to 22 Sluicegate Road. When the men in the delivery truck saw the house, they laughed and called out to Bill Bayo, "Here's the lumber you ordered. Would you like to order some dynamite?

Bill Bayo ignored them. He was pushing hard on one of the steel poles that Ernie had put in the ground the day before. The men unloaded the wood and left, grumbling about not getting a tip.

"Is this going to hold up?" Bill Bayo asked Ernie.

Ernie's face turned bright red and the muscles tightened in his jaw.

"Yup." Ernie replied through clenched teeth. He was a big young man – six foot two, around 240 pounds. Like Bill Bayo he was not yet old enough to be drafted (the Korean War was winding down) and probably would have been considered 4-F anyway because one leg was three inches shorter than the other. His huge bulk was rock-solid muscle. It was his misfortune to have neck muscles so massive that his head appeared to be disproportionately small. Some folks in town had taken to calling him "pinhead." It didn't help that he had lost all his body hair due to a childhood bout with rheumatic fever. The net effect was that of an off-kilter bowling pin. He wore a seemingly perpetual scowl on his face that could explode at any moment into instantaneous bouts of anger or laughter, depending on his reading of a situation. He had grown up on the fringes of town in an enclave called "Black Hole" by the more polite citizens of Eight-Cent-Nickel. Others in town preferred to call it by a more rude and insulting moniker. The cluster of small houses was inhabited by a select group of copper miners, mostly former railroad workers, officially designated in the county census as "Negroes."

Bill Bayo walked over to where the wood was piled and ran his hands over the roughly cut planks. He heard the sound of a vehicle starting followed by a loud crash. He ran back to where Ernie had backed his truck into the steel pole at 40 miles per hour. Ernie got out of his truck and inspected the pole.

"Didn't budge," he said. "Solid as a rock."

"What about your truck?" Bill Bayo said. Ernie didn't answer. He just got back in his truck and parked it across the street. He walked back to where Bill Bayo was standing.

"What's next?" he said.

That day Ernie single-handedly erected a huge steel framework in front of the condemned house. Positioning the base poles the day before had taken hours. Bill Bayo had stood in the middle of the street listening to the wind and directing Ernie to move the base structure back and forth, left and right, until settling on a final position. Ernie rarely spoke except to make a suggestion now and then and followed Bill Bayo's directions to the letter. On this evening when they had both grown weary he drove Bill Bayo home and did not speak at all.

Bill Bayo got out of the truck in front of the Oid house and called out, "See you in the morning."

Ernie didn't respond. Bill Bayo heard him gun the engine and peel out, followed by the screech of brakes, and the truck being thrown into reverse. Ernie hit the brakes again and came to a stop in front of Bill Bayo who heard the passenger side window rattling loudly as Ernie cranked it down and stuck his head out.

"I like my coffee dark and my doughnuts light," he said, and roared off down the street.

Ernie Benzini was the son of an immigrant Italian railroad worker and a Mississippi school teacher rumored to be the great-great-grand-daughter of a Sudanese Princess. Papa Benzini arrived in America with a large contingent of Italian men, all looking for work. He and several of his "paisans" got jobs working for a railroad the name of which they could not yet pronounce. He traveled extensively throughout the southern United States as a gandy dancer on a track maintenance crew. Since none of the white workers wanted to team up with "Eye-talian garlic eaters," Papa and his compatriots worked in mixed crews with "coloreds", "Polacks", and "greasers." His first day on the job he was paired up with one "colored" worker named Ike Banks, a short, stocky, ball of muscle with a nearly immobile deformed mouth. Nobody else wanted to work with Ike. He rarely spoke and when he did the words came out hopelessly garbled and accompanied by voluminous bubbles of saliva. Papa Benzini himself spoke a very broken, heavily accented English and it seemed the two were destined to dreary days of limited communication with hand signals and gestures.

One day, a few weeks after starting the job, the whole crew was taking a break in the shade of a huge cypress tree. Papa had forgotten his lunch so he sat quietly, sipping slowly from a canteen of water. Suddenly, he heard a rumbling next to him that caught him off guard.

"Yeeoh ika cahnreh?" Ike said, gently poking Papa Benzini in the arm. The sound of his voice came from deep in his belly: a low howling wind forcing its way through his tortured, immovable lips. Papa looked closely at his sweaty face for the first time since they had been paired together and was struck dumb with a sudden and hopeful revelation. He opened his mouth to reply but nothing came out.

"Yeeoh ika cahnreh?" Ike repeated. Papa Benzini smiled. Some of the other workers made fun of Ike and did exaggerated imitations of his unintelligible speech, but Papa did not hear them. He continued to stare at Ike and spoke as slowly and clearly as he could in his own twisted pronunciation, "Ayessa. I lika day corna bread."

Ike's mouth never budged but his eyes lit up and seemed to dance in their sockets. He reached into a paper sack and plunked right into Papa's hand a hunk of corn bread as big as a brick. Papa thanked him and waved the bread in the faces of the now silenced crew, took a big bite, and chewed. Ike let out what was probably a laugh and patted Papa on the back.

"Goo, huh?" he said.

Papa smiled and nodded his head. "Buon," he said, "Good."

The track gang traversed hundreds of miles of railroad over the next few months re-aligning rail, replacing rotten ties, and doing general maintenance as they went along. It just so happened that right around Christmas time they had worked themselves west to Jackson, Mississippi, Ike's home town. When the gang took a few days off for the holiday, Ike invited Papa Benzini to stay at his house and join his family for Christmas dinner. Papa gladly accepted, looking forward to his first home-cooked meal since getting off the boat in Norfolk, Virginia, many months before. There were several things, however, that he had not anticipated.

First, when he accompanied Ike to his house, he slowly became aware from the stares of Ike's neighbors that he was most likely the only white person in that part of town this Christmas. Second, Ike had a big family, and a very small house. Papa felt guilty when Ike insisted on giving him a room to himself, so that Ike and his wife ended up sleeping in another room, bunched up with their four youngest children. Finally, there was Audrey.

Audrey Banks was twenty-two years old and home for the holidays from teachers college where she was finishing her Masters in Education. She was bright, graceful, and to Papa, the most beautiful woman he had ever seen. She was also over six feet tall so she stood at least a full head over everyone in the household, including Papa Benzini. In later years he liked to joke that he always "looked up" to Audrey, but you could tell by the admiration in his eyes that he wasn't just referring to her height. Papa found himself staying as close to her as he could for the entire Christmas holiday, except, that is, for Christmas Eve.

The day before Christmas, Papa asked Ike if he could borrow some of his tools: specifically a saw, a hammer, and a chisel. He took the tools and disappeared, not returning until after the sun had gone down. Everyone was so busy getting things ready for Christmas Day that no-one even noticed he was gone; except Audrey. After the family had gone to bed she sat in a dark corner of the front porch and waited. Finally she could see the figure of Papa Benzini coming in from the street carrying a bunch of tools and something clumsily wrapped in newspaper. As he came up the steps she cleared her throat just loud enough for him to hear. He stopped with his hand on the front door knob, turned his head slowly toward her, smiled weakly, and made a feeble attempt to hide his package behind his back.

"Bongiorno, Missa Owdra," he said with a slight bow of his head.

Audrey folded her arms across her chest and looked away to hide her smile.

"And where have you been all day?" she said.

Papa took a deep breath and slowly took the newspaper-wrapped package from behind his back. He held it to his chest, his shoulders drooping, uncertain what to do next. Finally he held the package out to her.

"I...uh...I...," he said.

Then something seemed to pull his spirit together and with gentle but firm resolve he straightened up, held the package out to Audrey, and spoke in near perfect accent-less English.

"Merry Christmas."

Audrey got up from the chair, reached out and took the package.

"Mille grazie," she said in Italian. "Buon Natal."

Papa Benzini could not stop the corners of his mouth from stretching into a grin so wide it almost cracked his lower lip.

"Yes," he said, "Molto Buon Natal."

Chapter Four

The next day when Ernie picked him up, Bill Bayo had a box of Mother Oid's fresh-baked doughnuts and two thermoses of coffee.

"I'm sorry I didn't trust you," Bill Bayo said.

"Great doughnuts," Ernie mumbled as he washed a one down with coffee, "Java could be a little stronger."

Bill Bayo smiled. "What's that I smell in the back?"

"Varnish," Ernie said between bites, "Vertical oak will last a hundred years but if you finish the wood it will last darn near forever. I brought some dark stain too."

"I'd prefer a natural finish," said Bill Bayo.

"Well," said Ernie, pausing for a moment in his campaign to annihilate the doughnuts, "I think the wood should be dark. The house is old and faded and with the sky behind it a light color would get lost." He turned toward Bill Bayo, "You trust me on that?" Bill Bayo hesitated then nodded his head. "Listen," Ernie continued, "If I'm going to work with you we need to be able to trust each other. Do you get my drift?"

Bill Bayo thought for a minute. Except for the Oids, he had never met anyone as bull-headed straight as Ernie. On the way to the house he found himself telling Ernie things he had never told anyone except his family. He felt like any moment he would break out in a cold sweat as he talked about his past and his ideas for the future. Ernie was silent until they pulled in front of the house. Finally he spoke.

"You're loony," he said, patting Bill Bayo heavily on the shoulder, "let's get to work."

That evening, Postal Carrier Oid drove Marla, Carla, and Darla to 22 Sluicegate Rd. to see how the work was coming along. He was surprised to see Bill Bayo and Ernie lounging in the back of the pick-up truck, sipping the last of that morning's coffee. He pulled his car alongside and said, "That coffee must be mighty tasty by now." Bill Bayo and Ernie smiled.

"How do you like it?" Ernie said, pointing toward the house.

Postal Carrier Oid looked at it for a long time.

"Interesting," he said.

Bill Bayo burst out laughing. Marla and Carla giggled in the back seat. Darla, now twenty-two but still living at home, sat in the front and stared at the house.

Darla Oid had only recently been discharged from the U.S. Army where she had served as an operating room nurse with a Mobile Army Surgical Hospital for two years during the Korean War. Since her return she had remained uncharacteristically silent in sharp contrast to her former outspoken, never-at-a-loss-for-words self. Wallace and Mother Oid had tried to get her to talk but she continued to limit her conversation to one or two word sentences, when she decided to speak at all. So everyone jumped when she turned to Bill Bayo and blurted out, "What in God's name is that supposed to be?"

Bill Bayo stopped laughing. "What do you think?" he said.

About half way between the edge of the street and the front porch loomed a giant hollow wooden square. Completely framed within the square was the derelict house, now isolated and forlorn, which appeared from the street to be utterly detached from the world around it.

"Tomorrow I must bring Mother to see this," said Postal Carrier Oid, still recovering from the shock of Darla's outburst.

Bill Bayo sat motionless too, but not because of Darla. He felt a warm sensation in his cheeks but his clenched hands had suddenly gone cold.

Ernie turned and stared at him. The evening sun was an enormous orange balloon resting on the horizon and its rays painted Bill Bayo's face like a Monet tangerine. The backsides of the house and the frame were bathed in dark orange beams that made them appear to be glowing.

Bill Bayo seemed to go stiff all over. There was something there – a sound that he had detected earlier as soon as they had put the finishing touches on the frame. At first it was indistinct but now it had begun to take on a form that sent a chill to Bill Bayo's heart. Just then Postal Carrier Oid's car began to sputter and, as he pumped the gas pedal to keep it from stalling, the roar of the engine shattered the air and the sound disappeared.

"I had best get this thing home before it dies altogether," Postal Carrier Oid said.

As he began to slowly pull away Ernie yelled out, "Please thank Mother Oid for the doughnuts. They were out of this world!"

"Out of this world?" mumbled Carla in the back seat, "He ought to know."

"Now what do you mean by that?" said Postal Carrier Oid.

"She means," said Darla, "he's a space alien. Probably escaped from Roswell."

"A space alien?" said Postal Carrier Oid, "and here I thought he was a carpenter."

"He's a dumbbell," Marla said.

Postal Carrier Oid stopped the car and turned to the back seat.

"There will be none of that kind of talk in this family, young lady."

Marla sat back in the seat and pouted.

Darla said, "He is a dumbbell. All the folks in town say so."

"Now since when did you care what the folks in town say? Why..." something stopped Postal Carrier Oid from continuing

The girls in the back seat had started talking at the same time but Darla had slumped back in her seat, her lips pursed, her eyes staring straight ahead, focusing on nothing. Carla and Marla stopped abruptly when Postal Carrier Oid waved his hand.

"That will be enough of that," he said.

Postal Carrier Oid had been too young to fight in the First World War and too old to be drafted for the Second. But in his mind he could still see the hollow look in his father's eyes when he returned from France in 1918, having left his right arm in some forgotten shell hole outside of Verdun. He saw his father sitting at the dinner table raging against the tears, unable to cut his own meat. He remembered his death a few years later, the bitterness with which his life ended, and the good man that had never really returned from the trenches. Then he thought about his daughter, sitting miles away from him in the front seat of the car, and he prayed.

Muffled giggling welling up from the back seat brought him back to the present day.

"Now what's going on?" he said.

Carla covered her face with her hands and between giggles managed to get out a complete sentence. "Actually," she said, "I think he's cute."

When Ernie drove Bill Bayo home that night he spoke excitedly about the crazy thing they had done.

"Wait 'till the townsfolk get a load of that!" he said.

When they reached the Oid house Bill Bayo thanked him for all his hard work.

"Couldn't have done it without you," he said as they shook hands.

As he turned toward the house he again heard Ernie peel out, then a screech of brakes, the truck being thrown in reverse, and Ernie slamming on the brakes in front of the house.

"Hey!" Ernie called out. "See you soon, yes?"

Bill Bayo waved as Ernie gunned the engine. He heard the truck screeching around a corner as he stepped into the house where he was embraced by the warm air and the smell of Mother Oid's cooking. It was way past the Oid family bedtime so he removed his shoes and walked softly to the kitchen where his nose led him to a plateful of pork chops and garlic spinach that Mother Oid had left out for him. Bill Bayo sat down and was about to say a prayer of thanks when he heard the sound of someone crying outside in his garden. He left the kitchen and walked out the back door.

"Darla," he said, "What can I do to help you?"

"Nothing, Billy, but thanks for asking."

For a moment her weeping subsided. Then, with a choking sound from deep in her throat, a torrent of uncontrollable sobs poured out of her. She reached out and hugged Bill Bayo, burying her face in his chest. He patted her back and stroked her hair. When she had finally calmed down he wiped her eyes with the sleeve of his shirt.

"What was his name?" he asked.

"How did you know?" Darla said.

Since she was a little girl, Darla Oid had been the rock the other children had leaned on. She was outgoing, outspoken, and totally fearless. When they were out in the world she was their leader, confidant, protector, and disciplinarian. She grew into a mature and confident young woman and an indispensable help to Mother Oid who called her "my carbon copy." When she graduated from college she became a top-notch nurse, capable of showing kindness and caring to her patients but strong enough to bear their sorrow and pain, and sometimes their passing. She worked in the emergency room at the county hospital where she held up like a stone wall in the face of the most horrific injuries. The bloodshed in Korea had sorely tested her but her letters home were also filled with her observations of the beauty in the people she had met and the places she had seen. Then the letters stopped. When she returned home the whole family had decorated the house with her favorite flowers and made feast-sized portions of her favorite foods. But something was wrong, and try as they might, they could not get to the source of her pain.

Now Darla sat on the back steps of the house and looked down at the ground, her head swaying slowly with an occasional twitch as she tried to regain control.

"His name was David," she said. "He was an ambulance driver. So brave, so strong – he had these muscles in his arms. He could lift a loaded stretcher by himself. But when he hugged me it was like being wrapped in a pillow."

She pulled something out of her pocket and placed it in Bill Bayo's hand and began again to sob quietly.

"He gave me that three days before he was killed," she said.

Bill Bayo felt the ring she had placed in his hand. It was very light with a small but very sharp stone. He took Darla's hand and placed the ring in her palm, closed her fingers around it, and wrapped both his hands around hers.

"Oh my sister," he said. "Oh my dear sister."

She put the ring back in her pocket.

"The worst part," she said, slowly lifting her head to stare at the stars. "His ambulance got a direct hit from an artillery shell. They never even found his dog tags." Her voice began to trail off as she mumbled, "Not even a grave to visit."

Bill Bayo sat down next to her and put his arm around her shoulder. They sat that way for a long while. Finally, fading, tired, and numb, Darla stood up and, as she had done so many times in the past, playfully messed up the hair on Bill Bayo's head.

"That thing you made," she said. "It's kind of neat. Stupid but neat."

Bill Bayo smiled. He had a strange sensation in the middle of his chest like a small seed had been planted there. He shrugged it off, knowing that whatever it was would be revealed to him at the proper time.

"Doesn't amount to a hill of beans," he said as he walked behind Darla into the house.

Chapter Five

It was front page news. The Sunday edition of the *Post and Dispatch* featured a large photograph of the house on 22 Sluicegate Rd. with the giant frame sitting in front of it. The headline read: "Monstrosity!" Prominent on the editorial page was an expanded "Extra!" version of a regular column of opinion titled "By Heck," where the editor, a Mr. Heck Barnes, railed against the "new type of eyesore visited on our community by one Bill Bayo, recent purchaser of the property." "It's not bad enough we've got similar dilapidated structures all over the county," Mr. Barnes continued, "but now someone's got to focus attention on one of the worst examples."

Postal Carrier Oid read the editorial to the whole family that Sunday at dinner. "Well Bill," he said, "looks like you raised the hackles of Mr. Barnes. Front page picture and everything. I wonder who tipped him off?"

Bill Bayo tried with only partial success to suppress a grin.

"It's not even that Wallace," Mother Oid snapped then smiled sweetly. "The only person focusing attention on it is Mr. Heck himself. That boy has been a sore on this community since he was old enough to make a fist."

"I don't know, Mother," Postal Carrier Oid said shaking his head. "Says on the front page the Chamber of Commerce is ready to tar and feather old Artie Fuller for selling it to Billy. Says here they'll be," he read aloud, "'seeking an injunction to remove the offending structure until they can take the case to court on the basis of visual harm to the community.'"

Darla laughed out loud. "That's the least offending structure in this whole town!"

Hearing her laugh made Postal Carrier Oid pause. Then he smiled and turned to Bill Bayo.

"What do you think Billy?" said Postal Carrier Oid.

"I think I'll work in the garden now," Bill Bayo said and excused himself from the table. Everyone knew he was not in any way upset. They recognized that certain walk of his when he was laughing inside.

As the days passed it seemed like the whole of Eight-Cent-Nickel was in an uproar in danger of mushrooming out of control. Large groups of concerned citizens were showing up at Town Hall demanding some action be taken against this affront to the community. There was private talk among some folks about burning 22 Sluicegate Rd. to the ground. Finally, one night, a large mob carrying torches gathered in the town square. A few self-appointed leaders gave short speeches that fired up the crowd.

"We can't let this kind of thing go on in our own back yard," said one man.

"It's un-American!" said another.

"It's a communist conspiracy!" declared the final speaker, the bombastic Mr. Heck Barnes himself.

By this time the rabble was in enough of a frenzy that they set off for 22 Sluicegate Road with the intention of certain mayhem. A few blocks before reaching their goal they encountered a police roadblock where the Town Supervisor pleaded through a bull horn for everyone to just give him a few more days to rectify the situation. The crowd seemed to come to its senses, especially after a Policeman accidentally discharged his shotgun and blew the top off a pine tree. They dispersed amid loud grumbling and cursing. Two days later the Town Supervisor suddenly made an announcement that the whole thing had been settled amicably and that everyone should just calm down and get back to their own business. A rumor began to spread that someone had purchased all the other properties on the street including the old copper mine for an exorbitant sum and, in addition, had paid in full all the back taxes owed to the town. Though no-one could substantiate the rumor, it did seem curious that the

Town Supervisor soon thereafter purchased brand new Oldsmobiles for the use of Town officials, and ordered the renovation of the High School including the addition of an indoor pool and hockey rink. He also announced an across-the-board property tax cut of thirty percent. The citizens of Eight-Cent-Nickel were ecstatic and it appeared that the whole incident had blown over and finally come to an end.

It hadn't. Somehow the tale of the angry mob had filtered out to the rest of the state. Newspapers and radio stations were starved for sensational local news to offset the now boring daily reports from Korea where peace talks had stalled while both sides argued about the shape of the negotiating table. Once UPI and the AP picked up the story Eight-Cent-Nickel was again besieged by newspaper, newsreel, and radio reporters, and by film crews from the increasingly popular television news networks. This time, the major impact of all the attention was not national embarrassment for the town. Something totally unexpected happened.

Meanwhile, Bill Bayo went about his daily life as if nothing out of the ordinary had occurred. He seemed to relish the overblown reaction to his work but tried hard not to show it. He had settled back into his old routine of helping Mother Oid around the house and working his garden.

Bill Bayo loved his garden. It was a quiet place where he could think. A rock fountain he had built with Postal Carrier Oid provided a soothing, bubbling background sound. He enjoyed the variety of smells that came and went across his face with the breeze: peppers, cucumbers, squash, cabbage, and wild flowers. He would sometimes kneel quietly listening for the buzz of insect pests, snatch them with his bare hands, and dispatch them with extreme prejudice. In the fall he and Postal Carrier Oid would erect a temporary greenhouse so he could harvest things beyond their Montana growing season and keep the Oids in fresh vegetables for almost nine months out of the year.

A few days after the front page article had appeared and the town crisis was still building to its crescendo, he was working in the garden thinking about what he should do next. He had no money but felt that the next project should be much grander than "House at 22 Sluicegate Road". He was mulling over the germ of an idea when Mother Oid came out to the garden.

"Billy, there's a man out front who wants to speak with you."

A rotund little man in a Kelly hat driving a beat up Pierce Arrow had pulled in front of the house and rang the doorbell, asking if this was the place he might find Bill Bayo. While he waited he kept nervously turning and turning on the front porch, his hands jammed deep in his suit jacket pockets. Bill Bayo, thinking he must be a reporter, or a sheriff serving him with a summons to appear in court, stepped silently out onto the porch, folded his arms and waited.

"Are you Bill Bayo?" the man said.

Bill Bayo nodded his head.

"Oh the joy of it!" The little man started jumping up and down, causing everything on the front of the house to rattle, "The joy, the joy, the joy of it!" He finally stopped jumping and wiped his sweaty forehead with a dingy battered handkerchief. "I've been looking for you for months! For months!" In his overjoyed state he grabbed Bill Bayo's shoulders and started jumping again. "Don't you recognize me? Don't you know who I am?" He stopped abruptly. His eyebrows hunkered down in deep disappointment as he looked at Bill Bayo's blank expression.

His name was Aristophanes Marzipan, a famous eccentric and one of the richest men on the face of the earth. His smiling circular mug had been on countless magazine covers and newspaper front pages. His escapades had been the subject of uncountable newsreels and a character in a Hollywood movie had been based on his life.

"Sorry," said Bill Bayo.

Aristophanes Marzipan slowly regained his composure, though his hand still shook slightly as he stuffed the handkerchief back into the slightly torn front pocket of his suit jacket. "That's Ok. That's Ok." he said, "After all this is Montana. Listen. My name is Aristophanes Marzipan." He paused waiting for a reaction.

Oh," said Bill Bayo, "I have heard the name."

Aristophanes bewildered look was softened slightly by this belated recognition.

"Good. That's good. I would like you to accompany me," he turned toward his beat up old car and shook his head, "No. No. Not in that! Not in that! I'll bring a limousine and a driver. But please say you will accompany me to my temporary residence?"

Bill Bayo's unchanging expression was starting to unnerve Mr. Marzipan. He took Bill Bayo's hands in his and said, "Please say you will! Say you will! I can pick you up tomorrow at your convenience. I know how busy you must be. I promise you will not regret it."

"OK," Bill Bayo said, "Ten o'clock."

Aristophanes Marzipan yelled out "Wahoo!" and bounded down the steps, skipping all the way back to his car. "Ten o'clock! Ten o'clock! I'll see you tomorrow at Ten o'clock!" he called out as he jumped into his car and waved goodbye. The sound of his sixteen cylinder behemoth faded down the street.

"Oh my goodness! Him?" said Postal Carrier Oid at dinner that evening. He told the whole family the stories he had heard about Mr. Aristophanes Marzipan. It seems he had started life as an orphan and lived until he was 12 in a hell-hole of an orphanage in Erie, Pennsylvania. It was at that age that he decided he was tired of being at the mercy of others and had endured enough beatings, vermin, and horrible food for one lifetime. He was determined to make his own way in the world and ran away. He got a job hawking newspapers, slept in cardboard boxes in alleys, and ate food discarded in trash bins behind fancy restaurants. He not only managed to save some money but obtained an informal education from the newspapers he sold, reading them all from cover to cover. One day he stumbled upon an article about a quack inventor who was fighting eviction from his laboratory/apartment. He visited the inventor and found him working on mostly useless contraptions. One, however, caught Aristophanes Marzipan's interest. It was a device to be placed on the bowl of a spoon to prevent soup from leaking over the edge. He offered to pay the inventor's back rent if he would sell him the rights to the device. The inventor sold it to him on the spot.

"But what will you do with it?" the inventor asked, "I've tested it extensively and all the subjects say it makes the soup taste like iodine."

"I'm not sure, not sure" Aristophanes said, "but I do not plan on eating with it."

Aristophanes remembered an article he had read about a problem manufacturers were having finding a newer, better, cheaper design for ball bearings. It seemed that every new cost-saving design revealed the same fatal flaw: it was impossible to keep lubricant among the balls where it was needed with the result that they frequently overheated and failed. Aristophanes bought a new pencil and some clean paper and spent a few days making drawings of ball bearings incorporating the spoon bowl device in the bearing races (the inner and outer rings). He used his drawings to file for a United States Patent. As soon as his application was registered he tried to get appointments to demonstrate his device to the largest ball-bearing manufacturers in the country. None of them wanted to waste their time meeting with a twelve-year-old crackpot from Erie, Pennsylvania. So he brought his invention to a small local tool-and-die company he had read about that was struggling to stay solvent in the face of competition from the much-larger national companies. They had not paid their workers in weeks and had no money to pay him for his idea. He struck a bargain with them and they quickly created a prototype. It worked perfectly. The company went on to make a large fortune, selling the new ball bearings as fast as they could make them and eventually buying up some of the companies who had refused to even look at the drawings. Aristophanes Marzipan had negotiated his payment for the use of his design as a percentage of the gross unit price for every bearing sold and an option to purchase 51 percent of the company stock as soon as it went public. (He read the financial section of the newspaper as avidly as he read the rest.) Thus, before he reached his fourteenth birthday, Aristophanes Marzipan was a millionaire. He sought out the original inventor and explained what he had done.

"Congratulations, my friend," the inventor said, "you are a better scientist than I."

He refused to accept any of Aristophanes money but the boy insisted and set up a trust to ensure that the inventor and his family would be comfortable for the rest of their lives.

From then on, Aristophanes Marzipan spent most of his time traveling the world in search of strange and bizarre items he could then adapt to some useful purpose. The rest of his time he indulged in his one frivolous passion: he became a collector of art, usually purchased for exorbitant sums from obscure talents who, more often than not, eventually emerged as major artists. By the time he was thirty the value of his collection was over half a billion dollars and included works by Picasso, Matisse, DeKooning, and O'Keefe. That, combined with the royalties from all his patents, had made him the world's youngest billionaire at the tender age of thirty three. Now in his 70's, this was the man who had shown up at the Oid house looking for Bill Bayo on that quiet afternoon. Bill Bayo called Ernie, told him the story of the strange little man, and asked him to come along.

"I'm not sure what he wants but I would like you to be there," he said.

"Why not?" Ernie said, "Never rode in a limo before."

The next day a limousine arrived exactly at 10 a.m.. Ernie reached to open one of the back doors when Aristophanes Marzipan popped out of the other side so abruptly that Ernie snatched his hand back as if he had been burned by the door handle.

"The Driver will do it! The Driver will do it!" Aristophanes said, and just as abruptly popped back in.

The inside of the limousine was strewn with heavily pawed newspapers and magazines. Once inside Ernie sat by the window and turned to Aristophanes Marzipan,

"So where we going?" he said.

"I would tell you," Aristophanes said, "but I don't know who you are."

"What?" said Ernie.

Bill Bayo laughed and elbowed Ernie in the ribs, which he seemed not to feel at all.

"Mr. Marzipan," Bill Bayo said, "Ernie Benzini."

"The carpenter!" said Aristophanes. "Fine work! Fine work! Pleased to meet you!" He leaned over in his seat to face Ernie and smiled a big smile. "You know who I am, right?"

"Yep," said Ernie, and let out a big yawn.

Aristophanes Marzipan frowned and, facing forward again, addressed the Driver.

"Make a right up here," he said.

"That's the old copper mine," Ernie said.

Without turning, Aristophanes said, "Yep."

By the time they reached the entrance to the mine Ernie's laughter had dwindled down to a minor coughing fit. He started wiping the tears from his eyes with his shirt sleeve until Aristophanes dug under a pile of Montana newspapers and pulled out an old handkerchief. Ernie finished wiping and blew his nose.

"You got me!" he said, "You got me good!"

Bill Bayo started to open his door but Aristophanes stopped him. "The Driver will do it!" he said. "The Driver will do it!"

He led them into the old mine which no longer looked like a mine at all. What had once resembled a cave was now a vast grand hall adorned with chandeliers, statues, and fine furniture.

"This looks like a palace," Ernie said. "When did you do this?"

"Yesterday," Aristophanes said. He turned to Bill Bayo. "So, what do you think?"

The air was filled with music playing from a stereo system, a constant low wind howl coming from or going to unknown places deep in the earth, the tinkling of glass, and, curiously, the sound of a distant waterfall.

"Interesting," Bill Bayo said.

Aristophanes, now somewhat accustomed to Bill Bayo's muted mannerisms, grabbed him by the arm and dragged him over to a corner of the room. There was a black curtain hiding a large object.

"Now!" he said as he pulled a cord and opened the curtain, "What do you think of that?"

Bill Bayo stared blankly. Aristophanes tried to control his excitement but blurted out, "Don't you recognize that? Don't you know what that is?

Can't you see?"

"What is it?" Ernie said. "Looks like a piece of a wall."

"It is! It is!" Aristophanes said. "It's a part of the wall of the main hallway of the University of Montana's old College of Art building."

Bill Bayo walked to the object, knelt down, and ran his hands over a rough-hewn pine frame taped to the wall over an electric outlet.

"How did you get this?" he asked.

"I bought it! I bought it!" said Aristophanes Marzipan, "Well, I didn't exactly buy it. An artist friend of mine called me and told me about the hullabaloo your work created at the school and I immediately, immediately went to see it. I stopped them from removing your "Frame" with the offer of an endowment to the University of several million dollars, several million dollars to build a new art center. All I asked was that I be allowed to keep this part of the wall, to preserve it for posterity!"

Out of breath, he paused for a moment. "I hope you don't mind," he said.

Aristophanes Marzipan ordered a servant to bring out coffee and doughnuts. They all sat around a marble coffee table while Aristophanes finally meandered to the point of this whole visit.

"I wish to buy '22 Sluicegate Road'," he said.

Bill Bayo thought for a minute. "Not for sale," he said.

Aristophanes kept on rolling. "I've already purchased all the properties on that street and the surrounding area. I plan to preserve it just as it is. Just as it is. To make it, together with this old mine, into a new kind of museum."

Something clicked in Ernie's mind so he interrupted the conversation.

"I got an offer for some long-term work the other day," he said. "From a contractor who must be hard up for help because he likes me even less than I like him."

Aristophanes took a deep breath, turned back to Bill Bayo, and was about to continue when Ernie interrupted again.

"Seems there's going to be a new county home for orphaned children right here in Eight-Cent-Nickel. Private rooms. Gymnasium. Ball field. You know anything about that?"

"It was being discussed when I was at the Town Supervisor's office," Aristophanes said. "Now please let me continue." He turned back to Bill Bayo but Ernie refused to give up the floor.

"Is that you that's building that?" Ernie pointed at him. "Nobody seems to know where the money came from. The cheapskate builder who called me was actually offering decent wages."

Aristophanes composed himself and turned to Ernie who was looking him dead in the eye.

"All I can tell you is that I am familiar with the organization behind it. They are a good reputable charity known for creating a warm and nurturing atmosphere in their homes for unfortunate children."

He turned back to Bill Bayo and said, "I'll pay you a million dollars for it."

Ernie nearly jumped out of his seat. Bill Bayo was deep in thought, listening to the distant waterfall.

Aristophanes continued. "I'll even give you ten percent of the proceeds from all tourist-related income," he said. "Ten percent."

Bill Bayo sat motionless. Aristophanes tried to read what was going on inside his head but came up against a brick wall. Finally Bill Bayo spoke.

"I'll sell it to you," he said, "for one dollar."

Ernie went berserk.

"What are you crazy?" He began to jump around the room holding his head between his hands.

Aristophanes Marzipan held his hand up. "Calm down good craftsman," he said to Ernie.

Then, looking straight at Bill Bayo, he spoke in a soft voice, "I can't allow that."

"What?" said Ernie. He managed to move his shaky legs back to his seat and sat, still holding his head, his face redder than a Montana sunset. "Can't allow what?"

Aristophanes took out a handkerchief and wiped the area around his eyes. He patted Ernie on the leg and turned to Bill Bayo. "I cannot allow you so small a reward for your art, regardless of the nobility of your motive." He stopped wiping his eyes. "The facility in town will be well endowed. There is no need to short-change your talent." He searched Bill Bayo in vain for signs of a reaction, then continued quietly.

"I will pay you one million dollars but not for the work itself, just for the right to display it to the public. You may retain ownership and do what you will with your ten percent share of the exhibition revenues." Aristophanes wrote out a check for one million dollars. "You drive a hard bargain, young man. A hard bargain. So, what is your answer?"

Bill Bayo shrugged. "O.K." he said, and reached out his hand to shake on it.

Aristophanes threw the check to Ernie, took a hold of Bill Bayo's hand, and jumped out of his seat.

"Wahoo!" he yelled loudly. His cry pierced deep into the heart of the mountain, echoing in the distance for an unusually long time.

In the limousine on the way back to town Ernie held the check in his hands and gawked. He pushed it under Bill Bayo's nose.

"Smell that!" he said. "A million bucks! You're the richest man in Eight-Cent-Nickel!"

"I'll need a ride to the bank in the morning, if you're not busy," Bill Bayo said.

Ernie agreed to pick him up around 8:30 so they could be there when the bank opened.

At the bank the next morning Bill Bayo signed the check and handed it to an old woman behind the counter. While the woman was being revived on the floor, the bank manager handled the deposit.

"Aristophanes Marzipan!" the bank manager said. "I'll have to check on this."

Just then a clerk approached him. "You have a phone call in your office, sir," the clerk said.

The bank manager, grateful for the interruption and the opportunity to compose himself, excused himself and went to his office. Less than a minute later he came hurrying back, out of breath.

He handed the check to a teller and said, "Deposit this in Mr. Bayo's account, please." He smiled and shook Bill Bayo's hand.

As he started to walk away Bill Bayo called him back and handed him another bank form.

"I need to make a withdrawal," he said.

When the bank manager saw the amount he turned pale.

"We don't have that kind of cash available here," he said.

Ernie leaned over and saw the number $300,000.

"Wow!" said Ernie, "What are you doing?"

"Don't worry," Bill Bayo said, handing another form to the bank manager. "It's going right back in to another account.

He turned to Ernie and asked, "Do you have an account at this bank?"

"No," said Ernie, looking very confused.

"Well," said Bill Bayo, "You do now."

Postal Carrier and Mother Oid had been asleep when Bill Bayo came home from his meeting with Aristophanes Marzipan. So that next night at dinner he told the whole family of the adventure he and Ernie had the day before. He told them about the limo ride, the copper mine palace, and the section of wall from the University of Montana. Finally he told them about the check and his trip to the bank. After a stunned silence that lasted all of thirty seconds the house exploded with shouts and loud screaming laughter. Postal Carrier Oid congratulated Bill Bayo and hugged him. As he did, Bill Bayo stuck something in his back pocket. Postal Carrier Oid pulled a large legal sized document out and looked at it.

"Thanks, Billy," he said. He shook Bill Bayo's hand then showed the papers to Mother Oid. She smiled at Bill Bayo and kissed him on the cheek then turned to the girls and said, "I would like you ladies to calm down and thank your brother." She held the papers out for them to see. At the top was the word "Mortgage." At the bottom was a stamp mark with the words "Paid In Full."

Later Bill Bayo handed Postal Carrier Oid a savings account booklet with his and Mother Oid's name on it.

"You don't have to do this, Billy," Postal Carrier Oid said, "this is your money."

"No," Bill Bayo said. "This is our money."

He had kept enough money for himself to cover part if not all of the cost of his next "work." The germ of an idea he had conjured up while working in the garden had blossomed in his head during the visit with Aristophanes. Ernie, who now called Bill Bayo "partner," had already dived into the preliminary research while Bill Bayo worked in his garden and thought. His life, however, was about to be changed in an even more dramatic fashion.

(END OF EXCERPT)

ABOUT THE AUTHOR

"In the future, only people who are not famous will be famous."

"Chooch" is the gnome de plume of an unfinished scalawag years in the making. He is a musician, writer, and professional video maker who spent most of his life imagining; which explains his tenuous hold on reality. He has a BA in History and an MA in Communication and is retired after 30 years of producing epic training videos for a commuter railroad. In his rather mundane time upon this earth he has also worked in supermarkets, warehouses, mini-marts, and factories. His resume includes membership in several unions; a slew of country bands, rock bands, and country-rock bands; and other organizations too frivolous to mention. He has written and co-written screenplays, sitcom pilots, plays, and safety warnings featured on industrial cans of vegan lard. He is presently considering a career in professional wrestling, perhaps as a turnbuckle, and working on finishing a number of writing projects before he forgets the endings.

You can follow his exploits, explications, explanations, and exaggerations at iamchooch.com.

Peace to All Earthlings!

...and you.